the Spirit Box

the Spirit Box

■

Stephen Gallagher

SUBTERRANEAN PRESS · 2005

ISBN
1-59606-017-4

Subterranean Press
P. O. Box 190106
Burton, MI 48519

e-mail:
subpress@earthlink.net

website:
www.subterraneanpress.com

I couldn't have done this without the help of Marcie Kelso and Beth Petty at the Charlotte Region Film Office, along with Keith Bridges of the Charlotte-Mecklenburg Police Department and Ingeborg "Inge" Garrison, Trauma Coordinator for Presbyterian Healthcare. All gave me much more of their time than I had any right to ask for, and gave it generously.

For their interest and attention and their help in steering the project along its way, further thanks are due to Antony Harwood and Ellen Datlow, and to my wife Marilyn for coping with my notes and checking the finished work. And a big thanks to Howard Morhaim of the Howard Morhaim Literary Agency and William Schafer at Subterranean Press for faith and support.

And to my mother and father — this one's for you. You're never far away.

One

Tuesday, March 15

The young black security guard came out of the booth, took the card out of my hand, turned it the right way around, and swiped it through the reader. When the barrier started to rise she said, "There you go, Mister Bishop," and handed it back.

"Thanks," I said. My voice sounded scratchy.

The smile that she gave me was professional and courteous. No editorial content in it at all. If my appearance startled her, she didn't show it. If my minute of dumb persistence with the card had aroused her curiosity, she didn't show that either. She went back into the security hut and I drove on into the parking lot.

Macdonald-Stern. The company I'd spent three years helping to set up. The plant stood in a recently re-zoned piece of open countryside to the south of the airport, out beyond the Vietnamese church. Six years ago, there had been nothing here but woodland. Four years ago the state had put in roads and basic services. All over the USA they built these research parks like cargo cultists laying out airstrips on the beach, hoping to attract the spirits of prosperity. In some areas it didn't work, and you'd see some road named Technology Drive running off into nowhere with nothing along it but weeds and broken fences. Here it was different. Here they laid out the roads and the money came down out of the sky.

I cruised the Lexus around the parking lot. We had parking for a thousand cars in two secure areas. The lots were surrounded by birch trees and had video surveillance around the clock. The plant was a short walk away; you could glimpse it from here, looking like a Mayan temple buried deep in the jungle. From the roads outside you couldn't see anything of it at all.

We were a contract house offering analytical service to North Carolina's medical industries. They'd create the interesting-looking molecules and we'd tell them what, if anything, each new substance might be good for. The Mayan temple was one big state-of-the-art lab facility sitting on top of The Spirit Box, an enormous climate-controlled underground vault. In the vault were the test materials belonging to our various clients, kept under conditions of rigid security. Apart from the need to avoid cross-contamination, we based our procedures on the assumption that any one of those client substances might turn out to be the cure for cancer.

Something registered in the corner of my eye, and I felt a sudden shock. Christ, was that *me?* I'd caught sight of myself in the rearview mirror as I was backing into a vacant space. I managed to brake about an inch short of the Taurus in the next slot.

Then I had to take a moment.

When I'd locked the car I walked along the campus-style pathway to the admin building. There I went through the double doors into our entrance hall, and approached the desk.

"Hi," I said to the Security Man behind it.

He said, "Good morning, Mister Bishop."

I looked down at myself. I'd been wearing casual clothes to begin with, and now they were creased and rumpled from a day and a night's wear. There's casual, and there's casual.

I said, "You've got to excuse me. I didn't get time to change."

"You look fine to me, sir," the Security Man said. "Can I get you anything?"

"Isn't there somewhere I can get hold of a razor and stuff?"

"You can tell me what you need and I'll have it brought to your office. Or there's a vendor in the second-floor men's room in the west building."

"What kind of things does it have?"

"Razors, toothpaste, shoeshine…everything you need except the alibi."

"Thanks," I said. "And while I'm taking care of that, can you call Mickey Cheung in the Spirit Box and tell him I'll be with him in ten minutes?"

He reached for his phone.

"I'll do that," he said.

I said, "Thank you," and set off toward the west building.

I knew I looked bad and I probably looked as if I was hung-over. I caught myself walking unsteadily, and I wouldn't have blamed anyone for thinking I was drunk. But it was sheer physical tiredness. I'd gone around twenty-six hours without sleep and I wasn't about to stop.

I went through the connecting hall and into the west building, where I took the glass elevator up to the second floor. Four other people were along for the ride and not one of them betrayed any sign of having noticed me. They studied the floor, their wristwatches, the view outside.

In the men's room, to the sound of running water, I stood by the washbasins and emptied all of the money out of my pockets and onto the marble. I was able to scrape together enough change for a little vendor pack containing a toothbrush, a comb, floss, breath mints, a sachet of cologne, and a tube of toothpaste that was sized for a doll to use. The men's room lighting was discreet and the mirrors had that gold-tinted glass that makes you look tanned and better than you've any right to, but to my own eyes I still looked like a wreck. I shaved in hot water, washed in cold, combed my hair, cleaned my teeth, did whatever I could to tidy myself up. Someone came in and vanished into one of the toilet cubicles. I never saw who it was. He was still inside there when I left.

Everyone was going about their lives as if nothing remarkable had happened.

Heading back toward the management block, I did my best to walk straight and look steady. The cold water had done something for me. It had dragged me through the sleep barrier and into the new day. Not that the new day was a place I had any great wish to be.

From behind me, I heard, "John!"

I stopped and turned. I saw the boyish figure of Rose Macready. I'd just walked past her.

"Sorry," I said.

"You were walking along in a daze." Then she took a moment to study me more closely. "What happened?"

I wasn't sure what to say, so I just said a lame-sounding, "I had a bad night."

"You should have called me. I could have made it a better one."

"Rose..." I began, half-wanting her to be the first one I'd tell, but not even wanting to approach the moment where I told anyone at all.

"I'm teasing you, John," she said. "Come on. What's the order of the day?"

Rose Macready was only one step down from the top job in People Resources. In the old days it would have been called Personnel. She was single, around thirty-five years old, and was the only woman other than Sophie that I'd slept with since I'd been married. Rose and I had agreed to forget it. But I'd found that you don't.

The order of the day?

"I don't know yet," I said.

"Want to meet me for lunch?"

"I think I'll be out," I said.

"Okay," she said, and then as she was turning to walk on, she added, "Talk to me later if you change your mind."

Two

The elevator reached the bottom of the shaft, and I stepped out into the Spirit Box.

Actually, what I entered was the foyer to the vault's Master Control Suite, a subterranean room with the lighting plan of a flight deck and more processing power than a NASA mission. From where I stood I could see into the suite through three walls of glass that were variously angled like the facets on a diamond.

These places always look the same to me. It doesn't matter what they're controlling—a theme park, an Imax cinema, a couple of hundred channels of cable TV—they always have the same hardware, the same feel, the same one guy sitting in the middle of it all reading a newspaper.

Except that today, Mickey Cheung was already on his feet and waiting to buzz me through.

I don't know if it was his black-rimmed glasses or the fact that he spent so much of his working day underground, but almost everything about Mickey made me think of a mole. I reckon that nature had it mind for him to be small and round, but a twice-weekly workout kept him slim-waisted and chunky like a little Stretch Armstrong.

The doors slid open and as soon as I was through them I said, "You left a message on my service last night," I said. "You played me a recording of a girl crying. I didn't imagine that, did I? Yes or no?"

But he was staring at me.

"What happened to *you?*" he said.

"Never mind that. You *did* leave me a message?"

"Only after I spent most of the evening trying to get hold of you."

"Well, I'm here now. What was it all about?"

"Security got an anonymous tipoff," he said. "The caller said, if you want to know who's been stealing client samples out of the Spirit

Box, take a close look at an employee name of Don Farrow. I checked on Farrow, he's just one of the kids, basically a janitor. I got a master key and looked in his locker. His phone was inside. He had a dozen missed calls and a message waiting. That was the message I played out to you."

"It was a girl's voice."

"I noticed that."

"It sounded like my daughter," I said. "Did you notice *that?*"

He looked at me strangely.

"Not to me, it didn't," he said.

"Where's this Don Farrow?" I said. "I want to talk to him."

"Nobody's seen him since the weekend," Mickey said.

"How much substance is there in this?"

"Let me show you."

One of Mickey's assistants took over in the control suite, and I followed him through to the vault itself. The connecting tunnel was narrow-sided and round-ceilinged, and it was lit with an orange-white glow from stripes recessed into the walls. Walking behind Mickey, I found myself looking down at a pale scar on the crown of his head. It made a white L-shaped mark where the hair didn't grow. Mickey's hair was cut short, and it was dark like velvet.

Just like a mole's, in fact.

There was nothing supernatural behind the vault's nickname. A spirit box was the lockable case in which a Southern gentleman kept his expensive liquor. Once the name had caught on there were one or two attempts to attach urban legends to it — like a story of a construction worker killed and left buried down there during the excavations, completely untrue — but the name mainly stuck because of the vault's tight security.

It was a clean area with a filtered air supply, just like the environment where they make microchips. Everyone in there had to wear paper suits and masks. A thumbprint reader checked our authorisation and then lasered each of us a wrist tag like a new baby's, barcoded and single-use. As it was printing, we pulled on thin latex gloves and then we put the tags on over them.

Once through the airlock, we'd have to show our tags for scanning at all the automatic doorways. Otherwise they wouldn't let us through. All movements in the vault were logged on a hard drive and observed by video. Try to cheat the procedure and you'd start a lockdown and a big alert.

We came into the central hub of the vault, a wide corridor with a tight curve to it, and here we moved aside to let one of the suited assistants pass. Her heavy trolley had an electric motor assist. It moved on grey rubber tires and the motor clicked on and off as she manouevered it.

"Morning, Lucy," Mickey said.

"Hey, Mickey," she said.

She sounded young, and she was a slight figure. I glanced after her as she pulled the logged-out samples toward the lab exit. Seventy-five percent of the people in Mickey's department were the sons and daughters of company employees or contractors. For many of them, it was a first job. For the company it was an unofficial family-friendly policy. For all that this was a high-tech environment theirs was essentially low-grade work, barely a cut above stacking the shelves in a Wal-Mart.

We passed on. In the white light and spacesuits we might have been in some slow-moving science fiction Art Movie. The storage galleries were off to our left, radiating from the corridor like spokes from the hub. There were five levels, all but one of them exactly like this one. We were heading for an internal elevator bank that would take us down to the lowest.

How was I feeling? In turmoil, to be honest with you. On the outside I was moving normally while my gut and all the way up into my chest felt like a tight bag of snakes. Part of me knew beyond all logic that it was Gilly's voice I'd heard in that message. Logic suggested otherwise.

Another of the young interns went by with a trolley of samples for the labs upstairs. Most of them were bright kids, in my limited experience. They were straight enough, but I wouldn't have called any of them committed. Push the wagon, pull the wagon. What kind of a career would you call that?

We rode the elevator down to sub-level five. The elevator car was an odd shape, with a bumper rail at knee height. I could feel a pressure in my head. I don't know if it was real or imagined, but it wasn't pleasant.

This level wasn't quite like the others. It wasn't as bright, it wasn't as stark. It didn't have the same feel as the rest of them, either. When they'd dug right down into the red Carolina dirt they'd taken it all the way to the bedrock, and the bedrock they'd reached wasn't even. So the lowest level of the underground structure was fitted in with the contours of the substrate, which meant that there was less available space and its layout was eccentric. The main corridor wasn't a circle, it was a snake.

The levels above us were like a space station. This was more like a space station's crypt. Bare concrete, sealed. Bulkhead lighting. A painted floor. Of all the levels, this was the least-used. There was almost nothing down here but the old Russian stuff.

Lights flickered on as we stepped out of the elevator. They'd sensed our presence, and they'd power-down after we'd quit the area. Mickey knew where he was going, and led me around a couple of turns and into the second of three parallel galleries.

"Something here you need to see," he said.

The ceiling was low and the walls had a slight kink to them, so that the far end of the chamber ran on just out of sight. There had to be a thousand or more client samples on the shelves in this one gallery. They were all in packaging that was basic and low-tech. I saw a varied selection of scruffy boxes and jars, each item placed on its weight-sensitive pedestal and underlit like installation art. I could see at least one brown-paper parcel that had been vacuum-sealed into a thick plastic envelope, string and address labels and all.

"You're looking at the Soviet fire sale collection," Mickey Cheung said. "When it came to us, it arrived in fifty crates without a scrap of documentation. Our deal with the client is that we work on it at cheap rate when there's slack time in the labs. Barely two per cent's been touched, and nothing in that's been useful."

We walked down the gallery, and Mickey said, "Each individual sample is logged with a number and stands on a pressure pad recording its mass. The theory is that if any part of any sample gets removed without authorisation, it shows up. I've got five samples down here that defied the laws of physics and got bigger. We got variations of up to half a gram over recorded weight. That's too much of an increase for either oxidation or moisture to account for."

We stopped before the samples. There were five different jars, all with screw-on lids, and I could see that each had been topped up with a white powder that didn't quite match the contents of any of them. Something had spilled. I wiped a gloved finger across the shelf by the base of the nearest jar, and it left a clean mark.

"Talcum powder?" I said.

"At a guess," Mickey said.

"Anything here that's high-value?"

"The chemicals are probably worth less than the talcum powder," He said. "You'd hear rumors about the kind of things the Russians were working on, but we've yet to find anything startling to back them up. My guess is that it was mostly just Cold War propaganda. Bear in mind that all this stuff came from the labs that couldn't hack it in the free market. All the promising research found commercial sponsors."

"So the chances of pulling out a golden ticket are pretty slim."

"I'm not saying there's no possible chance of finding the chemical basis of a brand-new zillion-dollar product somewhere in here. The problem is that you're looking at everything from bug spray to voodoo juice, and nobody knows which is which."

"Voodoo juice?"

"Zombie cucumber from the parapsychology labs in Krasnodar. Imagine anyone being prepared to shell out a quarter of a mill for *that*."

"So why pick on these to steal?"

"Because if you look around, you can see that this is the only area the cameras don't cover."

We were finished, here. He'd made his point and there was nothing more of use that we could do. I was glad to get out.

As we were going back up in the elevator, I said to Mickey, "How would Don Farrow physically get the stuff out of the vault?"

"He wouldn't. Don Farrow's never had access down here. So we're probably talking about a team."

"That still leaves the problem of getting the stuff through the searches."

He sucked in and blew out a faintly exasperated breath, and the sides of his mask moved with the pressure.

"Well," he said, "you've seen the procedure. You strip to walk in, you strip to walk out. My guess is that ingestion or body cavity would be the only ways to go."

"You mean, swallow it?"

"Or stick it where the sun don't often shine. Personally, I'd swallow it. I wouldn't care to have a workmate stroll around the corner and find me in mid-insertion. There's no easy quip for an occasion such as that."

There was nothing more to see or say, so we returned to the surface. I was finding it hard to get my breath so I pulled my mask off in the elevator. I was aware of Mickey watching me. Studying me, even. I didn't look up or meet his eyes.

"Rough night last night?" he said after a while.

"May you never know," I said.

$\mathcal{T}hree$

She stood at the top of the stairs and called down to me, "Daddy, I've done something stupid."

And that really was the beginning of it.

I looked up from the box that I was packing. She was at the top of the big open-plan stairway that came down from the bedroom level and right into the living area. It was a huge house, the kind they mean when they talk about a place to die for. And rented, of course. We'd been in it for most of the three years. Gillian was holding the handrail and looking scared.

"No kidding," I said testily. "What now?"

There was a lot still to be done, and she hadn't exactly been of much help so far. She'd been moody and obstructive in the way that only a fifteen-year-old can. My immediate guess was that she'd been kicking at the doors or the furniture, taking out her resentment on the fabric of the place, and now she was worried because something had been damaged.

"Seriously," she said.

I can't tell you if she took a mis-step then or if her legs just gave out, but I could see her waver and then her foot missed the stair. Her heel clipped the riser and she sat down heavily, all at once. One hand was still holding the rail and she seemed to have no coordination. She slipped down onto the second stair and looked for a moment as if she might lose her grip and slide all the way.

I've no memory of laying down whatever I was holding, or of crossing the room. All I remember is that in an instant I was up there with her, steadying her onto the third step down. She let go of the handrail and she held onto my arm tightly.

"What have you done?" I said. A pallor had washed out her tan, and I could see the blue of the veins through her skin. Her touch was cold and very damp. Her hand on my arm seemed small.

"I took some pills," she said.

"What pills?" I said. "Where?"

"The ones you told me to clear out of the bathroom cabinet."

I tried to make it all compute. But it just wouldn't go. Pills. Bathroom cabinet. She'd done *what*? I tried to grasp the sense of it, the scale. But I was utterly unprepared.

"Oh, Jesus," I said.

I disengaged myself and left her there, and I went through the master bedroom to the bathroom. The bedroom had its own deck overlooking the lake, and a loft area which I'd been using as an office. The bathroom was carpeted, tiled, marbled, jacuzzied. The lighting alone would be enough to make you feel like you'd made it, that to live in a place like this you had to be up there with the rich. She'd left the lights switched on. The hidden fan was running.

The cabinet was directly above the basin. Its doors were wide open and the middle shelf had been swept clear of bottles and containers. As far as I could remember there should have been eight or a dozen of these, mostly over-the-counter remedies that had been bought as needed and then kept in case they'd ever be needed again.

All that remained on the shelf was the floss and the toothpaste, pushed over to one side. Most of the containers lay in the basin below, their childproof caps off. I sorted out odd ones at random, and shook them. Only one or two still had tablets inside. The rest were empty.

There were more medicines here than I could remember buying, and a few empty blister packs as well. Some we'd brought out with us from England. Others had the labels of various American drugstores. I'd never really kept track.

She surely couldn't have taken them *all*. Could she? But if she hadn't, where were they?

I went back. She was still on the third stair down. She was hunched forward with her arms wrapped around her middle and her head almost on her knees.

I sat beside her and showed her the plastic bottle in my hand. It was a twenty-five capsule pack of painkillers and there was one lone caplet rattling around inside it.

"Where's the rest of these?" I said.

"Don't shout at me," she said.

I wasn't shouting. Or I didn't think I was. But I needed her to feel some of the urgency that was beginning to overwhelm me. I was thinking that I wanted her to see it and remember it so that this would never, ever happen again.

I said, "I'm just trying to work out exactly what you've done."

She wiped her eyes with her sleeve, and obviously not for the first time. They were teary and red and sore.

"I told you," she said.

"You didn't tell me how many."

I waited.

"Oh, God," I said. "You didn't really take them all."

"I'm sorry," she said miserably.

Phone. Ambulance.

I tried to stand, and she clung onto me.

"No," she said.

I was about to say something sharp when I realized that she wasn't trying to prevent me from getting to the phone. She just didn't want me to leave her alone on the stairs again. She wasn't letting go.

"Come on," I said. "Let's get you downstairs. Stand up."

"I can't."

"I'll help you."

She wasn't exaggerating. I genuinely don't think she had the strength to stand up unaided. I had to take most of her weight as I walked her down the stairs while she moved her legs like a puppet does, brushing the ground and not really walking at all. We couldn't move anywhere near as fast as I would have liked.

"I want to go to a hospital," she said.

"I know."

"I want to go now."

"As soon as we reach the phone, I'll call an ambulance."

Down the stairs, one at a time, me taking the weight, both of us moving in slow motion.

"I feel awful," she said.

"Well," I said, "it was a stupid thing to do."

I got her down to the living room couch, where she rolled onto her side and curled up like a sick animal.

"Try to bring some of them back, Gilly," I said.

"No," she moaned.

"Put your fingers down your throat. If you don't do it, I'll have to."

First aid? I had no idea. Who does? They used to tell you to make a child drink salt water to trigger the vomit reflex. Now they say don't, because of saline poisoning. Throwing up helps. Or makes it worse. It all depends.

There had never been any time in my life when I needed help more. I picked up the phone, and it was dead.

Of course it was. I don't know why I was surprised. I'd arranged the line disconnection myself, less than a week ago. They'd asked me to pick a time and I'd said, off the top of my head, Oh, why don't we make it ten o'clock. I'd been assuming that we'd be done and out by then.

In spite of this I dialled 911 anyway, and of course nothing happened, and so then like an idiot I dialled it again, and then I slammed down the receiver because I'd remembered my cellular phone, hooked up to charge on the dashboard of the company Lexus outside.

Four

I'd moved the car off the driveway to make a clear space for the movers' truck in case they turned up early. Gilly and I were supposed to be closing up the house in the morning and then checking into one of those suite hotels later on in the day. Her mother had gone back to England ahead of us and Gilly had a ticket to join her in a few days' time, while I was to stay on and work out the last weeks of my contract.

It had been our first time living abroad. As far as Sophie and Gilly were concerned, it was supposed to have been understood from the beginning that I'd be working at a burnout pace and they wouldn't get to see too much of me. I'd argued that I was doing it for all of us, but I think we all knew that this was really for me. My moment.

I had no illusions about it. Landing this job had felt like finally making it into a team for the Olympics. In a perfect world, I'd be ten or fifteen years younger and it might have been the start of something. But I'd been around for long enough to know that it's never a perfect world. This was my high point, not my debut. At least I'd be able to say that I'd been there.

Afterwards, the plan was that we'd go home and I'd make it up to them. Not that there weren't compensations right here. The lifestyle, for one. We'd never known anything like it. Gilly went to a fee-paying school where, when they'd needed a graduation day speaker one year, they'd hired Mikhail Gorbachev. She made some good friends and she even started to pick up an accent. Sophie got the Mercedes sports car she'd always wanted and it took her two weeks to raise the nerve to drive it. The times when we had a rare long weekend, we'd fly somewhere. I fixed Gilly up with a company job for five weeks of that last summer, and it had started her thinking seriously about some kind of a medical career.

I didn't know the first thing about medicine. All I know is the medical business.

Which is ironic, when you think about it.

I got to the car. The phone was uncharged, but I'd a lead that I could plug into the lighter socket. The sky was dark, and there was a feeling of rain in the air. Carolina's one of those humid Southern states and when it rains, it really comes down. I sat in the car to make the call but I didn't close the door.

Our rented house was on Lake Wylie, west of the city. We weren't a long way out, but the nearest hospital that I knew of was at least half an hour's drive away. The house stood at the end of a lane, out on a small headland that we shared with four other properties, plus one still under construction on the last remaining waterfront lot. I thought of them as the Silent Mansions. Our private little area livened up at weekends and on holidays, but during the working week it was as if nothing moved.

So there was no point in me looking around for help. The only help was on the other end of a cellular connection.

"I need an ambulance," I said when I got through. "My daughter's taken an overdose. I need an ambulance for her right away."

"Your name, sir?"

Whoever talked to me, she was good. I was panicking and couldn't focus, and she anchored me and got all the details out of me without making me feel that time was being wasted.

She told me that a first responder unit would be with me ahead of the paramedics. This person would be a civilian volunteer from somewhere in the lake area. He or she would be carrying a jump kit of basic emergency gear and would be able to start an intervention. I was to co-operate and do whatever I was asked. I also had to get together all of the drugs containers and bring them along. The labels would help the trauma team to determine her treatment.

I went back into the house feeling reassured and even more scared, all at the same time. Help was on its way, but the danger had been given a new sense of scale and authority.

I imagined she could die. It could even come to that.

I don't know whether she'd done as I'd told her, or whether it was just her body rebelling against the cocktail of medicines that she'd swallowed, but I found her stretched out and leaning forward to retch onto the carpet. She was heaving like a dog and making the same kind of noises but the only product of her efforts, as far as I could see, was a thin spattering of bile like a patch of poodle pee. When I crouched by her, she gave up and flopped back. She lay there, breathing hard and shallow.

"The ambulance is coming," I said.

"When?"

"It's on its way right now," I told her. I was feeling her forehead; it was shiny with sweat but it was cold. I said, "Keep trying to be sick."

"There's nothing else to come."

She turned her head away from my touch, as if the pressure was an added discomfort. I dropped my hand to her shoulder and squeezed it, unable to give up the contact.

I said, "When did you take them?"

She was making a face with her eyes screwed shut and she didn't seem to register that, so I had to repeat it.

"About ten minutes after I went upstairs," she said then.

"Gilly," I said, "that was an hour ago. What were you doing?"

"Waiting for you to come and find me," she said.

I had to tear myself away, because there were things I had to do. First I went to the front door and pinned it wide open. When help arrived, I didn't want anything slowing it down.

As I was heading back across the living space toward the stairs, I called her name again. Her response was a faint groan. I couldn't see her over the back of the couch. I didn't want to leave her alone for any time at all, but I knew I had to.

The bathroom was exactly as I'd left it. I hadn't switched off the light or anything. If I'd been thinking straight, I might have taken along a bag to put the containers in. But I hadn't, so I started loading them into my pockets.

I glanced at all the stuff as I was shovelling it away. None of it was anything I'd ever bought. Yeast tablets. Herbal things with the look and texture of dried rabbit pellets. Homeopathic remedies. Nothing here that seemed exactly life-threatening. Then I came to some prescription antidepressants that Sophie had been on for at least half of our second year in the US. They might be a problem. And the painkillers were a worry.

Back down to the living area. That, too, was just as I'd left it. No-one had arrived yet. Gillian wasn't moving.

"Gilly?" I said, crouching before her and giving her a little shake. "Wake up. Don't go to sleep. They're nearly here."

Someone was supposed to be here.

That was when I went outside again, once I'd had a response out of her. I half-expected to find somebody cruising uncertainly around the turning circle at the end of the lane, trying to work out which of these half-million-dollar houses they were supposed to be looking for, needing to be hailed and waved in.

But I saw no-one.

I stood out there alone, the silent mansions at my back, the lake behind them, while ahead of me stretched the long and empty road that led inland.

"Fuck," I said.

Five

I can't tell you what it felt like. All the experience of the past three years just fell away and suddenly I was aware of nothing other than that I was a long way from home in an alien land, helpless and uncertain and tongue-tied and useless. Whenever we'd needed a doctor, we'd had the use of the company's on-site medical center. I'd never had to deal with a crisis. Certainly not alone. And whichever way you looked at it, you couldn't call this anything else.

I had to do something. I ran to the Lexus. Before I opened the door I could hear the cellular phone inside it ringing.

When I'd grabbed it up I said, "Will you get off the line, please? This is an emergency."

A voice that wasn't the same as the one I'd heard before said, "Mister Bishop, this is the ambulance control center. Our volunteer responder can't be reached through his pager. We'll keep on trying him, but I'm checking to see if we can get a helicopter out to you. How's your daughter now?"

There was more, but I didn't hear it. I said something I don't remember, but which I'm sure I'd regret if I did. I threw the phone down and then I started the Lexus and backed it all the way up the driveway, slewing from side to side and braking so late that I almost hit the house.

Back inside, Gillian stirred a little when I got to her. When I gave her shoulder a shake she reacted, wincing like a newborn trying to turn its face from the hard light of day.

"Come on, Gilly," I said. "We've got to go."

"Sleepy," she complained.

"No, Gilly, no. You mustn't sleep. I'm going to drive us to the hospital. Come on, now."

Trying to raise her from the couch was like trying to lift a sack. "You've got to help me," I said, and after a few moments she started to comply, weakly.

I walked her to the door. Why had I wasted so much time? If I'd put her straight into the car and set off with her right at the beginning, we might have been within sight of an Emergency Room by now.

I manoeuvred Gillian into the passenger seat and secured her with the belt. The phone was still hanging there on its lead, getting in the way. I turned the vents so that they were pointing at her face and then, once I'd started the engine, I boosted the air. It blew warm at first, but I knew that after a minute or less it would start to get fresher.

A minute was about the length of time it took me to reach the turnoff onto Rock Island Road, our first link to the rest of civilisation.

Rock Island Road was a fast and narrow country lane, with its split-rail fences and its old-fashioned roadside mailboxes and with dead-ended tracks running off it every quarter-mile or so. It was straight enough as these roads go, but with enough kinks and bumps to betray the fact that the land over which it ran had never quite been tamed in the haste to get it down. There was a lot of new development out here, but almost all of it was hidden away. Where Rock Island Road turned onto Shopton, there was a cluster of realtors' fingerpost signs pointing out toward the lake. They'd been hammered into the verge at the corner and they looked like the route markers for a bicycle race.

Shopton had a forty-five speed limit and just a few country homes along it. The verges were trimmed, the trees cut back, the roadside ditches kept clear. I looked across at Gillian. The cold air from the blowers seemed to have revived her a little. Her eyes were half-open, but she didn't look fully awake. They were like a cat's when it sleeps. She was breathing slowly, audibly.

I said, "Can you hear me?"

The sound of my voice seemed to raise her that last, short distance to the surface. I can't tell you exactly what the change was—it was a spark, something like that and no more—but the half-opened eyes seemed to take on life.

She gave a nod. It was so slight that it would have been easy for me to miss it.

I wanted to keep her engaged. I needed to keep her awake. Until I got her safely across the threshold of the Emergency Room and into the hands of a trauma team, I didn't dare let up.

"Why, Gilly?" I said. "I'm not angry. Just tell me why."

She took in a long, deep breath.

Then she said, "Nobody was listening to me."

"About what?"

"Nothing."

It was as if I'd had her for that brief moment but now she was turning away, slipping off again.

I said, "What, Gilly? Tell me." And when she didn't respond I said, "Gilly!" sharply, and sensed her coming back.

I didn't have to look at her or even hear her. I was simply aware of her presence, of its levels, of its distinctive texture within my own existence. I can remember when she was ten years old, and she went on a trip away with her school for the first time. We'd looked forward to a weekend without her. But the house felt as if it had been robbed of something, and we just moved around it like ghosts until we got her back.

She said, "You never care what I think. You never want to hear what I've got to say. The moment you see an opening, you jump in with the same old stuff."

"Now that's not true," I said.

"See?" she said. "You're doing it now."

I wasn't giving her my full attention because I was trying to work out where to head for. I knew of a couple of smaller hospitals with Emergency Rooms on the Pineville road south of the city, but close to the uptown area there were three of those huge medical complexes that resemble self-contained medieval cities. State-of-the-art places with all the high-tech backup you can imagine. The distance I'd have to cover would be about the same once I got onto the I77, but more importantly the Trauma Center exit was clearly signed and there would be less margin for error.

It was late in the morning. Traffic would be steady and it should be a straight run through.

I said, "Look, once we get you straightened out, we'll discuss it properly. I promise you I'll listen. If I don't listen you can punch me."

For a moment I thought she'd drifted again, and then she said, "But will it make any difference?"

"What do you mean?"

"We always do what you want to do. I never get a vote and I never have a choice."

We'd just passed the sign for the Charlotte city limit. There was still greenery all around us, but there were also power lines overhead and radio towers on the skyline. The less lovely it got, the happier I felt. Within the next mile or so we'd be crossing the Arrowood Industrial Park, and on the far side of the park was the interstate ramp. On the interstate I could zip straight to the heart of the city. It was about a five, six mile run on a fast road with no interruptions.

Seeing it all before me like that, I felt some of the terror recede and a sense of control returning. I was beginning to feel that I could handle this.

I said, "Be fair, Gilly. I've done my best for you. If ever a girl had a charmed life, it's you. You've never wanted for anything. Even coming here was the kind of adventure that most kids would kill for. Can't you see what an experience it's been? It'll set you up for life."

"You're doing it again," she said.

"What? Tell me what I'm doing."

"I barely get two words out and you spend the next ten minutes telling me how wrong I am and why."

We had to slow for a red light at York Road. It was the first major crossing I'd come to and some big tractor-trailer combinations were going through. There was nobody in the lane ahead of me and I started inching forward over the line, wondering if I dared run the light but seeing no opportunity to get through safely; then the lights changed anyway, and we took off and shot across into Arrowood.

"All right, then," I said. "I'm listening. Tell me what's wrong."

"I shouldn't have to," she said.

That kind of thing always makes me want to climb right up the wall and punch the ceiling. Sophie used to do it to me, until she finally accepted that we were wired differently and it was never going to work.

I said, "Don't punish me just because I fail to read your mind. If there's something you want me to know, give it me in plain English."

"I don't want to go back," she said.

"We've got to go back," I said. "The job's over."

"You get to stay."

"I explained that to you," I told her. "I can't leave until we clear up this business about the Spirit Box. It's part of my contract."

"I never signed any contract," Gilly said.

"We're British citizens," I said. "It's not like we had a…Ah, *Jesus!*"

"What?" she said, rising up in her seat so that her belt locked taut; my sudden curse had acted on her like a jab from a shock baton, and in an instant she was more awake than she'd been at any time since we'd left the house. She was looking around her like a startled sleepwalker.

What I'd seen was a helicopter, flying low and fast over the factory units to our left. I couldn't see any markings on it from this distance. It could have been the Air Ambulance or it might just as easily have been a local TV news traffic watch. It was heading in the direction of the lake.

It was gone already, but I told her about it. I said it looked as if I'd jumped the gun and that maybe it would have been better if we'd stayed where we were.

She said, "I suppose that's my fault, too,"

"No," I said. "It's mine."

The road through Arrowood had the same kind of feel as an airport perimeter road, and there was a rusty single-track railway line running alongside it. The sprawling park was mostly tenanted by chemical refineries and long, low factory units that looked like parcel depots. There was the I77, right ahead, passing above this road on a flyover.

I swung over into the left-hand lane to pick up the northbound ramp, and as we passed into the deep shadows under the bridge I was almost blinded for a moment when my vision failed to adjust.

It got better after a second or two. We joined a line of vehicles and I could hear interstate traffic booming on the concrete overhead as I waited to make the turn.

"Where are we?" she said.

"We'll be there in ten minutes," I said. "Just stay awake until then."

Her answer was a sleepy-sounding grunt.

"Do you want something to listen to?" I said. "You can listen to the radio. Do you hear me, Gilly? Stay awake."

"I heard you the first time," she murmured.

We were up and moving now, back into the daylight, putting on a burst of speed and joining the northbound flow. It was just as I'd expected. Traffic was steady, not too heavy. There were some tricky junctions up ahead, but I got into the middle lane and stayed there. The last thing I needed was to get sidelined into some turnoff that I didn't want.

I realized with dismay that my hands were trembling on the wheel. I held it tighter, and the tremors subsided. When I relaxed my grip again, they didn't return. But I felt queasy and guilty, the kind of guilt you feel when you know that any poise or skill you may seem to have is nothing more than blind luck, and that even if all turns out well in the end, you've been given a glimpse of the void that you'll never forget.

"My stomach hurts," she slurred, and I glanced across at her. She'd turned half-away and had the side of her face pressed into the seat.

And I thought, silently but with an unexpected viciousness that surprised me, *Just wait and see what it feels like once they've been pumping it out.*

We stayed there in the flow of the traffic, a buffalo herd of metal on its endless migration. We passed under bridges that swept with a dangerous grace overhead. This was going to be one big, wide run to the heart of town where I'd peel off on the south loop of the 277 and be able to leave within a couple of blocks of the big hospitals.

And there it all was, even sooner than I'd dared to hope, ahead and to the right; rising up in the distance all blue-misted like a set of mountains in a fantasy landscape, the glass towers of Charlotte's uptown district. One of the tallest of them seemed to wear a crown, like a crown of long thorns.

I took the ramp onto the 277 where it swept in around by the stadium, and that was where the traffic went solid.

Six

It wasn't just slow-moving, it had stopped completely. Bumper-to-bumper, door-to-door, backed-up like debris in a narrow drain. It was too late for me to do anything other than join on to the end of the line.

Once we'd come to a halt, I opened my door and got out. It felt strange to stand out on the highway. It's a place you instinctively feel you shouldn't be, like a dry river bed or a Women's Room. Looking ahead, it was as if I'd bobbed to the surface of a sea of car roofs, dotted with the reefs of jeeps and pickups.

I left the engine running and walked up to the car in front of me. It was an old Impala and its windows were down.

I said to the driver, "What's happening, here?"

And he looked at me and said, "Like I should know?"

Then I heard someone calling to me, and when I turned toward it I saw a man about two cars away. He was dressed for the office but he was in his shirtsleeves. For a moment I thought he was a cop in a shoulder holster but then I realized that what he had on was an under-the-jacket phone pouch in the same kind of design. The phone was in his hand.

He said, "My wife says she heard on the radio that there's a horse trailer turned over. The horse is alive but it's upside down. They've got the fire service there trying to work out how to move it."

Oh, *great*.

"Shit," I said. "I mean, thanks."

So we were all waiting for an upside-down horse. A couple of other cars had joined on either side, but there was no-one in the jam behind me yet. I'd be boxed-in if I didn't act quickly. I jumped back into the Lexus and put the automatic shift into reverse, and I did a screaming three-point-turn right there in the middle of the ramp and headed back down it the wrong way.

What else could I do? Walk a mile or more through backed-up traffic just to make myself known to the police at the head of the line?

My kid's back there. No rush. I reckon she'll be dead by now.

I scared the hell out of the drivers of three vehicles coming up, but I managed to miss them all. I registered the disbelief on each of their faces. At the bottom of the ramp I was able to go against the flow of traffic by staying on the concrete shoulder, swerving only to dodge between the shelled husks of burst truck tires. Then I probably knocked seven kinds of shit out of the underside of the Lexus when I crossed a low divider and cheated my way back onto the last uptown exit that I'd passed.

I think that was when I started to believe that I had some kind of divine endorsement for my cause.

I forget which street I came in by. It was College, Tryon, one of those. I had my foot right down and I felt like a canyon-runner as the high base walls of the business district's towers sped by. I knew where I was and I knew exactly where I needed to be. In a couple of blocks I'd need to make a right turn onto Trade Street, and Trade would take me straight down to Presbyterian Hospital.

In the seat beside me, Gillian gave a sudden, noisy shiver. She must have been taking a breath when it hit her, because she sucked in the air with a staccato gasp. I wanted to touch her but at this speed I didn't dare take my hands off the wheel. I can't really say whether I wanted to touch her for her own sake, or for mine.

The right onto Trade was a prohibited turn, but I made it anyway. The road dropped toward what I would have called a bus station, but which the locals called their Transit Mall. It was a huge and cavernous modern building, with an arched glass roof and a wide, open street entrance for the buses. I was passing the entrance when I heard the siren behind me.

I looked in the mirror and saw a white squad car of the Charlotte-Mecklenburg Police Department. I've never seen so many flashing lights on one vehicle. There were alternating blues and whites in the lightbar on the roof, and another set in the grille that flashed in a different sequence. In the widescreen frame of the car's windshield I saw an anonymous-looking lone officer, male. You see one of those coming up behind you at that kind of speed, and you don't mistake its purpose.

I debated whether to stop.

Then I decided that if I'd been sent him, I was obviously intended to make use of him.

Just past the Transit Mall there were some parking bays with meters, most of them unoccupied. I pulled the car over, and he came in right behind me. I started to get out. This, he didn't like.

"Get back in that car," he called, halfway out of his own, "Get back in that car." And so I got back into the Lexus and dropped the side-window and then sat with my hands resting in sight on the wheel.

When I looked in the door mirror, I could see him walking toward me. His uniform was a deep, midnight blue and his right hand was raised to his gun. Just touching it. Not quite going for it, just ready.

I guessed that by getting out I'd chosen exactly the wrong move and I'd thrown him into high gear. My license and car registration were in the glove box, but I didn't reach for them. For one thing, I didn't want to get shot. I'd made him edgy enough already. Under circumstances like these, they don't want to see initiative from you. They like you to follow directions.

As he got level with my open window he said, "Switch off the engine."

So I switched off the engine and he said, "What's the problem with you?"

I said, "My daughter's taken an overdose. I'm trying to get her to the hospital."

His attitude didn't change right away, but I could sense him stop and take this in. He crouched down a little so that he could see past me into the car and take a look at Gillian. He seemed sceptical. Not in a personal way, more like it was a kind of default setting that came with the uniform. I was starting to think that maybe I should have put my foot down and let him chase me all the way to the Emergency Room. It wasn't so far away, now, and this certainly wasn't getting us any closer.

"Miss?" he said.

She didn't respond. Her face was still turned away. She was in an awkward position, like someone trying to get a night's sleep in an airline seat.

"It's been at least two hours," I said.

"What's her name?"

"Gillian."

"Gillian?" he said. "Hey, Gillian. Can you look at me?"

"Some of the pills she took were prescription drugs," I told him. "I don't know what effect they're going to have. I called the paramedics out, but we couldn't wait. Please."

He was still studying her, putting everything into the balance. Me, the look of Gilly, the company Lexus, the distraught father's story, against whatever he'd seen of my reckless driving. Was there really any question that I was trying to lie my way out of a corner? Come *on*, I pleaded silently. At that moment Gilly gave another shudder, a real convulsion this time, and I reached over and tried to hold her and make it stop.

The patrolman said, "All right, follow me," and he went back to his car.

I pulled out right behind him. He held back on the lights and the siren until we reached the first crossing, and then he gave it everything and led me over to the other side. Traffic stopped and gave way, but the road didn't exactly clear before us. It was a grudging kind of compliance. More than one vehicle scrambled to make it through.

Bastards.

"It's all right, Gillian," I said. "It's going to be all right."

I can't say for certain whether she answered. She may have made a sound and the sound may have been, *No, it isn't*, but I couldn't even look at her to be sure.

"You'll see," I said.

We would see.

We were passing the Community College now. Young people with backpacks were dodging across the road, scattering like deer as they heard us coming. This was a narrow boulevard, with trees planted down its center. The trees were short and their branches hung out over the lanes, dense and low. The Lexus dipped in and out of the shadows as we headed up the street.

Just a few blocks to go, and then we were there.

~

Presbyterian wasn't an old building, but they'd designed the front of it to resemble one. Six stories of brown and red brick with a garden before it, broad and imposing in something like an old Colonial style. It looked solid, sober, reassuring, and classy. The entrance for the Emergency Room was around the back, where the parking was; we went around the block and my patrolman signalled a turn into the ambulance entrance and I followed him down.

Back here, the architecture was white and modern. It looked the way that every airport would probably look if all the flight passengers were Arab billionaires. The patrolman must have called ahead because they were waiting for us; we didn't go in under the canopy because there were at least five big ambulances blocking the lanes in the turnaround, but we stopped between the staff parking spaces and the entranceway.

Even as I was getting out of the car, two people were rolling out a stretcher while a third, a woman, was opening up my passenger door to get to Gillian. She quickly checked on a couple of things, but I couldn't see what. I saw her reach for a pulse but then the others were in my way and uncoupling Gillian's belt. You could see they'd done this kind of thing before. They had her out of there and back in through the entranceway in one fast load-and-go. Someone was shouting questions at her; someone else was talking to me.

I followed them in, and the patrolman followed me. Somebody asked for my car keys but they were still in the car. Because we'd come in from the ambulance bay, we'd bypassed the triage desk and the public waiting areas. After a double set of automatic doors we came through into a big, clean, well-lit space with a curving desk taking up most of the central area.

We'd hit them at a quiet time and there seemed to be very few people around, other than the team who were all over Gillian now. I saw at least three or four nurses and two physicians. You couldn't immediately tell who was who because they all had the same blue cotton uniform of loose pyjamas worn with sneakers, although one of the doctors had a white coat over his.

They stopped me there. Gillian was wheeled off to my left and into one of the acute treatment suites that ran along that side of the room. I glimpsed an area that looked like the kind of workspace where they assemble satellites, and then someone slid the glass door across and pulled a curtain behind it.

One of the doctors had stayed back. He wore a tag. I focused on it briefly and immediately forgot his name.

He said, "Are you the father?"

I said I was.

"Can you say exactly what it was she took?"

I was at a loss for a moment, and then I remembered and started to dig around in my pockets. I felt emptyheaded and suddenly lacking in all coordination, as if I'd just been led away from a week-long record attempt on a rollercoaster.

"These," I said. "But she couldn't tell me how many of each."

We moved over to the counter and I piled them up like stolen silverware. As the doctor was sorting through them and checking the labelling, a woman joined us. She was in her forties, dark-haired, wearing the tag of a Clinical Coordinator with nursing qualifications after her name.

The doctor said, "Did she vomit anything back up?"

"She tried," I said, "but nothing came. Can I stay with her?"

"Take a seat in the family room, Mister Bishop," he said. "Give us a chance to do what we do."

The woman was touching my arm, ready to guide me away. The doctor had moved off already and was sliding open the door to enter the acute room, giving me a brief and partial glimpse of what was going on inside. I couldn't even *see* Gillian. Then the door was closed and the scene was gone.

"You got her here," the woman said. "You did your job. You can't do any more than that."

She walked me to the place they called the family room. I thought it would be a public waiting room, but it was a small and private chamber just off the hallway between the emergency suite and the outer entrance. She asked me a few questions about Gillian on the way; any high blood pressure, diabetes, was she on any medication of her own.

"Please wait in here," she said. "Someone will be along to see you in just a couple of minutes."

"I need to know what's happening," I said.

"I know," she said. "I'm going to page Kate O'Brien. She'll be your patient representative."

"What does that mean?"

"It means we can keep you up on what's happening without anybody getting in the doctors' way."

She left me then and closed the door, and it was like she'd closed the door on a cell. The family room was about the size of one, and had a dead acoustic that gave an instant sense of isolation. It had low soft chairs and odd, high windows that were no more than horizontal slits and let in very little light. There was a TV set and a phone. The TV picture was on but the sound was turned low.

I dropped into one of the chairs.

I sat and I tilted my head back, and I gripped the arms of the seat with fingers that seemed to have no strength in them at all. I felt so relieved, I was almost sick with it.

But I'd done it. I'd done the job of being the dad. They don't give you any training for it and no-one ever tells you how hard it can sometimes be. This had to be about as extreme as it could get.

I had to sit there with the thought of Gilly only a few yards away being worked-over by strangers, but at least that was preferable to having her beside me in the car, ebbing slowly while the obstacles piled up ahead of us. I couldn't imagine any torture more exquisite. I couldn't imagine any predicament more cruel.

But we'd got through it.

Just.

That was the hard part. I didn't think I'd ever be able to forget it. You survive something, and the aftermath is more complicated than you can imagine. You don't just take the fact of your survival forward. Hey, great, we lived, I'm happy. The ghosts of near-disaster come along as well and continue to haunt you, in all their myriad forms. You're safe, but only by the skin of your teeth. You still think of everything that might have happened. Everything that almost did. It's like a door flaps open for a moment, and you see an infinity of demons beyond.

Wrung-out though I was, I couldn't relax. I couldn't take in what they were saying on the TV, although that was no great loss. It was one of those afternoon talk shows that are freak shows in disguise. Two hard and frightening women were arguing over the head of a sheepish-looking young man with an earring and a goatee beard. *He doan want you*, one of the two was saying. *He with me now*. It was the kind of human-zoo stuff that Gilly would watch all day, given half a chance.

I sat forward, put my head in my hands. I was startled to hear myself sob.

The door opened then and I was instantly composed. There were tears in my eyes and I couldn't so anything about that, but otherwise I hauled everything together and looked up.

I'd thought it might be the patrolman, seeking me out to do some follow-up.

But it was someone else.

"Hi," she said, checking out the room with a quick glance and finding only me. "Everything okay for you in here?"

I smiled and tried to say, "Sure," but my voice cracked and almost nothing came out.

"My name's Kate O'Brien," she said. "I'm your patient representative."

We shook hands awkwardly, and she sat. She'd brought along a clipboard and a number of forms, and some printed information leaflets for some of the more frequently-asked questions.

She couldn't have been much above five feet tall. She was fine and slight with great bones, a big shock of gorgeous red hair tied back in a bunch, and a redhead's fair complexion that didn't look as if it would take any sunlight at all. She was also seriously pregnant. I didn't quite have to help lower her down into the chair, but it was a close-run thing. I reckoned I'd probably have to help her out of it.

She said, "It's my job to keep you informed about your daughter's treatment. Think of me as a go-between. Have you any immediate questions that you need me to answer?"

"You mean apart from, how's she doing?"

"It's too early to tell you that yet. So far I can only say what's being done for her."

I steepled my hands in front of me and then turned them into fists and rested my face against them.

"'Kay," I said.

She said, "First thing they did was give her an airway and put in an IV. It's a large IV and they had to run it into her groin. They've been giving her a gastric lavage to take out her stomach contents and they've run a tube up through her nose and down into her stomach so they can put in liquid charcoal to deactivate the medicines and hopefully save her liver."

"Jesus," I said.

"She had a very irregular heartbeat when you brought her in. And those convulsions can be very dangerous. It's only fair to warn you about that. She's on several different drips. She's getting drugs for the cardiac disrhythmia and also reversing agents for some of the things that she took."

"What's a reversing agent?" I said. "Is that like an antidote?"

"You've got the idea," she said. "We've a dedicated computer here called a Poisondex. On that you can pull up every medicine on the market, including all the street drugs. It lists the symptoms, how you check for them, what the procedures are. The packaging you brought in saved everyone a lot of time. There's also a Poison Control number we can call. Poison Control have a more in-depth database. They also document and follow the history of every individual they ever get a call about. From today Gillian will have her own permanent file in their records."

"So," I said.

My mind was blank. The only question I really wanted answered was, when could I take her home? But I knew that it would be some time before I could know.

Kate O'Brien said, "When I left her, they were getting ready to put her on dialysis to take the toxins out of her blood. Did I say she was on oxygen?"

"Poor kid's really getting the works," I said, and I almost lost it then.

She put her hand on mine.

"Gillian's young," she said. "She's a healthy girl and she's got no co-morbid factors."

"What does that mean?"

"No ailments or complications that would have an effect on her chances. You've just got to hang in for her."

I nodded slowly.

"I'm going to be around the entire afternoon," she said. "I'll bring you all the information as I get it."

I think I managed a smile. "Thanks," I said. "Always feel free to come back and scare me some more."

She gave my hand a squeeze, and I was suddenly, almost overwhelmingly grateful for her presence. She was doing something more than putting a human face on a harrowing process. She was helping me to see a way through it. For me this was a completely new experience, but she'd done this before and she'd be doing it again. I was in a place that I didn't want to be, but at least I had a guide through the territory.

She said, "If you need anything and I'm not there, have them page me. Do me one big favor and don't try to go into the treatment room. Let the people work. It's not like on TV where everyone gets to stand and watch."

She started to rise. I jumped to my feet and helped her up out of the low chair.

"How long before the baby's due?" I asked her.

"Just over two weeks," she said.

"And you're still working?"

"That's my choice," she said. "He's in a breech position, but that's the only complication. My mother's the one doing all the worrying."

"Tell her I recognize the feeling," I said.

"Is there anything else you need right now?"

I glanced down at the phone.

"Can I use that to call a number in England?"

"You're welcome to try, but you could have a problem reaching an overseas operator."

"A pay phone, then?"

"Out the door, and down the corridor along the front of the building. Keep going and you'll find the rest rooms and the public waiting area. They've got vendors with every form of snack known to man. There's even a little microwave oven to heat them in."

"I may never need to go home," I said.

"No," she said, "but I know you'll be glad to."

Seven

I found the phones where she said they'd be, each one of them screened from the corridor in a cubicle of glass bricks. I made a call on my credit card, but I got my in-laws' answering machine and all that I could think of to say was, *It's me. I'll call again.*

The thought of putting on record a thirty-second summary of this worst of all days was simply beyond me. I didn't want to go scaring everyone, but I didn't want to play down such a close call, either. What I needed to put over was something like, *The dangerous part of it's over and Gilly's in the best hands possible,* but I was afraid it would come out more like *I just had the reaper breathe right down my neck and make every hair on my body stand on end, and I don't think I'll ever sleep soundly again.*

"You all done with the phone?" a woman said from behind me. I turned. She was blonde, middle-aged, expensively dressed and with her hair cut in a sharp bob. She was standing in the corridor a few feet away with a handful of change, not so close as to invade my space but close enough to stake a claim.

"Help yourself," I said, and left her to it.

Sophie was staying with her parents. She'd be there until our old house was ready for us to move back in. We'd let it out through an agency, on the same kind of arrangement as the place we'd been renting. The unmarried owner of the Lake Wylie house was working out a five-year contract in Alaska, living on a rig and saving his money.

Being unable to make the call gave me the itch of unfinished business. I wandered on down past the triage desk and through the public waiting room in search of the vending machines. The waiting area had soft armchairs and turquoise-blue carpeting, with big tiles of pink marble in the high-traffic areas. There was a fish tank and there were the usual TV sets, discreetly positioned and playing quietly. Of the dozen or so people scattered about, two were in hospital wheelchairs and looked as if they needed them.

I bought some machine coffee and walked back through. Some of those waiting were filling out patient forms on borrowed clipboards. Someone's cellular phone was piping *I'm Popeye the Sailorman*. My own was still in the car, and couldn't make international calls. I was hoping that one of the valets had moved the car for me, and that it hadn't been towed.

I sat there in the isolation of the Family Room and Kate O'Brien looked in after a while, with nothing new to report but just to see how I was doing. Because the room was right by the paramedics' entrance, I was able to hear the new ambulance cases arriving just outside my door. I counted three, and then there was a long gap, and then I heard voices that might or might not have been another.

Later on, I went out for a while. By now it was evening and the day was fading into an electric dark, all the sky in shades of neon. I stayed close to the automatic doors of the entrance, not wanting to stray too far, and I took a few breaths of unprocessed Carolina air.

Somehow over the past three years I'd lost my sense of the unfamiliarity of it all, and now it had suddenly returned. It was as if the past few hours had stripped me raw. I could feel every movement of the air against my skin, yet I could hardly feel the ground that I was standing on.

My first memory of my arrival here was of the airport at Raleigh; what I remembered of the terminal was just one long, low hallway with a tiled floor. It was cool and it was empty, as if it was a Sunday night and everyone had gone home. No waiting in line, no crowds to fight through, and plenty of spaces in the parking areas outside.

It's the America that most of us don't know. There are those crowded little strips on either coast making all the noise and getting all the attention, while the real places lie quietly between. The flyover states, I've heard them called.

The first thing that hits you in the Carolinas is a certain smell in the air; it's a kind of sweetness with a hint of rot, a distinctive odor of the South. You go outside, the ground's wet, but it's not actually raining, and it just feels as if there's so much moisture in the air that the air can't quite hold it all.

I could see across to the parking lot where I hoped my Lexus would be. I didn't know what had happened to the patrolman but his cruiser had gone, as well. In the lanes under the wide concrete awning of the pull-in, some of the ambulances stood with their engines idling. The ambulances weren't like the ones we had at home. They were enormous things, like bullion trucks.

I sat in my little room for a while longer and then I went back to the pay phone. If I got the machine again, I'd have to say something more than I'd managed last time. I started to work out a message as the call was going through.

But it was Sophie herself who answered.

"Yes?" she said.

"It's me," I said. I know it's a stupid way to start up a call, but with family it's a habit I've never been able to break. "I called earlier."

"I know," Sophie said. "I've been out at the house. I am getting straight on to the solicitor in the morning."

She'd caught me off-balance and I said, "What do you mean?"

"You want to see the state those people have left it in. I told you this would happen."

Already it was too late. She was telling me things about the house that I didn't need to know right now, and short of telling her to shut up I couldn't find any purchase to say what I needed to say. The longer I let her go on, the worse it was going to be.

"...and the carpet around the toilet is just literally rotting away," she was saying. "It's disgusting."

Finally I just had to break in and say, "Sophie, forget about the house and listen for a minute."

She took the interruption exactly the way I expected.

"Don't talk over me," she said. "I'm in the middle of telling you something!"

But I just plowed on into it.

"I've had a tricky situation here," I said, "but it's all worked out. Gilly took an overdose but she's fine."

Sophie wasn't usually one for being diverted easily, but at this she switched tracks in an instant.

"She did *what?*"

"She took an overdose," I repeated patiently. "The danger's over."

"How could you let her do that?" she said.

"Well," I said, "she found all those drugs you left behind. I'm at the hospital now. They're pumping them out of her. She was conscious all the way here. She's going to be fine. I'll call you again when she comes out. Where will you be?"

"She'll be all right, won't she?"

"Of course she will. Where will you be?"

"I'll be right here. Give me your number."

"There's no point. This is just a payphone. I'll have to call you."

"Which hospital is it?"

I was blank. I racked my brains.

"I don't know. Wait a minute. It's Presbyterian, the big one on Hawthorne."

I could hear her looking for something to write with and then noting it down.

"And you don't have the number?"

"No," I said. "I'll get it for next time."

"Can they get a phone to her? Can she call me herself?"

"Not yet. I'm not kidding you, Sophie, this has only just happened. They're still doing things to her. We've got to let them work."

"It's all right for you. You're there."

"You want to swap places with me? I've had the scare of my life."

"What are they doing?"

I told her what I could remember of the treatment details that Kate O'Brien had given me. They probably came out all wrong, but I did the best that I could. She asked me a lot of questions that I didn't know the answers to. Some of the things she wanted to know, even Jesus Christ with internet access couldn't have told her.

Mainly, she wanted to know what was going to happen.

And the only true answer to that one would have been, *So do I.*

At the end of it she said, "But why?"

And I couldn't answer that one with any certainty, either.

All I could say was, "I don't know. She started to tell me, but she wasn't making much sense. She says she doesn't want to come back. You know how she can be. But I think she scared herself as much as us. I reckon she'll be fine once we can get her home."

We ended the call and I headed back toward the Family Room. Being in there was rather like having the use of a business lounge in an airport. I don't know whether I appreciated the extra privacy, or felt oppressed by the isolation of it.

The fact of it was, I wouldn't have swapped places with Sophie for anything. It was bad enough being here, but imagine the agony of being half a world away.

Kate O'Brien was coming out of the treatment area just as I was reaching to open the door.

"Mister Bishop," she said.

"How's she doing now?" I said, and I moved to hold the Family Room door open so she could go in ahead of me. But she put her hand on my arm and gently manoeuvred me forward so that I went in first. Her touch was light and her scent made my heart race for a moment.

Nothing personal, nothing sensual; it just reached in and pushed the woman button.

When I got into the room and turned around, I found myself facing a small crowd who were shuffling in right behind me. They must have been somewhere close by, ready to gather at a signal. Leading them in was the doctor that I'd spoken to earlier. Beside him was a nurse, and in at the back came the dark-haired Clinical Coordinator. I was told later that they'd tried to get hold of someone from the chaplain's office as well, but there hadn't been time.

I suddenly felt outganged as they all arranged themselves into in that absurdly small space, and when Kate O'Brien then closed the door it was as if the entire world contracted to the stuffy cube within those four walls.

"What?" I said. "What is it?"

It was the doctor who spoke.

"Let's sit down," he said.

"I'm fine like this," I said. "What is it?"

He said, "I'm deeply sorry, Mister Bishop, but we weren't able to save your daughter."

I waited to hear what he had to tell me.

I knew he'd just said something, but I'd no idea what he meant by it.

He went on, "She'd already begun convulsions when we started the treatment. That was a sign that her brain had become swollen as a result of the tricyclic overdose. She went into a coma and we couldn't pull her back. We tried everything we possibly could, but nothing helped. I'm sorry."

I looked at the nurse who was standing beside him. When I'd noticed her earlier on I'd thought that she was curt and just a little bit pissed-off. Now I saw that she was young and her eyes were full of tears.

I said, "I'm sorry. I'm just not taking this in."

Kate O'Brien said, "Gillian died, Mister Bishop. Would you like to see her?"

Even that didn't do it.

"Died?" I said. It was a familiar enough word but I'd suddenly lost all grasp of its actual meaning.

The others moved aside to let Kate O'Brien through.

"Sit down, Mister Bishop," she said.

I didn't want to, but she guided me and I sat down anyway. I'd no resistance. The doctor took the next chair.

"Fuck," I said bleakly.

"We'll take you through to her in moment," the doctor said. "First I have to explain to you what you're going to see."

I realized then that Kate O'Brien was holding my hand. I hung onto hers like I'd known her for years. The doctor was talking and some part of me was listening.

He repeated some of the things that Kate O'Brien had already told me. About Gillian's treatment, about the feeder tube and the IV lines. He told me that they weren't able to remove any of these as she was now, in law, a Medical Examiner's case. He warned me that her face could be swollen, that she'd have rashes. They'd cleaned off the traces of the liquid charcoal as much as they could, but it was viscous and difficult to handle and it tended to get everywhere and leave stains.

And I just sat there and stared at them all.

They got me to my feet so they could walk me out of there. I tried to do it on my own, but my legs just gave way as I started to rise. I felt numb. I felt as if I was really somewhere else, although I couldn't have told you where. I bumped into the furniture, and felt nothing. Kate O'Brien stayed by my side and kept a tight hold on my hand, and I held it back with an equal, desperate pressure. Her hand was small and slender.

Her hand was exactly like Gillian's.

The automatic doors to the treatment area parted before us. I had a sense of people scrambling out of the way as we approached. I walked in the middle of my retinue, and the populace scattered. They might have been walking me to my execution. I felt drained and uncomprehending.

They'd moved her out of the room where they'd been working on her for the past few hours; time that had slipped by me in a haze while I'd wandered in and out, scratched, drunk coffee, looked up at the sky, tried to make calls, thought my stupid thoughts. They'd put her in one of the non-acute treatment rooms on the other side of the trauma area.

When the nurse slid open the door and I saw the end of the gurney, my heart almost stopped in my chest and I didn't want to go on. It was a threshold that I didn't want to cross.

But with Kate O'Brien still holding my hand, I somehow kept moving. Then the two of us were inside the room and, once again, the world contracted to the four walls within which I stood.

They'd closed the blinds and they'd switched off all the lights apart from the big medical spotlight on its enormous balanced arm, which they'd set low and turned to point at the wall. It made a soft, indirect glow. The room was like a bare, disused kitchen, clean but without any character. There were wall cupboards and a worktop with a sink to my left. The bed was against the wall on the right.

There was one chair set out alongside the bed. That was for me.

I didn't go to it. I just stood there.

I knew it was her, of course. She looked exhausted. Her hair was wet and pushed back from her forehead. Her eyes were closed, but not completely. Her lips were parted and dry. The nasal feeder tube was still in place but they'd taped it back to make it less conspicuous. If you'd told me then that there had been a mistake and that this was really someone else, and that Gilly was sitting in the next room sipping cold water from a paper cup, I'd have believed you in an instant.

Kate O'Brien said, "You should sit with her for a while."

It took me a few seconds to organize my movements. She pulled out the chair for me and I sat down.

I didn't know what to do. I was like someone about to start on a journey, but who'd forgotten how to walk.

"You can touch her," Kate O'Brien said.

Gillian's hand was lying on the covers. I reached out and took it. It was warm, but the tips of her fingers were beginning to darken. I looked at her face. The flush of life had already left her skin.

Kate O'Brien backed out and closed the sliding door. I never even heard her go. Everyone left us alone after that.

"Oh, Gilly," I said helplessly.

Within half an hour, Gillian had grown so pale that I almost wouldn't have known her.

I don't remember the passage of time. I was lost. It was as if I'd been following a track in the mist, and the track had suddenly gone. I was reaching forward blindly, finding nothing.

Every now and again I was aware of voices outside, but their reality was a world away.

Kate O'Brien came in and spoke to me at some point, and all I remember is that I shook my head and she left.

That was my day.

Eight

I don't remember the drive home from the hospital. What I can recall is standing there in the middle of the house with all the lights on, looking at the scene we'd walked out of and feeling bewildered and disbelieving. Objects lay where they'd fallen. Not one thing was different. It didn't make sense to me. I'd been hit with a change so profound that I couldn't take it in. My mind wouldn't accept it. Access denied.

There was a card by the door with a number to call, that was the only alteration. The movers had turned up and hadn't been able to get into the house. Everything else was just as we'd left it. I stood there useless for a while and then I started to stir.

Over the next few hours I finished all the packing, vacuumed every room, scrubbed every surface, disinfected every drain. I lugged all of the boxes down into the living room and stacked them. Their pattern didn't please me and so I rearranged them twice before throwing myself onto the couch, momentarily exhausted. From there I could see that one of the boxes was slightly out of line, so I had to drag myself up and move them all again. Once up, I carried on.

Gillian had hardly done a thing to her room, so I did it all. Her clothes, her books, her magazines, everything. I packed, not for a dead girl, but for my living daughter. She was still alive to me. She couldn't die.

I wouldn't let her.

I'd no real and immediate sense of loss. But loss was a speeding truck at my heels, so close behind me that I could feel the heat of its grille at my back. The moment I stumbled, I'd be under it.

And grief? I felt no grief. What I felt was a terror of grief. Grief was a betrayal. Grief meant she was dead.

The first thing we'd done when we'd started the packing had been to strip all the beds and take the linen down to the big washer in the basement utility room. The linen wasn't ours, it belonged here. It would still be downstairs, the machine's cycle long finished, the sheets beginning to go stale in the drum.

I descended to the basement, switching on more lights as I went. The machine was silent but its red indicator was still on. I pulled the sheets and loaded them into the dryer, and then I looked to the bedcovers that we'd left heaped on the floor. Something in me wanted to protest. I'd been working flat-out for some hours now and I was starting to slow down, dragging myself through the motions. When I picked up the cover that had been on Gilly's bed, something fell out of the bundle and onto the floor.

I stooped to pick it up. It was Gilly's gingerbread lady doll.

This was a handmade rag doll in a gingham dress, looking exactly like a gingerbread figure with currant-button eyes. It had come from an indoor market in Wilmington. Gilly had always had a serious soft toy habit. With every one of them it was point, buy, and promptly forget, and the discards got heaped up in the corner of her room like diseased cattle at a furnace. The waste of it used to send me up the wall.

We'd been trying to change her ways with a general ban, but we were always caving in and making exceptions. This had been one of them. The dolls were handmade by the stallholder's wife. He told us how he'd met her on a blind date and they'd been married for thirty-two years. She gave the dolls names, and never used the same one twice — she kept a list and crossed names off it as she went along. She also sewed a little red heart onto every one. You had to pull the dress up like a pervert to see it, but it was there. Each doll was meant to be as unique as its owner.

Well, that just did it. You might as well have walked in and harpooned me. I sat down on the basement floor and put my face into the bedcover. I rocked back and forth but as hard as I tried, I couldn't get a sound out. It stayed locked-in and I felt as if I would burst, like a stoppered cannon.

I don't know how long this went on, but it was paused by a faint sound from upstairs.

I could hear a ring tone. It came from my cellular phone, recharged from its time in the car, and it was still going when I reached it. The phone lay on a chair where I'd slung it, along with my jacket.

I started to say, "Hello?" but it wasn't a person, just the message service. When the message started I heard a half-familiar voice say something like, *John? Just listen to this.* It wasn't a brilliantly clear connection but I could just about make out what came next. What came next was a girl's voice. I couldn't hear what she said first.

The signal got better as I took a couple of steps to move closer to the window. Outside, the first streaks of daylight were appearing in the sky over the lake.

"*Nothing's working,*" I heard her say then. "*Nothing helps. Oh, God, what have I done? It hurts. It hurts so much.*"

I felt as if I'd been punched in the stomach and it had gone right through.

Now I could just hear a deep, shuddery breathing, the sound of lips only inches from the receiver.

"*Why aren't you here?*" she said.

My head spun and I put a hand out to steady myself, just in case I fell. Not looking, misjudging the distance, grasping at the air before I found something solid.

Then there was a lot of fumbling with the phone and I could hear that she was starting to cry, but quietly.

"What isn't working?" I said, forgetting that I was talking back to a recording. "Where does it hurt? Where are you?"

"*I want Daddy,*" she said.

The call ended.

"Gillian?" I was saying as the signal cut out. "Gillian, if it's you, speak to me. It's daddy."

I moved again but it was no use, the message was over.

Then came a man's voice. This next message was brief and to the point. He just spoke and then hung up.

"You don't have to panic yet," he said. "She didn't die."

Nine

People go mad, of course. The mind starts to dictate its own reality. They see coded messages in the soap operas on TV. There are secret instructions in the license plates of passing cars, placed there by God for their eyes alone.

There's nothing irrational about it.

At least, not to them.

Was I trying to impose meaning on a world that suddenly had none? I'd heard what I'd heard, and some sneaking part of me clung to a belief in the impossible. My daughter was dead. I knew exactly where her body lay right now. If this was being mad, there was something awesome in it. Something like ecstasy.

I caught sight of myself in an elevator mirror on the way up to my office. All that registered was that my eyes were like a couple of lasers in deep, dark holes and the knuckles on the hand clutching Don Farrow's phone were white.

My office was on a corner of the fourth floor at the top of the admin block. All of the other consultants had moved out and their suites were being refitted. Even though the building had hardly been up for five minutes, there was a definite end-of-an-era feel about this entire section of it. The pictures were off the walls and there was new furniture in the empty offices.

Miranda started to say her usual good morning as I went through, and I heard her falter as she looked up from her keyboard and saw me.

"Mister Bishop..." she said.

"Miranda," I acknowledged. "Can you get Rose Macready for me?"

I went into my office, and sat heavily in my leather chair. It sighed, expensively. The cheap ones fart.

Miranda buzzed me and I picked up the phone. A couple of seconds later, I was talking to Rose.

"It's about a Donald Farrow," I said. "I need some info. Can you give me a home address and anything else you have?"

"I'll zap it over," she said.

During the call I was aware of Miranda moving into the doorway and watching me. When I hung up, she said, "Is everything all right?"

I could have told her.

I almost did.

But even as my mind took a run at it, I felt it shear away from the challenge like a stunt rider who knows that he just doesn't have the speed for the jump.

Miranda returned to her own outer office, and I sat back in the chair.

If I'd been able to explain it to anyone, Miranda would have been the first person I'd have turned to. She was my in-house ally and confidante. I don't know what her age was. The only ungenerous urge I'd ever had toward her had been to tell her that the hair color she used had no counterpart in nature, but I'd managed to keep that to myself.

I glanced at the photograph of Gilly and Sophie that I kept on the corner of the desk. It was just a snapshot in a stand-up cardboard frame. It didn't hurt me to look at it and I marvelled at this, a little. The way you do when you get a local anaesthetic and you can watch them cut into your skin while you feel nothing. You almost want to take the knife yourself, and cut some more. Even though you know how sorry you'll be later.

Miranda buzzed through to me then.

"It should be with you now," she said.

I swung the chair around to face my desktop terminal. A couple of clicks and my password brought up the intranet file that Rose had sent over. It was the barest information about Donald Farrow, a janitorial technician for the deep materials storage area known as The Spirit Box. Date of employment, place of residence…it was little more than an electronic Rolodex card. From this it looked as if he was a low-paid bottle-washer in the vault. He worked below-ground but he didn't have clearance for the stacks. Not much status and no responsibilities.

Miranda was back in the doorway.

"That's all they can let us have," she said. "You'll need special clearance to see the personal data."

"This is fine," I said. "It's exactly what I needed."

Miranda said, "Is this something I ought to know about?"

"No," I said, rising. "Don't worry about it. I'm going out."

"Now?"

"I don't know how long I'll be," I said.

~

I drove North out of town on Tryon Street and found myself on a long road of old businesses in old brick buildings, of closed-down properties, of wide-open acreages where factories had once stood and now truck trailers were stored. Here were all the old industries that had sprung up along the railway lines, most of them now withering and dying. Used-car dealers had moved in because the land was available and the area was cheap, but they had to safeguard their stock behind railings and razor wire. Most of the stock didn't look worth much protection anyway. You could buy coal, ice, used tires, lumber. I saw a church that was like a shack long overdue for demolition, with a basketball hoop on its end wall.

Somewhere out here I'd find Don Farrow's house. And if he was home, I'd find Don Farrow. If he wasn't…I don't know. I wasn't stupid. But it seemed that nothing I'd ever considered certain could be relied upon any more. Part of me was desperate to know what he might tell me, another part of me wanted to stay in a place where no explanation existed. In this solid world of rust and rails and barbed wire and weeds, I felt as if I was chasing a wraith.

I made a turn off the road and, within a few hundred yards, found a set of disused-looking railroad tracks. I went under a low trestle bridge and came out into a wooded lane. There were more buildings out here; an entire settlement of them, in fact. My guess would be that this had once been dense woodland and they'd cleared as little of it as they needed to get the houses in. Most of these were one-story and inexpensive-looking, with open front yards and shaded porches. Some had immense mature trees springing up out of the ground no more than a couple of yards from their front doors.

The area certainly had an atmosphere. It was the kind of housing I always think of as your standard American, flag-over-the-porch, car-on-the-lawn, junk-in-the-yard eccentric. You see it deep in the country and on the fringes of every American town or city. No two properties are ever the same, and for variety you can add a big satellite dish, or some concrete lawn animals, or some lounge furniture for sitting out on. I reckon the lounge furniture and a barbecue are mandatory items. It's as if the life explodes out of these places like the stuffing out of a sofa, and nobody's too concerned to keep it back in. They're places of weed growth, rickety security, young families, cracked asphalt, and the mournful score of distant freight trains.

I cruised the area like a kerbcrawler. I looked at every building I passed. They were all in different styles, some of them fenced and painted and well kept-up, the ramshackle and the respectable co-existing side by side.

I couldn't see any people anywhere, but I could hear dogs in every back yard. As I rolled along with my window down they glimpsed me through the gaps in the houses, and a kind of Mexican wave of their yelping rolled along with me.

You had to look hard to be sure that some of these places were even inhabited. I passed one with a notice nailed to it declaring it to be unsafe, its furnishings piled up along the sidewalk as garbage for collection, and it didn't look all that different from the rest.

I located Don Farrow's house by the names on its mailbox.

The front porch was enclosed by mosquito wire screens. The woodwork needed paint and was streaked with sap from the branches of an overhanging tree. I pressed the bell and peered through the wire. Nothing happened. Now that the dogs had shut up, I could hear a radio playing somewhere.

A car drew up in front of the house next door and let out a middle-aged woman in matching pink top and trousers. Then it drove off. The woman was carrying a lunch-counter sandwich. She saw me trying the bell again and, as she was stepping up onto her own porch, she called over, "You can usually find someone around the back."

"Thanks," I said. "Do you know if they've got a dog I should watch out for?"

"If they ever did," she said, "it moved out in disgust. Are you their landlord?"

"No."

"Pity. He's long overdue a visit."

I went around the side of the house. The yard behind it wasn't enclosed, and despite the neighbor's reassurance I kept a wary eye out for anything with teeth and a turn of speed.

What I found was two boys in lawn chairs, and no lawn. The grass all around the sides of the yard was overgrown but in the middle was just bare dirt, worn smooth. In the middle of the bare patch stood a red Chevrolet truck, raised up on a jack and with its transmission on the ground beside it.

I don't know if the boys were supposed to be working on the truck, or if they were just thinking about it. There were some tools lying around, but the boys certainly weren't getting their hands dirty. One had thick glasses and wore a red bandanna on his head, like a pirate. The other was dark and wore long shorts under a big T-shirt that read *Pittsburgh Steelers Research Triangle Fan Club.*

The radio was on the ground between them, as was a small stack of empty beer cans. Beer at this time in the morning? I couldn't have faced it. The radio was on a long power lead that went all the way back into the house.

My appearance took them both by surprise. The one with the bandanna said, "Help you?"

"Is either one of you Don Farrow?" I said.

"What's it concerning?" the other boy said. He seemed the sharper and more wary of the two.

"Is that a yes or a no?"

"Don isn't here," the first one said.

I said, "I'm with his employers. He didn't show up for work and I really need to talk to him about something."

"He's been around," Bandanna Boy said. "But he isn't here now."

"He isn't sick, then?"

I watched the brows of the two of them knot as they computed furiously. I could guess what they were thinking. What would get Don into trouble, what would keep him out of it? They weren't the brightest of specimens, although my guess was that they'd both had an education. I wouldn't have been surprised to learn that they and Don Farrow had been classmates. Live cheap, share the rent...it's something you can carry on with after graduation. For a while.

I said, "It's not a trick question. I'm not the company truant officer. Can't you say where he is?"

"Nobody knows," the boy in the T-shirt said.

"He isn't sick," the other said. "But he's busy. He comes, he goes, is all I know. It's been a few days."

"I'd like to take a look in his room," I said.

"You can't do *that,*" Bandanna Boy said. "Where do you think you are?"

"Look," I said reasonably. "I need to find him. I'm going to walk into the house and look in his room whether you think that's a good idea or not. I don't have the time or the inclination to explain my reasons to you. If you're worried about what he'll say, tell him I made you some kind of a threat that scared the shit out of you."

"Like what?"

"I'll leave that to you," I said. "Whatever you think he'll believe. All I'm saying to you is, look into my eyes and tell me if you really think this is worth giving me a problem over."

From what I'd seen in the elevator mirror that morning, one such look ought to do the trick.

As it seemed to.

"Shit," the boy in the T-shirt said plaintively, and he looked at the other. "What are we gonna do?"

"Call the cops if you like," I said. "But before you do that, be certain there's nothing in the house that you wouldn't want them to see."

The screen door was closed, but it had no latch and the main door behind it was wide open. This led into a short, dark hallway with rooms leading off. The two boys crowded in behind me, but they stopped abruptly and almost collided with each other when I swung around to face them.

"Which is Don's room?" I said.

"You've got some nerve," Bandanna Boy said.

"Think about this," I said. "It's happening, you can't stop it. If you don't tell me which room's his, I'll just have to look in them all."

He saw the logic. Sullenly, he pointed to one of the nearest doors. I tried it, but I couldn't open it because it was locked.

That made him grin.

"*Now* what are you going to—" he began, but before he could finish speaking I abruptly threw my weight up against the door and it popped right open, as if the frame had warped so much there was no more than an edge of metal to hold it shut. It took no great violence.

I could hear them outside, talking in low urgent voices as I prowled around Donald Farrow's room. There were more clothes strewn around the floor than there were in the closet, and the place stank like a wrestler's trunks. I looked through the drawers, I opened the cupboards. Farrow's main assets appeared to consist of an X-Box, several hundred science fiction paperbacks, and a wall poster of Sarah Michelle Gellar.

There was a writing desk with several unwashed mugs and a lot of days-old crockery being used as paperweights. I shifted some of these aside to see what they covered. The two boys had gone quiet as I was doing this, and without having to check I knew with certainty that they'd moved into the doorway and were watching me. I could almost feel the weight of their gaze as it fell on my back.

Without turning or looking around, I said, "Did Don ever mention the name of Gillian?"

"Gillian who?" Bandanna Boy said.

I looked back at him. "Did he?"

The boy shrugged and said, "his girlfriend's name is Rachel."

I spotted something then. The Buffy poster was on the wall alongside the doorway and I could see that there was a corner of white sticking out from its lower edge. Nothing huge, but enough to catch the eye. I went over, and worked a single sheet of notepaper out from behind it. The wall was flimsy and the poster was held up by glue-tack. Farrow had hidden the paper there and my bursting through the door must have jarred it down.

It was Macdonald-Stern company notepaper, or a scan of it. If he'd left it out in plain sight amongst the rest of the mess that littered the room, no-one would ever have noticed it. I started to glance through what was written there. After the first few lines I felt the hairs on the back of my neck begin to rise.

I held it up and looked at the boys again.

"Do you know what this is?" I said, but both of them shook their heads and neither looked shifty or guilty about it.

I folded the letter twice and stowed it safely in the inside pocket of my jacket.

"I reckon I can fairly call this company property," I said. "So I'll be taking it with me."

Ten

The rock terrace was an extensive indoor garden in the Macdonald-Stern building's atrium. The atrium was so high that it had felt like the outdoors even before we'd put in the natural-stone waterfall and piped in the jungle sounds. We'd given it different levels and semiprivate areas, like something out of the Swiss Family Robinson. It was designed to be a common working space, but an informal one. A natural focus for everyone on the site. It was manned by two stewards with a servery that offered coffee and soft drinks, but no alcohol.

The stewards were like the Pool Boys on an expensive ocean liner. Young, tanned, cheerful. They even dressed the part, in blue Hawaiian shirts and white knee-length shorts. One of them saw me and said, "Good morning, Mister Bishop."

"I'm here to see Bill Nickles," I said.

"He's on the palm deck. Can I bring you anything?"

"Thanks. I don't think so."

Bill Nickles had taken over a table in the shade of some transplanted coconut palms, and it looked as if he'd been combining work with a long, late breakfast. He'd been brought in from Seattle to replace Brice Jernigan after Jernigan's near-fatal heart attack only three weeks before, and he was still working to get up to speed. I could see from some way off that he had stacks of papers all over the table, along with an empty cafetiere and a plate of doughnuts. It was the kind of breakfast that had almost done for his predecessor. I saw that someone was with him already and I recognized Mike Munn, our Area Recruiter.

Mike was talking earnestly. Bill Nickles was listening and nodding, reading something at the same time. As I waited, I tried for a calm attitude and tried not to hold myself like a dog who's impatient to dive into a fight.

Nickles was a broad, avuncular figure in a loud checked shirt. I'd glimpsed him before this, but I hadn't met him properly. He didn't look like your regular CEO. He looked like someone who ought to have been running a lumber yard and letting his grown-up sons do all the lifting.

I wasn't sure whether to approach or hang back, but then Nickles looked up and caught my eye. He called to me by name, even though we'd never been introduced, and beckoned me in.

Mike Munn belatedly caught on that his part of this was over, and gathered up his stuff. He nodded to me as he went.

"John," he said, and I saw his eyes take in my rumpled clothing. I got the sense that his hadn't been a good meeting. I moved into his place.

"I'll be with you in one second," Bill Nickles said, and continued to scan his way down the piece of paper that he was holding in his hand.

Then he dropped it into a file and closed it, pushed the file aside, and turned to me.

He said, "Unbelievable amount of detail. I hardly have to tell you about that. Given that you're probably responsible for most of it."

"We design you a system, Mister Nickles," I said. "We don't tell you what to put through it."

"Call me Bill," he said, and he made a gesture with a circling finger to indicate our surroundings. "Whose idea was all this?"

"You like it?"

"I'm still trying to decide."

"It's to encourage open association. Informal but creative."

"You think that up, or steal it?"

"I'll tell you straight, Bill, we steal everything. We don't believe in making our mistakes at your expense."

"That's a good line," Nickles said. "I've got another one for you. Give people the chance to dick around all day, and they'll never go to work."

"That's why the coffee's free at your desk," I said, "but out here you pay for it."

He picked up one of his files, didn't find what he was looking for under it, and moved to another.

"So, what's the Spirit Box?" he said.

I said. "It's what everyone calls the secure vault where we store the client materials."

"And what's happening with it to justify me squeezing you into my schedule at twenty minutes' notice?"

"This," I said, and I took out the paper that I'd found in Don Farrow's room.

He studied it for a few moments and then started sorting through his files with a new purpose. When he'd found the one he had in mind, he drew out a sheet of facsimile paper and laid it alongside.

He looked from one to the other. For me they were upside down, but it was obvious that the content of the two was identical. They'd been printed in a loopy italic font that was hard to mistake. The absent Donald Farrow was clearly up to no good.

What I'd placed before Nickles was the original of an anonymous letter, an offer of goods that read like a ransom note. The address for reply was just a box number and a zip code. I wasn't all that well up on zip codes, but I could see that it wasn't for anywhere local. There were several spelling mistakes in the text. You can't exactly call it bad typing when a thing's been written on a computer, but the style and the layout gave it that kind of feel. Everything was crammed up at the top and the message was one long ramble.

After the offer came a list. There were six of the number codes that we used in classifying and assigning materials to their places in the vault. These were the identifiers that we attached to every sample in our care. All of those listed appeared to come from the same basic group. I was certain that the numbers would belong to the cut samples I'd seen earlier that morning. Next to each was an asking price of two hundred and fifty thousand dollars.

When he'd done comparing, Bill Nickles looked at me directly. His eyes were a very pale blue and his gaze was unblinking. Whatever else his manner might be saying, these were don't-fuck-with-me eyes.

"Where did this come from?"

I told him where I'd found it, but I didn't tell him anything about Gillian or the phonecall or why I'd gone out there.

"What about yours?" I said then.

"Last Thursday, one of our Vice-Presidents had a call from a friendly body in a rival company. That company had received a fax offering them a selection of chemical samples out of this company's vault. Then we heard that Pfizer and Glaxo got the same document. This document. Give me your assessment."

"Well," I said. "On the one hand, these are low-grade and low-priority materials. We're holding them for a client who picked them up cheap about ten years ago in the former Soviet Union. They're from labs and University departments that went to the wall under democracy. It was like one big fire sale and the documentation is nil. We don't know what any of it is, we don't know what any of it's for."

"And on the other hand?"

"For all anybody knows, there could be cures in there for diseases that the CIA hasn't even invented yet. But aside from that. Suppose a man walks into your house while you and your family are asleep, and he takes a glass of water and walks out again. Is it fair to say that the cost of the water is not your biggest reason for worry?"

Nickles looked at me. "So?"

"Let me have whatever I need to find Farrow," I said. I neglected to tell him that I didn't give the proverbial rat's ass about the company, its secrets, or the security of its vault. All that I wanted to know concerned that message.

"Understand this, John," Nickles said. "No police, no press. We're in the confidence business. The last thing we need is for something like this to get back to our clients. This is strictly within the family. Do you understand me, John?"

"Strictly within the family," I said.

~

It was all over in fifteen minutes or less. After I'd left Bill Nickles I went into the nearest washroom, locked myself in a cubicle, and sat there holding my head in my hands as if I could keep it from exploding.

I don't know for how long.

What did I think I was doing? There was a serious possibility that I was on the point of losing my mind, here. Even worse, the prospect wasn't an entirely unattractive one. What I yet had to deal with was just too enormous to be embraced, and I had no will to embrace it at all. How much easier it would be just to lay it all down, never even engage with it, and retreat into some soft-sided retirement home of madness.

I was tormented. I don't know of any other word that can describe it more precisely. As if the fact of losing her wasn't bad enough. I'd held her dead hand, yet she'd called to me. Or something had called in her voice. I didn't know what, how, or why. I didn't believe in ghosts, although I think I might have been ready to.

When I closed my eyes, I could see her.

I can see her even now.

Imagine this.

You're dreaming you're on a train, and the train is in motion. It's night. You look out of the window, and there's another train on the next track. You're looking straight over into a moving carriage that's only a yard or two from your own.

What you see there is a separate and self-contained world. The carriages seem to weave in an uneasy, disconnected way as the two trains roll onward.

But there she is. She's in there alone. A traveller on a different journey. Eyes averted, otherwise engaged. She isn't aware of you. You can shout but she won't hear.

If she'd look up, she'd see you. But she doesn't. Perhaps you've been forgotten. Perhaps she has no will to find you.

Now the tracks begin to separate.

Slowly the other train begins to peel away into the night, and there's nothing you can do to stop it or call it back. It has some other destination.

There were all kinds of things you might have said back there on the platform, but you passed up the chance.

Framed by the window, her figure grows smaller until it's lost from your sight. Never once did she look out. Now it's too late. Now she's too far away. The carriage windows are like a stream of tracer bullets arcing away into the darkness.

You keep on watching.

You keep on watching even though there's nothing more to see.

~

I came out of the cubicle wiping my eyes on a handful of toilet paper. I went over to the basins and, after I'd splashed myself with cold water for the second time that morning, I examined myself in the mirror. This time I tried to be honest with myself.

I looked awful. My face, never exactly pretty to begin with, looked like a bag of rocks. I took a deep breath, pulled everything in, and found that if I counted to ten, then my mind would start to clear and my hands would grow steady. It was a trick, no more. It was as if all the secret stuff inside was a burst and ruptured mess, and but with this effort I could hold the broken shell together around it.

I went back to my office. I didn't dare look at Miranda as I passed her desk.

"Can you ask Rose to come over?" I said to her, and then I dived for cover where I hoped she wouldn't follow.

~

Rose Macready looked at me closely and said, "You really did have a lousy night, didn't you?"

In my mind's eye I saw myself asking her to close the door, and then sitting her down and telling her everything. I knew that she'd listen if I did. In fact, she probably wouldn't forgive me if I didn't.

I wouldn't exactly say that we'd been lovers. We'd been friends and then we'd got drunk once and it had become physical. I couldn't call it a mistake because after that it had happened a few more times. Too often to pretend there was no real intent. I'd felt guilty for a while, but perhaps never as guilty as I ought.

It wasn't a looks thing. She was attractive in a businesslike way when in makeup, but she could be quite plain without it. She believed herself to be a little on the plump side, and didn't like to be naked with the lights on. All kinds of things interested her, and for a while I happened to be one of them.

What had taken place between us had been entirely in the present tense, with no thoughts of a future. Even while it had been going on, I'd never felt that I was standing at the beginning of some startling new path I might have followed. It had changed nothing in my life. It had been more like a safety valve that had allowed me to carry on with things as they were, at a time when things hadn't been all that good.

She said, "So what's happening?" and the moment passed, taking the urge to confession with it.

I gestured toward the L-shaped meeting area in the corner of the office, two good sprawling sofas and a coffee table, and as we moved over I said, "I'm trying to get my hands on our missing janitor."

"Don Farrow?"

"He's the one."

I flopped down wearily but of course, a professional woman in a business suit doesn't sprawl. She perched herself on the edge of the other sofa with her knees together and made me feel like Orson Welles in a hammock.

"Did you try the address I sent you?" Rose said.

"First place I looked," I said. "They haven't seen him since the weekend. Got to be careful on this one, Rose. He's offering stuff for sale out of the vault. It's worth nothing but it makes a nonsense of our client guarantees."

"I can guess what Bill Nickles is thinking," she said. "It's like being in a company that gets hit by hackers. I was with an outfit once where someone broke into the system and triggered a half-million loss in business. Security tracked him down, but they didn't prosecute. They bought him off and sat on the story. The accountants covered the damage and that was that. The last thing you do is admit you were ever vulnerable."

I pinched the bridge of my nose between my eyes. They were hot and they hurt.

"Whatever," I said. "To be honest with you, Rose, I just want to find this Farrow boy and talk to him."

"So," Rose said. "What more do you need from me?"

"All the detail we've got on him," I said, "plus anything on his co-workers and all the rest of that department. Refer any clearance questions up to Bill Nickles. Does that sound okay?"

She took out a little PalmPilot and made a note.

"I'll put Marcie on it," she said. "Anything else?"

"Yeah," I said. "Just fix my life for me."

I'd meant it as one of those throwaway lines, but it came out sounding more heartfelt than anything I'd been intending.

It was too late to take it back. She looked at me, and I avoided meeting her eyes. I scratched at the back of my neck and felt as if I was squirming under the inspection of someone who knew me far too well for comfort.

"John?" she said. "John, why don't you tell me what's wrong?"

"I'm sorry, Rose," I said. "If I was able to tell you, I would."

$\mathcal{E}leven$

Even with traffic, it rarely took more than twenty minutes to get back to the lake house at the end of the day. A short enough journey, but today I didn't want to make it. There was nothing for me there.

On the other hand, I had nowhere else to go.

I hadn't slept in thirty-six hours. Gilly had been dead for less than twenty-four. I hadn't called Sophie to tell her but I was sure she'd have heard it from the hospital by now. It was wrong of me, but I couldn't help it. The unanswered calls and messages on my phone were all from her. The longer I left speaking to her, the more impossible it felt.

As I sat there holding the wheel while most of the cars around me were pulling out of their parking spaces, I realized that I hadn't eaten anything in most of that time, either. I still had no appetite, but I had an unpleasant aching feeling that stood in for one. I'd been feeling dizzy for a while. Now that I'd settled into the seat, I felt sick as well. Empty sickness. All acid and bubbles, and a pain as if a live rat was trying to claw its way up into my chest.

It didn't seem right that I should eat. It didn't seem right that I should do anything that was for me.

But what else *could* I do?

Instead of heading out toward the lake I headed into town, looking for somewhere. Fast food, a coffee shop, I really didn't care. I put the radio on to fill out the silence. There was the usual choice of Christian Broadcasting, Country music, or rock stations where everybody sounded like Aerosmith. Within a few seconds there came a static blip from the speakers like an eardrum tearing, and then a few seconds later I heard an accompanying thunder in the distance.

The sky grew dark and I switched on the lights. As I passed under a road bridge the rain came down out of nowhere, and so I dropped my speed and turned on the wipers.

Then I spied a place, just beyond a roadside store that sold transit-damaged furniture. It wasn't part of any chain or franchise and so it didn't have the usual enormous see-it-a-mile-away sign in its forecourt, just a board on the front of the building.

I pulled into the parking lot. There were a number of vehicles there, pickups and sedans, but there was space just a few yards from the entrance.

The rain was really pounding down now. Even with the wipers going at full speed I could barely see to park. It sluiced down the windshield in rivers and, as I waited for the downpour to ease off, the restaurant's lights shone through it and cast a slow-moving pattern over the car's interior. I looked down at my hands, and it was flowing over my skin like something molten. It was an effect that I'd seen in movies. They do it when they want to make you think of tears. To me it looked as if I was deep underwater, drowning and feeling nothing.

The rain just kept on coming, and so after a while I got out of the car anyway. In the half-dozen strides it took me to get to the door, I was soaked. Unlike the thunderstorm rains of August, this was cold. And then, when the air conditioning inside the restaurant hit me, it was like a shock that went all the way through to my bones.

I don't know what had happened to the owners of all the cars, but there couldn't have been more than five people in the place. It proved to be a small diner with a B-grade sanitation certificate and an elderly man at the register making change in slow motion. There were little ornamental knick-knacks everywhere, the kind you might win on fairgrounds. They'd even put the certificate in a gilded frame, as if it represented something they'd really struggled to achieve.

But the coffee was hot and the steak, I think, would have been exceptional if I'd been in any mood to appreciate it. As it was, I just sat there and put it away. When the waitress came around giving out refills, she stopped by my table and as she was topping up my cup, she said, "I like what you've done with your hair."

I looked up at her blankly. She was shaped like a cottage loaf and reminded me of a schoolteacher I'd had when I was small.

"Excuse me?" I said.

She put out her free hand and stroked me like a cat, not hard.

"Those highlights," she said, and moved on with her flat shoes slapping on the vinyl floor.

Along with the menu and all the other stuff on the table before me, there was a sugar jar with a chrome spout. I picked it up and angled it so that I could see my reflection.

Highlights?

"They're not highlights," I said. "It's just grey."

But she'd already forgotten me, and was now exchanging a few pleasant words with another unaccompanied man a few tables along.

"Just grey," I said again quietly.

I stared at my distorted image in the chrome for a while longer, and then I set the jar down and pushed it away.

~

The rain had stopped and it had gone dark when I started to drive back. I wasn't going particularly slowly, but it seemed as if every car on the road was anxious to pass me. They'd come up behind, their lights would stay close on my tail for a while, and then they'd pull out at the first opportunity and speed off on a mission to God knows where.

My headlights threw long shadows from the realtors' signs at the end of the approach road, and the shadows zoomed across the grass as I made the turn. I could feel my heart hammering in my chest, as if I was closing in on some intimidating appointment.

Then, within minutes, I was home.

No. Not home. I got out of the Lexus, and I looked at the unlit house. I could hear the wind in the branches, the calling of some night bird out across the water.

I felt as if I needed someone to help me through this part.

But there was no-one.

Gilly had loved this house on sight. But I think at twelve years old we could have shown her anywhere with its own boat house and swim dock and a speedboat on the water, and she'd have fallen for it just as hard. Lake Wylie and Lake Norman had been created some years ago when Duke Power had flooded the Catawba River to serve two nuclear plants. That had worried me when I'd first heard it—did I really want a child of mine swimming in that stuff?—but it didn't seem to worry anyone else.

Everyone's idea of a dream home was a two hundred year old house overlooking the lake. But this was as close as you'd get to it. The fact of it was that all of the old houses were at the bottom of the lake and everything on the shore was brand new.

I stopped by the mailbox and took out the key. That morning I'd called the movers' twenty-four hour number and left a message to say where they could find it.

There was no mail, but there were a couple of other things. By the hallway light I saw that one was a business card with the blue hornets'-nest logo of the Charlotte-Mecklenburg Police Department over an officer's name and contact number. The other was a note from Kate O'Brien, urging me to call her and enclosing a leaflet for a support outfit called Kindermourn.

The movers had been back. All of the boxes were gone, and the living area looked startling and bare. They'd taken everything but my suitcase. Gillian was supposed to pack a bag as well, but she hadn't. I went upstairs to see if there was anything that had been missed, but our mark on the place had been thoroughly removed.

I stood in the bathroom before the empty cabinet, and I closed my eyes. This was where I'd stood. The exact moment was still there before me. If I opened them, perhaps it would replay and I could handle it differently this time.

I opened them. But nothing had changed and she still wasn't there.

What was that?

Someone had called out my name downstairs.

I was too worn-out to feel surprised or even concerned. I wiped my face on my sleeve and went to see who it was and what he wanted.

There was a policeman standing in the middle of my living room. He wasn't searching the place or even looking around, he was just waiting there.

"Mister Bishop?" he said. "You left your door wide open."

"Did I?" I said. "I'm sorry." I don't know why I was apologising. "I'm finding it hard to think straight," I said, and then I heard myself saying, "My daughter died."

"I know all about that, sir. I escorted you to the hospital."

I looked at him properly, then. At him, not just at the uniform. But I didn't actually recognize him. I had a memory of the part he'd played, but otherwise I was looking at a stranger.

I reached into my pocket and pulled out the card that I'd found in the mailbox.

"Is this you?" I said, showing it to him, and he inclined his head in confirmation. It was amazing to me that I couldn't remember his face or his presence at all.

"Forgive me," I said.

He waved that away. He said, "Your wife's been calling the department. Nobody knew where you were."

"I went to work."

He didn't actually show surprise, but I think that it threw him for a moment.

It took him a second or two to pick up again, and then he said, "Well, I don't believe any of us thought of that one."

I looked around helplessly. "I can't take it in," I said. "I know I should be dealing with it…but I'm walking around like…"

I tailed off because I didn't know *what* I was walking around like. What could I tell him? That the newly-dead call like sirens from the mist, and then vanish when we run toward them?

If I was looking for any sense of support or familiarity from the room, it wasn't there. Last week, this had been home. Now it was once more someone else's house. No part of what I'd lost was to be found here.

The patrolman said, "Is there anyone I can call for you? I mean, anyone who can come over?"

I shook my head.

"I feel as if everything's stopped," I said. "Nothing's going to move on for me until I can agree to what's happened. And the moment I do that…well, I can't do it."

"Why's that?"

"Because," I said, "it means walking out of the life with her in it and into a place where I just don't want to be. I know I need to face it, but I can't. I can't tell you how hard it is."

He thought for a second or two, and then he checked his watch.

"Excuse me for one moment, Mister Bishop," he said, and went outside.

I looked through the window and I could see him at his cruiser. He was standing by the open door of it and talking on the radio.

I switched on the outside light and then went out to join him. I stood there on what had once felt like my driveway, my hands in my pockets, waiting for him to finish. The night air seemed clean and washed-out. I couldn't understand how I could express myself so openly to a total stranger, and yet I couldn't find the words to call my wife.

When he'd finished on the radio, he came down to me and took my arm.

"Come inside with me, John," he said. "I want to talk to you."

We went back into the living area and we sat on the couch, a couple of feet apart. I touched my hand to my forehead. I couldn't sit back or relax.

He said, "Are there any other children?"

"No," I said.

"I've got two. One's more grown-up than I'd like her to be and the other one behaves like she'll never grow up at all. But it should have been three. We lost a boy at eighteen months to leukaemia. I'm not going to draw any comparisons, but I'm going to tell you this. People are going to tell you that time heals and you'll get over it. I'm saying that it doesn't and you never will. What's going to happen is that you'll make a life around what you've got. You'll fight it every inch of the way, because accepting it will feel like you're betraying your daughter. What I'm telling you is, that's all right. That's how it is."

"I'm not sure I'm feeling anything at all," I told him.

"I've seen this before," he said. "You're like a deer. His heart's blown out but his legs are still running 'cause his head doesn't know it yet."

"I just went to work and spent the whole day like there was nothing wrong."

"You don't look right, John. If nobody said so, they were being polite."

I had to concede that he was probably right. I'd thought that I'd been getting away with it, but I was sure now that I hadn't.

"What am I going to do?" I said.

"Well," he said, "there are some things you'll *have* to do."

I found that as long as the talk was about immediate and practical matters, I was fine. I was almost grateful to engage with those. It would probably take no more than a couple of days for the Medical Examiner's office to release her, he told me. Gilly's was not an unattended death, so it was very unlikely that a postmortem examination would be necessary. In place of one, all of her Emergency Room charts and notes would be passed along for the Examiner's attention.

I hadn't even thought of that. Could the prospect of my kid getting a post-mortem have made the last couple of days any worse? It was hard to imagine how, but it might.

When she was finally released, I'd have to decide whether I wanted to deal with her here or to ship the body home. Either way, I'd have to select a local mortician. There would be forms to fill in, declarations to sign. It was a big deal even to move a body across a state line, let alone across international boundaries.

Had she carried a donor card? I started to say no, but then I had to admit that I didn't know for certain. I guessed not. She was idealistic enough, but not that organized. I remembered Kate O'Brien at some point asking me whether it was something we'd ever discussed. I'd said that I couldn't think, and could we talk about it later. I realized now that this was as good as a refusal. Later was no use.

They couldn't have taken her major organs anyway, not after an overdose. I know it wasn't the right thing to feel, but a part of me was relieved that I hadn't had to decide.

It was getting so I didn't want my patrolman to leave; I wanted him to stay here and keep talking, filling the silence with detail.

But eventually he said, "Will your wife be coming over?"

"I don't know," I said.

I knew I couldn't talk to her. Not yet. Especially not since my last words had been a reassurance that the danger was over and all was well. We'd end up blaming each other, and I'd have the harder time of making it stick.

"Don't be alone," he warned me.

"I'm fine," I said.

"No," he said. "You're not."

~

I wandered the house for a while when he'd gone. Not occupying it. Haunting it. Strictly speaking, I was supposed to be in the hotel by now. Two rooms had been reserved. One for me, and one for Gilly.

Exhaustion was always one step behind me, waiting for me to falter, ready to invade.

In the end, I dropped onto the couch and curled my legs up underneath me. Don Farrow's phone was in my jacket. I'd kept it close to me all day, although it hadn't rung again.

It didn't ring now.

Twelve

Wednesday, March 16

Miranda said, "Some files came over from Rose Macready's department. I put them on your desk. She says the main stuff's in your mailbox and there's more to come."

"Thank you," I said.

"You didn't check your e-mail yesterday."

"I'll do it now."

I could tell from the way that Miranda was acting around me that I'd made a better job of my self-presentation this morning. She could still sense that something was wrong with me but she was a little more relaxed, a little less apprehensive. I have to say that I'd worked for her approval. I'd spent a half-hour under the shower and I'd dressed in laundered clothes from my suitcase. I'd shaved with my own razor, and with rather more care than yesterday.

You're like a deer. His heart's blown out but his legs are still running.

Because his head doesn't know it yet.

I spent a few minutes checking the inbox on my screen, glancing at the e-mails and skipping the jokes, most of which I'd seen in some form before. There were messages from my real bosses back in England as well as the routine stuff being circulated around Macdonald-Stern. There was one from Rose Macready with a big file attachment that I moved over into my documents folder to open and read later.

Then I looked at the paper files that Miranda had left for me. They were all marked Confidential but there was nothing too exciting in any of them. They were the employment details on everyone in Mickey Cheung's department who had access to the vault. All of them told variations on the same story. Everyone here was young, college-educated, inexperienced, and had a parent or other close relative who worked either at the plant or for one of Macdonald-Stern's associated companies. Or if the relative didn't work for Macdonald-Stern, there was some connection with the plant as a contractor or supplier.

There, separately, was Donald Farrow's job application form and details. I took out the letter that I'd found in his room and looked from one to the other. The form was handwritten and the letter was typed. But even on the briefest read-through, something was obvious. Don Farrow was not the author of the letter. Don Farrow was articulate, and he could spell.

The author of the letter managed neither.

Could the style have been put on? I didn't think so. It had the flavor of genuine ignorance, and I wasn't so sure that genuine ignorance could be faked. Like an adult can never match the spontaneity of a child's painting. You see it sometimes when they try to imitate children's art in magazine ads and posters, and something inside you sees it and always knows.

There was a basic conundrum, here. Someone had got it into their heads that anything, absolutely anything out of the Spirit Box must automatically be worth big money. Which suggested that they knew nothing of the realities of the setup.

But then, only someone with access could have taken the samples out.

And anyone with access would know better.

It dawned on me then that things only began to make any kind of sense if there were at least three separate people involved. The crude intelligence that had dreamed up the plan and composed the note; the person who'd actually lifted the substances; and Farrow himself, perhaps acting as some kind of a go-between.

Three, as a minimum. I was thinking along these lines when my phone rang.

"Hi, John," she said. "It's Rose."

"Thanks for the stuff," I said. "I'm looking at it now."

"There's more to come," she said. "Those are the active employees, but there's been a lot of churn in that department."

"I'll take whatever you've got."

"Marcie apologizes for the time that it's taking. Will you be at home tonight?"

"I'll be in some hotel," I said. "Wherever they've decided to put me. I was supposed to be out of the house two days ago."

"Okay," she said. "I'll see you."

"Yep," I said, and we both hung up.

~

"Mister Bishop. It's Kate O'Brien. How are you doing?"

"Hello, Kate. How do you *think* I'm doing?"

"Have you talked to your wife yet?"

"No."

"I have. She needs you now and I imagine you'll need her. Why aren't you returning any of her calls?"

"I don't know what I'll say."

"What does it matter?"

"She'll blame me because I was here and I'll blame her because she wasn't."

"Well, that's in no way a unique scenario, John. At least make a start. You've got a lot to deal with and there's a limit to how far you can run from it."

"Let me run from it until I'm ready."

"I don't seem to have any answer to that."

"How's the baby coming along?"

"He seems to be doing fine. He's got a kick like Jackie Chan. Thank you for asking."

"No problem."

"There's some paperwork you'll need to take care of. I'll be happy to help you with it, but it needs you to read it and sign. Will you come to me, or shall I come to you?"

"Does it have to be now?"

"It has to be soon. I can help you through it but I can't do it for you."

"Don't come out. I'll call in."

"Any idea when?"

"Soon. As soon as I can"

"Today?"

"Yeah. Today. Or tomorrow."

"I won't be in tomorrow. I'll be here today until six. Ask for me at the desk. If you don't come in, John, I'm going to come looking for you. There's something I've got to ask. Can you bring some of Gillian's clothes?"

"...?"

"Some of her clothes, John. Whatever you want her to be dressed in. Pick some things you know she really liked."

"Clothes. Right."

"I'll see you soon."

"Right."

Thirteen

Kate O'Brien led me into the bright and private corridors behind the ER on the way through to her office. It wasn't too busy out in front, but it seemed deserted back here. The corridors were wide, the light was soft and white, the floor an off-white vinyl tile with a pale green pattern let into it.

The office was a windowless room deep in the building that Kate shared with a couple of social workers and the other Patient Reps on the staff, none of whom was around. Three or more people would have crowded the place out. It was small like a ship's galley, and they'd had to fit it out like one. Instead of desks it had a shallow counter that ran all the way around the walls. Above the counter was a run of wall cupboards. At the back of the room were a PC computer and an inkjet printer, and beside them a well-used coffee maker with paper filters and a glass jug.

She pulled out a chair for me, and I sat. She explained all the forms and I listened and nodded. She gave me a pen and I signed. She gave me copies to take away with me, and I sat with them in my hand.

"Kate?" I said. "Can you tell me something?"

"As long as you're asking me something I know."

"How long did I stay with her?"

"You sat with her for nearly six hours."

"And after that, they took her away? To where?"

"To the hospital mortuary. She's there now. Do you want to see her again? I can arrange that for you."

I told her about the call, and the strange message that had followed it. I repeated them both word for word, as best as I could remember. *Don't panic yet. She didn't die.* I was fairly sure that my memory of them was exact. I told her about the turmoil I'd been experiencing ever since.

"Oh, John," she said, looking at me, lost for the words with which to respond.

"Don't pity me, Kate," I said. "You don't have to feel sorry for me. I know how it sounds. I don't know what to think of it either. I could be mad, I could be wrong. I just don't know."

"Come with me," she said, and started to get to her feet.

I followed Kate to the nearest elevators, slowing my pace to match her walk. Although she was small and slight, she was as game as any heavily pregnant woman I've seen. I felt a twinge of shame at her being involved in this part of my life when she had so much to think about in her own.

One of the doctors was waiting by the elevators. He was wearing the fatigues and the headgear and a surgical mask that he'd pulled down under his chin, and there was more beard sticking out in front of him than most people have hair on their heads.

Kate said to him, "Hi, how are you doing?"

"I'm not as pregnant as you," he said.

"I ain't pregnant," Kate said. "It must be something I swallowed."

The down elevator came and we took it, leaving him waiting to go up.

The hospital mortuary was in the basement. They didn't keep the bodies in those slide-out drawers you always see on the screen. There was one door, and it was like the door on a meat safe. To get to it you had to go through an anteroom where records were kept and the administration was done. On the other side of the door was a walk-in cold room, into which the cadavers were wheeled on their stretchers and laid on sheet plastic.

I got as far as the door, and I stopped.

I got right up to it. I even put my hands against it and closed my eyes and touched my forehead to the cold metal while Kate O'Brien waited with quiet patience.

But when it came right down to it, I couldn't face the thought of going in.

"Please," I said. "I can't do it. Can you check on her for me?"

Kate called the mortuary attendant. I should have thought harder about what I was asking her to do, but at that moment I was only thinking of my own pain. I realized my error when, a minute or so later, she came out of the cold room looking pale and shaken, and I was ashamed. Had I imagined that I was the only person in the world who could be distressed by Gilly's death?

"Nothing's changed, John," she said. "She's exactly the same as she was when you left her."

"I'd better see," I said, and I went inside alone. Kate was right. I saw what I had to and came out again.

"All right?" Kate said, and I nodded.

She was carrying a blue see-through sack that was tagged with Gilly's name.

"These are her clothes," she explained. "You can see why I had to ask you to bring in some others. These are pretty much ruined. The ones that weren't soiled had to be cut off her. When the time comes to move her to a funeral home you'll need something decent for them to dress her in."

"I'll have to buy her something," I said. "Everything else got packed away."

"Do you know her size?"

I shook my head.

Kate put the bag on a steel trolley, and the attendant pulled the items out one by one. He was gaunt and bony and brown-eyed, and I guessed that his head was newly-shaved because the skin uncovered by the cropping was grey. The rubber gloves he wore looked like the regular kitchen kind.

I may barely have been able to face the presence of her body in the cold room. But if I needed some tangible evidence of the hard reality of Gilly's death, here it was.

The first thing out was the T-shirt she'd been wearing. It had been raggedly cut with scissors and stained with the liquid charcoal they'd been putting into her. It had stiffened as it had dried, so that it was like something that was part-cloth, part-cardboard. It made a sound as he carefully prized it apart.

Kate and the attendant put their heads together to decipher the sizes on the labels, and I wrote them down. Her shoes came out last. By the time we'd finished, the entire outfit was laid out along the trolley. We must have looked like archaeologists analysing the remains from a dig. Her watch, her ear studs.

All hers, beyond question.

I could tell that Kate was watching me closely, but I focused on the task in hand. Most of what Gilly had been wearing on that day came from The Gap. I wouldn't even have been able to guess at the sizes myself. The numbers meant nothing to me. When it was all done, we left the attendant shovelling it all back into the bag. I'd have liked to have kept the jewellery — though cheap, it was hers — but nothing could be taken away until the Medical Examiner's release.

On the way back up, Kate's pager started to beep. She glanced at it and then switched off the noise and said to me, "How could you go to work?"

I looked down at her lump.

"How can you?" I said.

"It's not the same thing, John."

"No, I'm sorry," I said. "I know it isn't. I'm a mess, Kate. I'm not ashamed to admit it. I'm in a place I don't want to be and there's no road that'll lead me out of it."

"Did you call Kindermourn?"

"Yes," I lied.

"What did they say?"

"Just stuff," I said.

"You haven't called them."

"Leave me to do this, Kate," I said. "Please. It's hard enough. Everybody's got an idea of how I ought to feel, but nobody can walk in and take it all off me. And if they can't do that, then they can't do anything."

"John," she said, "I can't force you to accept help. But if you think you can do this on your own, you'll make it even harder than it already is."

"Difficult to imagine," I said.

"Believe it," she told me.

~

Back on the main floor, she went to find a phone and I went out to my car. It was in the visitors' lot and I had to walk past the entrance to the hospital's Cancer Center to get to it. They had a couple of benches set up outside the entranceway and someone had come out of there to smoke.

It was too late in the day to think about going back to the plant. What I had in mind was to drive down to the Southpark Shopping Center and see if I could find a branch of The Gap, where I'd get the help of some assistant to pick out replacements for everything of Gilly's that had spoiled. I didn't feel adventurous enough to go choosing new things for her. The last time I'd bought her clothes, she'd been about eight. And that was only because we'd been on a river and I'd somehow managed to tip the rental boat when we were getting out. We were miles from home and I remember squelching up the main street with her hand in mine in some little Yorkshire Dales town, looking for a clothing shop that would take one of my wet credit cards.

Now here I was, shopping for her again. Whatever else might happen, no-one would lay my kid out naked in a sheet. Life and death didn't come into it. Voices from beyond didn't come into it, either.

Even a doll can get a new dress.

Especially the kind which has your heart stitched onto it.

Fourteen

As a key contract worker on his way in, I'd merited a prestigious hotel near the University. Now that I was on my way out I got a Bel Air Inn behind a strip mall, with the South Boulevard traffic roaring by less than two hundred yards away. There was a coffee shop on the premises, and a Bojangles chicken restaurant a short walk across the parking lot for any gourmet resident who might happen to mourn the absence of a handy KFC or Dairy Queen. The motel was no more than a couple of years old and had internal corridor access, rather than the traditional design where your car's right outside your door.

I left the Lexus in one of the visitor spaces and went to check in.

The clerk at the desk said, "We were expecting you yesterday," and the sniffy way he said it made me bridle straight away. But he was young and I gave him a chance.

"I know. I'm sorry."

"I don't know that we've been able to hold the rooms," he said, shaking his head and moving things around on the part of the counter I couldn't see.

"No," I said, letting a warning note creep in, "but I'm sure your supervisor can find out for me."

I was in no mood for mind games. The rooms were on the company account and would be paid for whether I'd turned up or not. I didn't need to bring my excuse in a note.

He typed something on a keyboard, scrolled through a couple of pages on a screen.

"One-eighteen and one-twenty," he said. "They're adjacent."

"I'll only need one of them."

"It appears to be a confirmed booking."

"Bill the company however you like, but just give me the one key."

One-eighteen was on the ground floor on the far side of the building. I could use my key card on the door at the end of the main corridor. It was dark outside, but the parking lot was brightly lit. Out beyond the strip mall stood the usual mass of high-striding roadside neon.

As I was moving the Lexus I passed a twelve-seater Ford Clubwagon with Michigan plates. The driver had just got out at the front and his seven or eight passengers were getting out at the back. He was in his sixties, genial and rotund, wearing a dark baseball cap. They were all young men with the air of immigrant workers, and they had their shirts hanging over the backs of their jeans. They looked sheepish and uncertain. He was obviously bussing them to or from a job somewhere, and this was an overnight stop.

I could hear them all moving down the corridor as I looked around my room a few minutes later. I threw my case onto the farthest of the two queen-sized beds and my loose papers onto the bedside table. The connecting doors between this room and the next had been propped open. I went over and closed them, locking the one on my side. I had a brief glimpse of the other room as a mirror-image of the one I was in.

Should I shower? Should I eat? I didn't know. Whatever it took to keep the engine going. I put on the TV and didn't bother to change the channel. I didn't care what it was playing. I just wanted the noise.

It wasn't a bad room. Good carpet, nice lighting. Lots of space. A serious bathroom with a huge shower stall.

I sat there for a while and then I went out to find my way to the coffee shop.

I was in the coffee shop when Rose Macready found me about half an hour later.

~

"Hi," she said, standing over my table, and I must have looked like some kind of an idiot as I gawped up at her.

"Rose?" I said.

"Miranda told me which hotel. Are you on your own, or..." She tailed off, as if she hadn't thought quite far enough ahead to imagine what the exact opposite of 'on my own' might be, and then she wound it up lamely with, "Or not?"

"I'm on my own," I said.

She slid into the seat opposite me.

"I brought over the rest of what you asked for," she said. "It could have waited until morning. But what the hell. I thought I'd come looking. I'm going to miss you when you're gone."

"Thanks," I said. The waitress came by with a menu, but Rose waved it away.

"Why don't you have a coffee or something?" I said.

"I don't want to mess up your plans."

"I don't have any."

She looked down at my bacon cheeseburger then.

"That looks disgusting," she said.

"And it looks better than it tastes. What did you manage to get for me?"

"I left it to Marcie. It's all in my car," she said, leaning back and stretching as if to get out all of the kinks from a long day at the office.

Rose had once told me how, after her third 'other woman' stint, she'd concluded that there must be some signal she was giving off to married men. I'd told her that I could confirm it. I'd felt it from the beginning, whenever she'd walked by.

She seemed happy enough with her life. From her commitment-free partners she got exactly what she needed, and no more. Maybe things would change for her when she met the right person but until now, the right bells hadn't rung.

I said, "And where's your car?"

"Right out front." She reached for my keycard folder, which was lying on the table beside my plate, and turned it around so that she could read the number on it. "I'll put it in your room for you," she said. "Take your time."

"I've spent all the time on this I'm going to," I said. "I'm done."

We drove the couple of hundred or so yards in her sports BMW, the engine a bass rumble, its tires crunching on the loose gravel at the edge of the lot where the blacktop was starting to break up.

She said, "Marcie burned you a disk rather than print everything out. Have you got your powerbook?"

"No," I said. "I don't."

"You can use mine."

She parked her car in the slot alongside my own and went around to get the computer out of the trunk. I led the way into the building, and then at the door to the room I stepped aside so that she could enter first. I'd no worries about how it would look. I hadn't spent enough time in there to mess it up yet.

Once we were inside, Rose handed me the powerbook and said, "You'd better plug it in. The battery's almost out. Can I use your bathroom?

"Sure."

Rose told me her password and went into the bathroom while I set up the machine on my dressing table. The room lights were low and the screen was nice and bright. I slid in the gold-colored CD that her assistant had created at the office for me. Once it was up to speed a directory appeared, and I gave it a quick check-over to see the range of the information she'd put onto it. I noted that it included most of the detail that I already had but it went a lot further with employee grades, employment histories, medical records and a lot of other confidential information that I couldn't have accessed before.

After a few minutes I glanced past the powerbook's screen to the dressing-table mirror, where I could see the strip of light that showed under the bathroom door.

Rose seemed to be taking a while. I could hear the sound of the loud fan running inside there, and after a moment I heard the toilet flushing.

I opened the odd file, just to see if anything jumped out at me.

I heard the door opening before I saw anything.

She'd switched off the bathroom light, although the fan inside it was still running on a delay. I looked up at the sound and in the mirror I was aware of the blur that was Rose Macready, barefoot and naked and with her clothes held before her, crossing the room in an instant and then dropping the clothes and sliding into the bed.

It was a swift and lithe move, made only a little inelegant by the way she'd used the bundle for modesty. If modesty's what you can call it.

I turned in my chair and looked back at her. She'd pulled the covers right up to her nose; after a moment she dropped them a few inches so that she could speak. I'd thought she was wearing nothing at all, but I was wrong. She was still wearing her pearl ear-rings.

"Well, say something," she said. "If you don't want to play, I'd at least like the chance to start piecing my dignity back together."

"Sorry, Rose," I said. "You just took me by surprise."

"Well, make up your mind. The surprise won't keep for ever. Please don't tell me I read it wrong, John. I know how you feel about sleeping alone."

"I need a couple of minutes," I said.

I went into the bathroom and sat on the toilet lid in the bright overhead light. My heart was sinking like a deep-sea probe. I didn't know what to say to her and I didn't know what to do. I could have told her that I'd been sleeping alone for most of the past year, making do on a fold-down while Sophie made an early retreat to the bedroom and pulled up the drawbridge behind her. But that wouldn't get me out of this situation. If anything, it might get me in deeper.

I could smell her expensive perfume. The fan hadn't cleared it yet. Her shoes were on the other side of the bathroom, lying where she'd kicked them off.

How on earth could I deal with this?

But the problem was solved for me when I heard, muffled by the heavy door, her astonished cry of "OH my *GOD*..."

And I realized that this could only mean one thing. While I'd been sitting in here she must have grown bored and curious, and my guess was that she'd started to read through some of the hospital papers I'd left on the bedside table.

Wearily, I got up from the toilet and opened the door.

I wasn't wrong. She was sitting up with the form copies in her hands. She was looking at one for a second, then another, working through them as if she couldn't believe what she was seeing.

She looked up at me, wildly.

"Is this true?" she said.

I nodded.

"When did it happen?"

"Monday night."

"And you're just..." She shook her head. "I can't believe you're going around like nothing's wrong."

"Don't shout, Rose," I said.

"You should be the one who's making some noise," she said, and she threw back the covers and swung herself out of bed. "There's an appropriate response to something like this, John."

She grabbed up her clothes and started to dress.

"Thanks for letting me come down here and do something I can always be ashamed of," she said as she stood and pulled up her lingerie pants. The elastic made a sound as she snapped them into place.

"I'm sorry," I said.

"Sorry doesn't do it. And you're telling the wrong person. I think you're sick."

"You could be right."

"Then get help." She snapped her bra on backwards at waist-level, and then swung it around and put her arms through the loops one at a time like she was shouldering a pack. As she reached down for her blouse she went on, "Don't use the rest of us to help you pretend there's nothing wrong."

I brought her shoes out of the bathroom for her. In the time it took me to get them, she was back into her skirt and all but ready to go.

"Why are you doing this, John?" she said, zipping it up at the side. "Can you tell me?"

"No, I can't."

"Fuck you," she said. "I thought I knew you. I want to feel sorry for you, but fuck you."

She grabbed the shoes from me and tore out of the room with them in one hand and her jacket in the other. Ten seconds later I heard the crash of the outside door at the end of the passageway. Shortly after that I heard what had to be the BMW taking off, tires squealing like pigs at slaughter.

She'd left me with her computer. I closed it down. Somehow, I hadn't the heart to carry on right now. After staring at the TV for a while I undressed and climbed into bed and switched off the lights. When I lay back into the dent on the pillow that Rose had left, her perfume seemed to rise up around me. It was as if she was still here; not just the illusion of her, but some part of her presence itself.

Childless Rose, you could have no idea.

Could Gillian have known anything of our affair? Could she? I was sure I'd never let anything show or slip, but I knew she wasn't stupid. There were other signs than perfume, other traces that could cling. Could she have read me, regardless of what I was trying to hide?

I didn't even know I was dozing until I snapped awake at the sound of someone moving in the next room.

Gillian's room.

I heard a young woman's voice and I heard a young woman's laugh. It sent a faint shock right through me.

I lay awake and listened for a while, but it was simply that the clerk had relet the room to someone else. That was all.

I couldn't get back to sleep after that, and so I got the recharged powerbook and brought it over to the bed. Marcie had been thorough. Many of the files carried a digital mug shot of the relevant employee, photographed at interview. I looked at Farrow's and saw an unremarkable youth with freckles. I stared at his face for a while and his face told me nothing. I lay there scrolling through the meaningless data, knowing that I'd be able to make no use of it until I'd decided on something to look for, some pattern to seek.

Then one name caught my eye. The feelings I had about my discovery were seriously mixed.

Hadn't one of those boys said that Don Farrow's latest girlfriend was named Rachel?

There was a Rachel who worked in the Spirit Box.

Fifteen

Thursday, March 17

Mickey Cheung was late getting in that morning, but I was trying his number so often that I got him before he'd even had a chance to look at the messages I'd been leaving.

"Mickey," I said, "I need to speak to Rachel Young. Is she working today and is there anything you can tell me about her?"

"Give me ten minutes," he said. "I literally just walked in the door. I'll get back to you."

"Ten minutes," I said in a way that I hoped made him realize that I meant it, and mentally making a note that I'd call him again in five.

"Miranda," I called out then through the open office door. "Can you come in for a moment?"

Miranda came in. She didn't exactly seem eager. Her face was set like a mask, her lips a pencil-slash. I reckoned I probably knew why.

I said, "Sit down." She half-glanced at the chair but didn't sit; when she looked back at me I said, "My daughter died on Monday."

The mask began to slip.

"Oh God," she said.

"You already know this."

"Everyone's been talking about it this morning. I didn't dare say anything. I'm so sorry."

"Nothing we can do about it," I said, and I shook my head and all the breath just seemed to run out of me. Saying it had done something to me. It left me feeling soft-boned and helpless.

"I don't know what's going to happen," I said.

"You shouldn't be here."

"What's everyone saying?"

"Everyone's saying that you shouldn't be here."

"I've got reasons for that," I said. "If this makes you feel awkward, I'll understand."

"It's not about *me*," she said. "It's about you. Don't turn it around."

"Look," I said, and I reached for her hand and held it in both of mine. "We've worked together for three years. Without you I'd have been flat on my face by the end of day one. I don't know what you think of me, but I know you deserve better. What I'm asking is, if you can, just try to see me through this. It won't be forever. I'll be gone before too long."

I held her then, and she put her arms around me. I could feel her fingers raking up bunches of material on my back, she was clinging so tight. I think this was the first physical contact we'd ever had. In modern-day business you're in constant fear of a lawsuit if you so much as pass too close in a doorway.

She wouldn't meet my eyes as she turned and left the office. Her own, I could see, were red.

My phone rang. It was Mickey Cheung.

Without any preamble, he said, "Rachel Young has been absent from work all week. Same time period as Don Farrow. We've had no calls and no explanations. She didn't answer the phone when I tried her home just now."

"Any other absences in your department?"

"I'm ahead of you, there. One. Same days as the others. Name of Bob Mechanic."

"Bob Mechanic..." I repeated slowly as I typed in the letters.

"It's a real name," Mickey said.

"I know it is. I'm calling up his file."

During the few seconds that it took for the file to appear, Mickey said, "Apparently you say it different to a car mechanic, but I don't know how."

"So what do you call him when he comes in?"

"Just Bob," he said. "He's employed right alongside Farrow in our janitorial services. They sterilize the carts and run the laundry."

I looked at the picture that came up. A square-jawed and healthy-looking boy with a hint of a squint. Just-Bob the jock. Could he be my missing link? My Third Man? Mentally I tried to picture him along with freckly Don, and with blonde and willowy Rachel Young.

"What's their work like?"

"Same as any graduate student getting their first taste of paid employment. You have to lead them around like a chimpanzee in a diaper. They're not stupid, but at that age your mind's on other things."

"What I'm saying is..."

"I know what you're saying, John. You want to know if any of them could have choked down five bags of client property and walked them out of the vault. To that I have to say, I don't know. Rachel's the only one with access, but she's also the least likely candidate for criminal behavior."

I switched files and went to the picture of Rachel Young. What did I see?

Someone else's babysitter. Some girl who might work at the library. Somebody's girlfriend at a party who smiles but hardly speaks and whose name you never catch. I'd stared at her image for most of an hour last night, and I still didn't know. Mickey was right. She was about as unlikely a candidate for a drugs mule as you could imagine.

But.

"Thanks, Mickey," I said. "I'm onto it."

I called Security. I explained my authority and told them that I wanted to search certain of the staff lockers, and arranged to be met in the services block by someone with a master key.

The someone was a big man named Sharon. I swear it. His name tag was almost at my eye level.

I said, "I need to see inside the lockers for Don Farrow, Rachel Young, and Bob Mechanic."

"I need the numbers," he said.

"Well, check for them."

"How am I supposed to do that?"

I lowered my voice so he had to bend toward me to hear what I was saying.

"Listen, Sharon," I said. "The way I feel like now, I'm like toxic waste and the shell's about to crack. I appreciate your position. But make an effort and help me out, for both our sakes."

He scowled.

"The name's Jim," he said.

"So what's that about?" I said, pointing at his name tag. He took it and turned it as far around as it would go so that he could read it.

"Fuck," he said. "They did it to me again."

He snatched off the badge and walked away, muttering darkly.

While he was making the necessary call, I took a look through the area. I knew where Farrow's locker was. For the others I needed guidance.

I think I'd once been in here when it was half-built, but never since. Back then it was a hard-hat site with no windows in the frames and a drainage problem. Now it was coat room and personal storage for about five hundred of the lower-grade employees. The ceiling was false and the hidden lights were fluorescent, and although the fittings and the banks of lockers hadn't been cheap, they'd already been mistreated enough to look it. The locker room itself was a mixed facility but there were separate-sex shower and changing areas somewhere off at the back.

Gilly would have been assigned a locker in here, during her summer work experience. There had been a company youth program with others just like her, mostly children of management, doing mailroom jobs and running messages during the school vacations. They were given tasks where they could do no harm, nor come to any. I'd given her a ride to the site every morning, and Sophie had picked her up on the days that I'd had to stay late.

I'd had to drop her at the parking lot. I was forbidden even to walk in with her. Walked to your first job by one of your parents? That was a serious lapse of cool. She'd said she enjoyed it, but I think she found it a mixed experience. The few times I saw her around the site, she'd looked lost and uncertain.

I'd had to let this pass. Or risk another serious lapse of cool.

Big Jim came back about five minutes later, carrying a torn-off strip of paper with three numbers written on it. Holding it up before him so that he could refer to it, lips moving silently, he led me through the maze of lockers until we reached the big alcove he was looking for.

"This one's the lady's," he said, pointing, double-checking against what he'd written.

It was a corner locker in the next section to Farrow's. Each of the doors had a card-holder on it for the owner's name, but most hadn't bothered to use it. Rachel had. Her name was on pink card hand-lettered in a pale blue ink.

"Open it up," I said.

I didn't feel comfortable prying, but it had to be done. Jim who-wasn't-Sharon sorted through about thirty keys to find the appropriate master, and then he opened the door and stepped back.

There wasn't much in there to look at. A change of shoes. A spare sweater on a hanger. Up on the shelf, some items of makeup and a few toiletries including tampons and a talc shaker. Two thrift store paperbacks and a ropy-looking orange. I touched nothing else, but I picked up the container of talcum powder. It was a drugstore's own-brand product, unscented, and from the weight of it the container was almost empty.

I set it back on the shelf, exactly as it had been.

"Okay," I said.

Big Jim stepped back in and relocked the door, and as he was doing it he looked over his shoulder and indicated the opposite row with a nod.

"The two boys are across the way," he said.

We went over. I felt a tingling. The lockers allocated to Don Farrow and Bob Mechanic stood side by side. I don't know why but almost immediately I could imagine the two of them standing there, heads together, voices lowered, far enough from Rachel Young for them to discuss her score on the babe-o-meter and close enough for her to guess they were probably doing it.

And what would she do then? Cut them down? Color up and pretend not to hear? I'd have to know her to be able to say.

Bob Mechanic's locker door had a circular mark on it where a sticker had been peeled off but the adhesive had stayed behind. Beside Farrow's locker hung the phone charger wire, running from a power point on the wall somewhere behind.

"They know they're not supposed to do that," Big Jim said.

"Let's have a look inside," I said.

Don Farrow's locker was piled deep with unwashed clothing. There was a bottle of Listerine mouthwash, about a dozen CD cases featuring bands I'd never heard of, and a Discman with its earpiece leads tangled up in a puzzle-knot. I dug down through the clothes but I found nothing.

Bob Mechanic's locker was empty. Not empty as in, nothing much there; empty as in, cleaned out completely and looking abandoned.

"Okay," I said to Big Jim, "you can close them up again."

As Big Jim was resecuring the lockers, I stood back and looked around. Anything else to be learned here? I was about to leave when my eye was caught by something.

Two doors down from Don Farrow's was a locker with a name card in its slot. This one wasn't handwritten; it was a home-made job from a computer. I couldn't read the name from where I was standing, but there was something very familiar about the typeface.

I moved in closer. On the card I read the name *Cyrus L Behan* and, centered below that in bold capitals, *PRIVATE – KEEP OUT*.

"I also want to look in this one," I said to Big Jim.

"I don't have all day to go through every damn locker in the place with you," he said.

"Last one," I said.

I couldn't have told you the name of the font, but it looked awfully like the loopy italic style used in the letter that I'd taken from Farrow's room.

Sixteen

That didn't necessarily mean anything.

The same font was probably available to anyone with a computer that ran the most common standard software. The contents of Cyrus Behan's locker had told me nothing, other than that he had an outdoor job in the grounds. All that I found in it was his workwear and a lot of dried-out grass cuttings. So he didn't even work in the same department as the others, or anything close to it. The nearer I got to my desk, the less I felt I'd made any kind of a discovery.

When I got there, Bill Nickles was in the outer office. He was just turning away from a conversation with Miranda.

"John," he said when eyes lit upon me. "I was looking for you. Let's talk inside."

He walked in ahead of me, and I followed. It looked as if the Seattle man had been making a few concessions to his new surroundings. He was wearing a suit and tie today, and he didn't look right in either. He looked as if he'd turned out for the funeral of a fishing partner.

Miranda hovered in the doorway and asked if we needed coffee. We didn't. Bill Nickles looked around the bare walls and said, "Looks like you cleared everything out."

"Job was nearly over," I said. "I was getting ready to go home."

That was it for the small talk. After that he got straight down to it.

"Why didn't you tell me about your daughter?" he said.

"That's harder to do than it sounds."

"I've got a message from your wife. She's given up trying to reach you and she's flying in tonight. I'm quoting her exact words, now. You either drop everything and be there or you go to hell."

"And what do you say?"

He didn't take me up on that. He started to pace the room around me, massaging the back of his neck as if to work on the tension I'd been causing him.

He said, "I never would have let you go ahead with this if I'd known the situation."

"Am I off the job?"

"If you need someone else to make the decision for you then, yes, I'm taking you off it. Mainly for your sake but partly out of self-interest because I'm just not sure I can rely on you to do this right, John. You've got other things you need to think about. Stop using work as a place to hide."

I said, "I was just starting to get somewhere, Bill."

"Than you'll have made life that much easier for whoever takes over," Nickles said. "Let me do the same for you. Go see your wife and start dealing with your grief. I want you to spend the afternoon having a long talk with someone from health and welfare. Her name's..." He waved, vaguely. "Wendy something. She's a bereavement specialist. She's waiting for you to call. If you don't call, I've told her to come looking."

"What do I do?" I said. "Pick up the phone and ask for Wendy Something?"

"*Doctor* Wendy Something," he corrected. "John," he said, "if this had happened to me, I wouldn't run from it."

"*Has* it ever happened to you?"

"No."

"Then you don't know, Bill. And I hope you never will."

It was awkward for a few moments while he shook my hand and told me it was all for the best, and did the *If there's anything I can do...*line. I said I'd call him if I thought of anything, and he went.

I sat in my big chair, swinging it gently from side to side, massaging my temples. I became aware of Miranda again. I didn't even have to look in her direction. I just knew.

"Mister Bishop," she began. "John..."

"Just give me a couple of minutes," I said.

"Wendy Blood's on the line. She's..."

"I know who she is. I'll call her back."

I swung around to face my keyboard. Intranet. Password. Behan.

Miranda waited uncertainly for a few moments longer, and then she withdrew.

I'd been right. Cyrus Behan was a greensman, twenty-seven years old. He was one of a dozen or so workers who kept the acreage around the plant looking trimmed and civilized; cutting the grass, running the leafblower, lopping the trees when they needed it. The acreage was enormous and the job called for some heavy equipment and the skills to operate it. The same department maintained the tropical foliage on the indoor rock terrace, and a couple of its workers came around the admin block once every week or so to spritz and feed the houseplants.

I couldn't say that I'd ever seen Behan on houseplant duty. From his picture, he looked overweight and pasty and he had one of those straggly beards that look like long armpit hair. I could see him driving a backhoe but I couldn't imagine him tripping around giving little squirts from a water spray.

By now I was all but convinced that this line of enquiry was taking me nowhere. It was a hunch and it hadn't worked out. At least nothing had been lost by it. One last thing to check up on, and I could put it out of my mind altogether.

I put in a call to the groundskeeping supervisor. He told me that Behan wasn't available and hadn't reported in all week. He hadn't called to give a reason for his absence. He hadn't been contactable at all. Nobody had seen him since before the weekend.

Same as the others.

When I tried Behan's home phone number, it rang and rang and no-one picked it up.

I sat for a while, thinking.

My time here had a limit on it. I'd no way of knowing how long it would be before they cancelled my passwords, took me off the site access list, and walked me out of the building with all the deference due to someone who'd become a sudden embarrassment to all. It might be a week or more. It might be a matter of hours.

Or even less. On one occasion when we'd had to fire someone, I think the record from warm chair to parking lot was about twenty minutes.

I put the summary pages from the four files into a print queue and went out to get the sheets as they emerged from the Laserjet machine alongside Miranda's workstation. Nothing beats hard copy. When the dust's cleared after Armageddon and we're all living in caves with no light or power, we'll look pretty stupid if everything we need to rebuild civilisation is on DVDs and Zip drives. I didn't have my own powerbook, and I'd had Rose Macready's laptop returned to her. When they cancelled my passwords I'd have no access to records at all. Old-fashioned hard copy was the only way to go.

Out they came, page after page. Don, Rachel, Bob Mechanic, Cyrus Behan. Not their entire employee records — I'd have been there an hour — but just the top sheets with their basic personal information. I was now convinced that, separately or together, the four of them had a story they could tell me.

I'd also a powerful feeling that the torment of my uncertainty was about to be replaced by something more solid. I ought to have welcomed that. But I'm not sure that I did.

After all, to lay a ghost is to drive it from your life.

Miranda said, "Shall I return Doctor Blood's call now?"

"Hold off a while longer," I said.

I got all my papers together and left the office. I don't remember what I told Miranda on my way out, but I'm sure that she didn't believe it.

I remember almost running down the corridor. The elevator took too long to arrive and so I went down by the fire stairs. The walls seemed to be pressing in on me and I had an overwhelming sense of being pursued by something. I wasn't, of course. The only things that followed me were the strange looks I was getting.

I burst out into the foyer and I did start to run, then, heading for the exit doors. But all the papers that I was carrying slid out of my grip and scattered at my feet and in my wake. It was like a bad dream, but it was real. I'd never really had a panic attack and I couldn't have told you what one was. But I imagine that what I was experiencing was something like it.

What brought me out of it was a sharp call from the guard at the reception counter.

"Can I help you, sir?" he said, and it was that way of saying it that security people use, the one that makes it into a challenge without giving you anything to throw back at them.

I was crouching down and trying to grab all my papers together when he reached me. He recognized me then, and said, "Mister Bishop?" and I looked up at him apologetically.

He was the one who'd told me where to find the shaving kit. I wondered why he hadn't recognized me sooner, and then I decided that I probably didn't want to know the reason.

"I'm sorry for this," I said. "I just...I realized I was late for something."

I'd got most of it by now, just gathering up the dropped pages and shuffling them together with no thought for their order. I could sort them out later. He squatted by me and handed me a couple of sheets, and passersby gave me odd ones that had sailed off even further.

I got back to my feet. "Thanks," I said to everyone. "Thank you." And I went on my way.

They were watching me. Everyone was. That wasn't paranoia, it was the consequence of making a spectacle of myself. I tried to act calmly from there on, and after a few seconds I started to get a grip.

It wasn't easy.

I felt as if I was on the brink of depriving myself of the one thing that had been holding me up over the past couple of days. I felt like a scarecrow about to fly apart. The hurricane was getting closer and I could feel its first effects, small disturbances rolling ahead of the main event, little exploratory pokes and prods at my fabric prior to the great blast that would blow me asunder.

And there was nothing I could do about it, other than go on.

As I was walking up the open-air pathway to the parking lot, the cellular phone in my pocket began to ring.

I reached for it thinking that it was my own, and then I realized that it couldn't be. My own was switched off, somewhere, as part of my mute avoidance scheme for dealing with Sophie. This had to be Don Farrow's phone.

I took it out, thumbing one of the buttons on the keypad to take the call, and put it to my ear.

"Hello?" I said cautiously.

And a male voice that I recognized from that one time before said, "It's me. She's got worse. Get back here."

The breath had stopped in me.

I thought quickly.

"Where are you?" I said.

I had enough presence of mind to realize that the caller thought he was talking to Don Farrow. I'd no idea what Farrow's voice was like, but I'd tried to make it sound as if I could be anyone.

"Don?" the voice at the other end of the line said, suspiciously.

"Uh-huh," I said, trying to reduce my exposure even more.

There was silence for a moment, and then he hung up.

Seventeen

From there, I went to Rachel Young's address. I had to go right into the middle of town, where I drove north on Plaza and turned east to enter an area of wide, well-kept streets where every house was the size of an embassy. This was Victorian Charlotte, the buildings all gothic and gingerbread with immaculate gardens and great oaks lining the lanes.

I walked up a path of herringbone brick to the house where Rachel was supposed to live. The address seemed right, although it was hardly the kind of place I'd expect to find a girl in her twenties on starting-out wages. I knew it wasn't the parental home; her father was a manager with one of our suppliers out in Gastonia. This house was a white clapboard colonial, and it was enormous. It had a colonnaded porch at the front and shutters at the windows. I saw a built-out study on the side of the house and an outside stairway going around the back of it. Up at roof level, there were attic windows in the Dutch style.

I couldn't see any life through the ground-floor windows and so I went around to the stairway. It was wooden with a carved balustrade, painted white in keeping with the rest of the house. It appeared to lead up to a separate entrance for a duplex apartment. The apartment had its own mailbox at the foot of the stairs.

This made more sense. At the top of the stairs I knocked on the door, and then I peered in through the window beside it. What little I could see had a museum-like look of desertion.

Then I had an inspiration, and took out Don Farrow's phone. After some inexpert fumbling I managed to bring up the menu of stored numbers and started to scroll through them. Farrow had logged all of his numbers by initials or first names. There were two Bobs (Bob1,

Bob2) but only one Rachel. I pressed the call button while Rachel's name was onscreen.

A few seconds later, I could hear the phone inside the apartment begin to ring out.

I let it ring for a while, just in case there *was* anyone who might answer, and then I shut it off. I looked around. You could see quite a lot of the neighborhood from here. Very nice. The gardens weren't huge but they had classy features like arbors and rose walks and hedged-in secret corners. I could hear a mid-distant buzz of traffic from a few streets away, but below me nothing moved.

I descended the stairway and tried to take a peek inside the mailbox, but I couldn't see to tell if there were deliveries backed-up or not.

She wasn't here, and there was no-one who could tell me where she'd gone.

I went over and sat in the car.

~

There was no Cyrus listed in the memory but I tried the phone trick again for the two Bobs. The first number rang out for so long that I was about to give up, when someone came on the line and said, "Hello?"

"Bob Mechanic?" I said.

"Bob who?"

"Sorry to have bothered you," I said, and rang off.

When I tried Bob2, I could hear the phone being picked up in the middle of laughter and then a young-sounding woman came on. She still had the laugh in her voice as she said, "Yes?"

"Hi," I said. "Who am I speaking to?"

"This is Jean. How can I help you?"

"I'm trying to get hold of Bob Mechanic."

"I'm pretty sure he's gone. Just a minute."

The phone went muffled, the way it does when someone puts their hand over the mouthpiece at the other end, and I could hear an offline conversation without quite being able to decipher it. Then everything went clear and loud again and she said, "Yeah, he's gone."

"Where am I calling, Jean?"

"This is the Y."

"The YMCA?"

"Yeah," she said. "I never can spell it."

"Has Bob been living there?" His file had only shown a street address.

"He put all his things in a van and moved out last week. If you can give me one moment I'll see if he left anything I can tell you."

This time there was the clunk of the receiver being set down and another offline conversation where I heard *what do I have to press?* and then suddenly I was on hold with music. The music sounded like an electronic glockenspiel and reminded me of the musical lights on our last Christmas tree.

She came back on again after about a minute.

"You still there?" she said.

"Yes."

"Hello?"

"I'm still here."

"There's a number for his parents. I think that's all there is."

"Is that where he went?"

"I wouldn't know. Do you want the number?"

"Please."

I was stretched across the car, rummaging for the pen that I knew was in the glove box. When I found it, it wouldn't write, and I had to ask her to repeat the number while I scribbled the ballpoint into life on the corner of one of my sheets.

When I'd got it, I thanked her and rang off.

I called the parents' number straight away. Something was odd about the call. I heard it ring, and then it seemed to ring again in a different tone as if it had been rerouted.

And after all that, I got through to a machine. I heard a woman say, *"You've reached our number, now please leave us yours and we'll get back to you."*

After the beep I simply said, "I'm trying to reach Bob. I'll call again later. You can tell him it's about what happened in the Spirit Box."

After that, I sat in the car and thought for a while. I leaned my head back against the headrest. All the way down the empty street before me, the tall oaks with their arching branches made a cathedral-like corridor. I could imagine it here in summer or fall. Then it would be lush. Right now it was kind of severe.

I'd a powerful sense of being close to something. Pretty soon I felt I'd know what it was. I wasn't here because I placed the company's interests above my own grief. I was here because there was a great hook in my heart and it was pulling me forward. Someone had called to me in my dead daughter's voice. When that happens, your choices are limited.

One more place to look.

Eighteen

Behan's address was at the Thrift Efficiency Apartments along Wilkinson Boulevard to the west of the city. I came down a steep driveway from the main road to get to it, and I took the time to give it the once-around before I stopped. The place looked exactly like you'd expect from its name; like a stalag. A single building three stories high, with outside deck access to the rooms on every level. Small windows, grey metalwork. The building was painted and maintained, but there was something terribly grim about it.

I imagine that's what you're always going to get with cheap accommodation for single working men. No frills whatsoever, rock-bottom rent, a dead Pontiac in the parking lot, and unlimited Krispy Kreme Donuts within strolling distance if the litter on the grass was anything to go by. The Pontiac's front end was stoved-in and its passenger window had been replaced by a billowing trash bag. The doughnut wrappers made a trail to Red Star Food and Beverages across the way.

I'd seen a sign for an office on the front of the building. I found the entrance and went inside. There was a dingy hallway and the office was behind glass, like the space behind a teller's window. Apart from me, the only other things in the hallway were a humming Coke machine and a board with a set of printed rules on it.

There were a *lot* of rules.

I had to rap on the glass to be noticed. There was no buzzer. Through the glass I could see a young man sitting with his back to me, over on the other side of the room. He was typing away on a laptop computer, rattling along as if his life depended on it. He was a fast typist and he was using all his fingers. But at my knock he stopped.

He didn't look at me. He looked over to his left, and reached for a switch.

"Yes?" he said, and his voice came out of a box somewhere in the room with me. He was still looking to his left and I realized that I was on a security camera and he could see me on his monitor.

"I was given this address for Cyrus Behan," I said.

"He's in thirty-five."

"Do I just go on up?"

"Sure."

So much for the screening process. He went back to his typing and I went back outside.

Stairways at either end of the building linked all of the floors. The rules were repeated on every level. *Non-paying guests are not allowed. Stay off balconies. No loud noises, visiting other guests or alcohol outside the rooms. Keep your entrance door closed. Do not knock on other guests' doors. Take trash to the dumpster and close the door. Not a full service motel.*

No kidding.

I went up to the top floor and found unit number thirty-five. I knocked on Behan's door and got no reply. I tried the door, but it was obvious that I wasn't going to get in. I knocked again, just in case. As I was waiting, I heard a sound behind me.

When I looked back over my shoulder, I saw a man coming out of one of the units farther down the balcony. Our eyes met briefly, but he quickly looked away. He didn't look like the kind who'd have much conversation, and I didn't try to engage him. He headed off toward the stairway.

I went all the way back down to the office and knocked on the window again.

"He isn't there," I said.

"Better luck next time."

And that was it; he switched off the intercom, returned to his laptop, and carried on speed-typing like there was some kind of a record to beat.

I knocked again, harder. This time he took a while to stop. Then, wearily, he reached for the switch and threw it with a gesture that was no doubt intended to show me how much I was intruding on his valuable time.

I said, "Any chance of checking the room?"

"Nope," he said, and he was starting for the switch again when I saw the place where the pickup microphone was taped alongside the glass, and reached up and flicked it hard.

I don't know how loud a sound it made on the other side, but he jumped as if he'd been goosed by a hot spark. He swung around to face me, and he didn't look pleased. But then, you can act as pissed-off as you like when you're behind toughened glass.

I said, reasonably, "Do we have to talk through this? I don't bite."

"What's to talk about?" he said. I could see him properly now. He was long-necked and long-haired. He looked a little bit like a bird puppet.

I didn't answer him. I just indicated the door in appeal.

He cut the intercom, turned his back on me, and carried on typing.

But he wasn't ignoring me. He was making a show of ignoring me, and that isn't the same thing. I just stood there watching the back of his head. Every now and again his fingers stumbled or faltered, and every now and again I saw him cast a quick glance in the direction of my image on his closed-circuit TV monitor.

I think he lasted maybe all of two minutes.

In the end he came over and opened the door.

He stood there looking at me with a sullen expression and I said, "What I meant was, is there any chance of *you* checking the room. Nobody's seen him for days."

His eyes were dark-ringed. Their whites had a touch of yellow. He looked well-fed, but badly-nourished. He was no younger than twenty-three or four, no older than thirty.

He said, "Are you a cop?"

"How many cops have an accent like mine?" I said. "I'm with his employers. Do you know him?"

"Cyrus?" he said. "Yeah. Not as a friend. He tried to get me to help him sell his comic books one time. As if I knew anything about it."

He put a well-used little *back in 5* card in the window and then locked up the office behind him.

We went upstairs. The young man knocked on the door exactly as I had only a few minutes before.

"Manager," he called.

Despite his possession of the magic word, his results were no better than mine.

Nothing.

"Mister Behan?" he called again.

"I tried that," I said.

He looked at me. He seemed to have been struck by a troubling thought.

"What if he's in there?" he said.

"Open the door and take a look," I suggested.

"No, I mean…what if he's *in there?*"

I realized then what he was saying. He was looking pale and unhappy. Scared, even. What he meant was, what if we walk in and find that he's died in there?

I held out my hand. "Give me the key," I said.

Even if Behan was just a pair of boots and a maggot farm, it would be as nothing to me. I might feel it, but it wouldn't break me. I'd had that already, much closer to home.

He gave me his passkey and backed off as I unlocked the door. With my hand on the door handle, I prepared myself to enter by drawing in a deep breath and holding it as if I was about to plunge into a roomful of toxic air.

"Oh, shit," the young man said, and turned right away in real fear.

I actually thought that the chances of Cyrus Behan having died in his apartment were pretty slim. For one thing, I was convinced that the voice I'd heard on the phone was his. For another, according to his employee record he drove a big V8 Dodge Ram truck, and there had been nothing like it in the parking lot.

All I really wanted was the chance to look through Behan's apartment without the manager at my heels. If the prospect of something unpleasant kept him out of the way, then fine.

I stopped holding my breath once I'd stepped inside.

There was one main studio room with a dining counter and small kitchen area at the back of it. There was a separate bathroom. The daybed had been folded back and there was a deer hide for a rug before it. There was a stale smell of clothing overdue for the laundry. At first I thought it might have been coming from the deer hide, but it came from no one place in particular; it just hung in the air.

I hadn't much time. I did a very quick and silent check of a few drawers and the closet. A glance around the kitchen, a look at the shelves. Behan was a photographer; or rather, he was a photography hardware nut with no sense of what made a picture. He had a couple of Nikon bodies and a range of lenses, while on the walls there were a lot of no-good snapshots that could have been taken by anyone with no eye and indifferent equipment. Some had been taken on what looked like a hunting trip, showing empty landscapes with the dot of a bird in a washed-out sky. Another was a shot of a tank of fish, made with an electronic flash. The glass side of the tank had reflected the flash and ruined the picture. But you could still see one or two of the fish, so…up it had gone.

I didn't see any books. Just hunting magazines. I flicked through one, found nothing of interest, and put it back with the rest. Stowed under the table were an old, unbranded PC computer and a printer.

He owned a Zenith TV and a no-name VCR. A small microwave oven. I looked in the refrigerator and checked on the milk. It was solid in the carton.

From outside the open doorway I heard, "What do you see?"

"You're safe to look," I called back. "He isn't here."

I moved to the bathroom doorway, to make it look as if I'd been checking back there and was just coming out.

"Thank fuck for that," the young man said as he stepped inside.

I said, "I take it he's not in your friends and family program."

"I don't wish him harm or anything," the young man said, glancing around at the meagre display that was Cyrus Behan's effort at making a home for himself, "but I don't know what it is. There's just something about him that puts you on edge."

"Like what?"

"You make some throwaway remark, you know, the way you do in conversation? And he jumps on it and wants to know everything you meant by it."

I nodded, still looking around myself, trying to soak in every scrap of odd detail so that I could review and analyze its significance later.

"How well do you know him?" I said.

"I don't know him at all. That one time was the only time I had to deal with him."

"So did you help him sell his comic books?"

"Even I could see he'd nothing worth selling. He came down to the office with a box of stuff he'd had for years. I don't know what made him think I was the person to ask. They were all messed up, drawings on the covers, creases, coupons cut out of them…I tried to explain it to him. Certain hot titles have a value, yeah. In mint condition, yeah. But what he had was just yard sale garbage you could pick up anywhere for pennies. These fanboys keep their choice stuff in mylar bags and only look at them by moonlight. Cyrus didn't get it. He'd go, like, what do you mean? They're the same stories, aren't they?"

"That's interesting," I said.

"He wouldn't believe what they told him at the fantasy bookstore, either. Everyone was out to cheat him. We'd better go."

"Sure," I said. We'd enjoyed the guilty pleasures of trespass for long enough.

"Want to leave him a message?"

I reckoned not. We moved back out onto the deck, and the young man relocked the apartment behind us.

"Does the room have a phone?" I said. I hadn't noticed one.

"No," he said. "There's a pay phone on every floor."

That explained why I'd had no reply.

Where at first he'd been uncommunicative, now this so-called Building Manager couldn't stop talking. He kept at it all the way back down to the office. I realized that he hadn't just been nervous, he'd been genuinely shaken by the mere possibility of what we might have found.

God help him, I thought, if and when he *did* have a body in one of the apartments to deal with on his shift. It was bound to happen sooner or later. A place like this might have been built with lonely deaths in mind.

On he chattered. He told me of something that had happened a few days after the comic books incident, how he'd been writing in the office and felt a prickling on the back of his head; he'd turned and seen Behan watching him through the glass much as I'd done — a level stare as if to say, *I know what you and your friends at the store are trying to pull.*

"Are you studying?" I said.

"Me?" he said. "No. I'm done with all that."

"So what's all the typing about?"

"I'm writing a novel."

"No kidding," I said. "Seriously?"

"Yeah."

I didn't know what else to say to that. So I said, "What kind of novel is it?"

"Extreme Horror," he said.

I thought of how he'd been, upstairs.

"Got much experience of that?" I said.

"It's all I ever read," he said.

Nineteen

I was starting to see it now. Cyrus reminded me of a great-uncle of mine who'd been convinced that anything old was antique and that every antique was priceless. Totters and ragmen came to your door and offered you pennies for your old rubbish, which they then sold on for thousands in auction houses. Which is exactly what *did* sometimes happen in the working-class backstreets where he'd grown up, so he was impossible to argue with. He hoarded everything. When he eventually died and they had to break into his house, it's said that they opened one of the cupboards and found two years' worth of his bowel movements, each one wrapped in newspaper and dated.

All right, then, maybe he was an extreme case. But I reckoned I could see how Cyrus Behan's mind might be working. He was no better-informed about the pharmaceutical world than he was about the comic book market. But he knew what he knew. What he knew was that they kept all that stuff in the vault and they made billions out of it. Anything else they told you was just clever-clever blather to put you off the scent.

I felt as if I'd covered a lot of ground in a short time, but now I'd stalled. Don Farrow had touched base and flown again, Rachel's phone rang in an empty apartment, and it looked as if Cyrus hadn't been home in days. None of them could be pinned down.

Bob Mechanic's behaviour hadn't been like the others. He'd actually planned ahead, packed up his gear and moved out. I didn't know whether this meant anything. I tried his contact number again, got rerouted again, hung up when I heard the same woman's voice giving the same recorded message. I guessed it was his mother but I couldn't say for sure.

It was early in the evening and I could feel myself running down. Sophie's flight would be due to land at Douglas International sometime within the next hour. If I watched for every light in the sky, I'd probably see her plane coming in.

What had she instructed Bill Nickles to tell me? Drop everything and be there, or go to hell.

Well, I knew I couldn't face her, so hell it had to be. I couldn't imagine what we might say to each other if we met now. Gillian had been the pin that had held us together, but Gillian was gone.

Only the siren echo that I'd been chasing now remained.

I'd never been much of a drinker, but I felt the need of something. Something to help brace me while this moment slid by. Coffee wouldn't do it. There's only so much coffee you can take before your heart runs away from you and your brain threatens to explode. The next bar that I spotted, I pulled in. It was a joyless-looking place and I reckoned it was probably as good as I deserved.

It was two low, conjoined buildings with a gravel parking lot to the side. The gravel was all churned up with the red dirt showing through. The buildings looked as if they'd been hastily thrown up in cinderblock and then topped off with clapboards and a double red shingled roof. On the roof, a couple of shiny tin air extractors turned in the breeze. The boards had been holed and patched and repaired several times, and the entire structure had been slapped over with a coating of cheap grey-blue paint.

When I walked around to the entrance I had to step over wheel ruts that had filled with rainwater. One of them was so deep that there was a bottle floating in it, neck-upwards like something out of Robinson Crusoe.

I'd thought it was going to be one of those sports bars with a big TV and some memorabilia around the walls, but it wasn't. It had a small dance floor and a revolving glitter ball, and there was slow music playing. No-one was dancing, though. It was too early in the evening for that. As far as I could see I was the only customer in the place. I sat at a table where you could see the marks of the cloth that had wiped it, and when somebody came I gave my order for a Jim Beam and water. The Jim Beam arrived on a paper coaster and the water came in a little jug with a piece broken out of its spout.

I don't remember the taste of it or any effect it had upon me. I'm not even sure that I touched it. I think I just sat there with my forehead against my knuckles and my eyes screwed shut.

I was thinking back to how we'd made the family deal. How Sophie and Gillian were going to give me these three years, and I was going to work my guts out with total job focus. The promise was that after the ambition had been achieved and the money was safely invested, I'd stop prioritising my career and be around more. I'd pick and choose the jobs, I'd travel less, I'd be around for anniversaries and birthdays.

To be honest, I'd known all along that it was never going to work out exactly as planned. Very few people get to pick and choose their jobs in any competitive field. I suppose that making the deal was like lying for sex. I'd have said anything, knowing that three years down the line we'd be different people in a different world. You can't plan in detail for that. I knew it even if they didn't. Everything's a leap in the dark.

Everything.

It had been quite a time. There was all the exhilaration of money coming in and out in breathtaking amounts; flights, new clothes, cars, the house rental, Gilly's school fees at Charlotte County Day. Even with me putting in sixty or seventy hours most weeks on the project, we were still able to make the most of the opportunities that came our way. Time in the mountains, time on the coast, weekends out of state whenever I could get away. Gilly pined for her friends and then made new ones. Sophie couldn't take to being a company wife. I wasn't much of a sympathetic listener. I was working flat out and everything I did was for all of us, wasn't it?

Well, I'd been wrong about many things but I'd been right about one. It had been a leap in the dark, for sure.

What we had here was the darkness of the pit.

"Dance with me?"

I looked up blankly. I hadn't been aware of anyone approaching. I couldn't even have told you what she'd said, but then she repeated it.

I said, "I'm not here to dance. Nothing personal."

She was standing over me and when she spoke, it was in a near-mumble. She had a seriously bad complexion and she was as skinny as a pole. She was wearing some kind of a see-through crocheted dress over black underwear. The effect was supposed to be seductive, but instead it was achingly sad. She looked about seventeen but was probably older. I assumed that she was employed here to work the customers. I didn't imagine that she'd spotted me and been drawn to my irresistible good looks.

She said, "I'm gonna get fired today if no-one says yes."

I glanced around. There was no-one else out here to say yes, no, or anything at all.

"What kind of place *is* this?" I said.

"Dance with me?" she repeated in her mumbling monotone. "Please? Just once. He's watching."

I looked across to the bar, where a man with a fat neck and a white shirt was setting up his working space for the evening. He was laying out shot glasses, jiggers, shiny chrome shakers on clean folded towels. His back was toward us but I imagine he could have been watching us in the mirrors. I thought I saw his reflection glance our way, just once.

I went onto the tiny dance floor with her because I hadn't got the heart to say no. Five minutes of my time to save her lousy job. Which was probably just a line that she'd been told to use on everyone.

It wasn't really dancing. It was no more than that slow-shuffle that you do to music. We didn't talk and she didn't look at me. She was a sad wreck of a girl, and there was almost nothing to her in my arms. We moved awkwardly, almost in embarrassment, our bodies barely touching.

I closed my eyes, and for a moment I tried to lose myself.

Dad, I heard her say. *Dad, I was trying to tell you. There wasn't much time and you still wouldn't listen.*

My eyes snapped open. I was facing the bar and we were turning into the light. I could see us in the mirrors. The glitterball cast its diamond patterns across us, giving us the look of the dancing drowned. She was lifting her face up to look at me and in that moment I saw —

But no. Overwhelming and real as it was for one instant, the certainty flickered and went.

Such things were not, and could not be.

I stopped the dance before the music ended. She waited as I pulled out my wallet and took out some bills. I tipped her far too much. She gave me a perfunctory thanks but her expression didn't change. The way she acted, it was as if the life was all gone from her. Nothing could please her, nor disappoint. I didn't return to my table or my drink; right now I didn't want either. As I was leaving the bar, I was aware of the man with the fat neck swooping for the money.

Outside, facing the road, I took a deep breath. The night air was cold, a blade in my head. It hurt and brought tears to my eyes. I opened my eyes, and they more or less cleared.

I picked my way across the ruts to get back to my car. Once I missed my step and splashed into some of the rainwater, but here it wasn't so deep. I looked for the stars reflected in the pools, but all that I could see there was the lights of the club behind me.

What do we wish for our children? The usual things, the simple ones. Happiness. A few answered prayers. A safe place to live. Some place where the star that they wish upon doesn't turn out to be the lights of a police helicopter. More than anything we want them to outlast us, so that we can let go at the end with the belief that they'll carry on for ever.

However you wanted to read it, I surely had failed her.

I sat in the car. When I closed my eyes, it was as if that momentary vision from the dance floor had been flash-burned into the backs of them and was taking a slow forever to fade. I tried to summon back its details, but too many of them were gone. All I could see were the dark shapes and their auras. Too little of them to read the full truth of it.

I could not tell you whether in that moment I'd seen my daughter alive and in my embrace, or myself dead and in hers.

~

After a while — I don't know how long, it could have been an hour or more — I remembered to try the Bob Mechanic number again.

Again, I could hear the signal being rerouted, a simple echo of enormous distances and complex technology. But instead of my getting the machine, this time a man's voice answered. Thrown for a moment, I forgot my own name as I was starting to introduce myself. I had to begin it again.

He said, "I'm Daniel Mechanic. I'm Bob's father."

That rang a bell. I had Bob Mechanic's papers on my knee, and tilting them to the glow of the Lexus' interior light I saw that Dan Mechanic was a senior lab technician who had moved his family to Charlotte for the startup of the plant, but had been forced to give up the job two years later due to ill health. The reason wasn't given. He was down here in the paperwork as a referee for his son's employment application.

I said, "I hope you're enjoying your retirement, sir."

"We got your message," he said. "I'd have called you back, but you didn't leave a number."

"I'm not as organized as I ought to be," I said. I was about to go on, but what Dan Mechanic said then was enough to make me catch my breath and hold it.

He said, "Bob and I have been having a long discussion. He says he's ready to talk to you."

It would be very easy for me to blow it right now. I chose my words with care.

"Fine," I said.

"Any problem to you if I sit in?"

"That's fine as well."

"We'll meet you anywhere you want to say."

"That won't be necessary," I said. "Tell me where you are and I'll come to you."

Twenty

Friday, March 18

Of course, when I said this, I was assuming that I could be there within the hour. Then Dan Mechanic had explained how on his retirement, he'd cashed in his benefits and bought a second home in the form of a beach house on the Outer Banks. They'd been spending most of their time there. Most of their friends knew where to reach them but for anyone who didn't, they'd arranged to have their calls rerouted from their home number. Bobby was out there with them now.

Bobby was ready to talk to me. The implication was that he had something he needed to confess. I was already ninety per cent certain that it was Bob Mechanic who'd made the anonymous call setting Mickey onto Don Farrow. The way I read it, he'd probably been dragged part of the way in and then got scared. He'd run for the safety of home like a bear cub scrambling to get behind his parents' legs.

I really hoped that nothing would happen to make Bobby change his mind.

I'd set out for the coast, knowing that I wouldn't reach Cedar Island in time for the last ferry but driving as if I was working to a deadline anyway. I stopped in Havelock for a meal that I quickly regretted, in a restaurant where they were stacking the chairs on the tables all around me as I ate. Somewhere between there and Beaufort I found myself snapping awake just in time to swing on the wheel and prevent the car from leaving the road.

After that I took a turnoff and found a dirt lane where I could get myself out of everybody's way and attract no unwelcome attention. There I locked the doors, dropped the seatback as far as it would recline, settled myself in with my coat for a blanket, and slept.

I don't think I dreamed; I don't think I even moved. It was as if I was catching up for every lousy night I'd ever had. When I awoke to the grey twilight of the pre-dawn, I felt boneless and drugged and too heavy to rise. I also felt a weird kind of bliss, but that faded as I rubbed at my eyes and then struggled the seatback upright and generally tried to get myself going again. When I got out of the car to relieve myself, I caught the scent of the ocean. Not from the pee, I mean from the breeze that was blowing inland.

Daybreak proper came as I was driving through Beaufort.

Most people's mental picture of the Carolina coast is of hurricane winds stripping the buildings, seen through the rain on a news camera lens. See it at any other time, and you begin to understand why, after every evacuation, people emerge from the schools and the shelters where they've been waiting out the storm, fix up what needs fixing, and carry on. There's something about a seacoast. I can't say exactly what — the grass is coarse and unlovely, the sand's a nuisance, everything rusts, and nothing you can build will ever last. But think of all that and a sunrise across tidal flats, and you'll know what I mean.

I reached the Cedar Island terminal in time for the first ferry of the day. They boarded me with about a dozen other vehicles, leaving space for another thirty or so on the car deck. Ahead of us, way across Pamlico Sound, stood the Outer Banks, one long ribbon of offshore islands curving out into the Atlantic like a bow. Thanks to boat services and connecting bridges, you could drive for most of their length and return to the mainland some seventy miles to the north.

The waters in the Sound were exceptionally calm. A hefty flock of seagulls followed in our wake for a while, and then dispersed. It was well into the morning when we entered the picturesque harbor at the southern tip of Ocracoke Island. Like all of the others in the chain, Ocracoke is one long, narrow spit. In places it's so narrow that you'd think it was just two beaches, back-to-back.

It was almost eleven when I reached the filling station that I'd been told to look out for.

The sign looked as if it dated back about forty or fifty years. The pumps were the old-fashioned kind with the moving numbers and they were all rust-stained and pitted, like dumped household appliances. The place appeared to be closed for the off-season. I left the Lexus here and followed a path through low scrub trees toward the dunes and the beach. The sand underfoot had fine broken shells in it, and there was the occasional crack of plastic as I came across half-buried litter.

There was only one house on this part of the beach. Shingled and on stilts, with a railed deck all around it and a stairway up the outside, it stood three stories high and looked like new unpainted timber in an age-old style. Oceanfront gothic, the Psycho house on legs. In the space underneath stood a Range Rover and a speedboat on a trailer. There was no garden area, nothing to differentiate the house and its grounds from the surrounding scrubland. It had an outside shower, and two air-conditioning units that stood apart from the house like beehives.

Up on the deck, I could see a solitary figure framed against the sky. Waiting.

And as I drew closer, this young man called out, "Mister Bishop? Would you like to come up the stairs?"

"Good morning, Bob," I said, squinting up at him.

"I'm glad you're here," he called back. "I'm sorry for the trouble I'm causing you."

"I know," I said.

"I hope this is the right thing to do."

"It is," I said. "Don't be scared."

I climbed the stairs to the deck, and we went inside to meet his parents. Now that I saw him close-to, Bob Mechanic was at least a couple of years older than his file photograph. In that, he'd looked like a boy. An athletic boy, but fast rather than strong. He'd filled out since. Now he looked strong rather than fast.

The rough beachcomber architecture was mostly just set-dressing, and the house interior was like that of any other well-planned and expensive American home. Dan, the father, apologized that he couldn't shake hands. He had support braces on both wrists and I realized that it was probably arthritis that had put a premature end to his working life. Other than that, he was tanned and trim. Beach life obviously agreed with him. His wife I recognized from her voice on the answering machine, and she was exactly as I'd have pictured her.

We sat in their family room with its big picture-window view of the ocean. Nothing separated the house from the sea apart from a low bank of grassy dunes. I could hear the Atlantic rollers thundering in gently on the other side of the glass. Bob sat in the middle of the sofa, between his parents. He was subdued and respectful.

He said, "How much of it do you know?"

"I believe that there are four people involved, yourself included," I said, "and that Cyrus Behan is one of the others. Am I right about that?"

"Yes, you are," Bob said.

"Did Cyrus have an unrealistic notion of what some of the material in the company's vault might be worth to a competitor?"

"It isn't quite so straightforward as that," Bob said. "None of us knew what he had in mind at the beginning. It started with a bet."

I waited.

"Cyrus Behan wasn't a friend," Bob went on after a while. "We didn't know him and we didn't work with him. He just happened to have the locker next to Don Farrow and me. You could always tell when he'd been around. You could smell cut grass and sweat. Don and I worked together and we used to go a little bit crazy sometimes. I don't think either of us saw much of a future career as glorified janitors, which is all our jobs really amounted to. We sterilized the carts and we laundered the towels. Trained monkeys could have done it.

"We used to make fun of this girl from our section that we saw every morning. Not so she could hear, just between ourselves. I guess Cyrus knew what we were doing. Her locker was just across from ours. It was Don who noticed that she always did the same things in the same order. Like a little ritual."

I'm not sure what I sensed coming, but I spoke more sharply than I'd intended to when I said, "What was her name?"

"This was Rachel Young," he said. "I suppose you'd say she was a kind of ugly duckling. Squeaky-geeky. The way she dressed, it was like her mother had chosen everything she'd ever wear in her life and picked them all out on the same day in nineteen seventy-three. Don said she probably held a Bible between her knees as a contraceptive."

"Robert..!" his mother interrupted, as if for a moment she'd forgotten that he was no longer ten years old and apt to forget himself in company, but Bob just shrugged.

"I'm just saying how it was," he said. "I'm not saying it was right. Fact of it was, she was just ordinary. Nothing about her particularly stood out. That seemed to irritate Don. He had something against her type. But I don't think he could have told you why."

"How long have you known him?"

"Since I was about thirteen years old. But all of this happened in the last couple of months. So there we are, watching Rachel and having some fun. Then Cyrus is there with us. Joining in like we all know each other. From being just this shadow in the background, suddenly Cyrus is saying to me and Don that it's all very well for us to laugh, but he didn't for one minute believe that we could ever get her to go out with one of us. He started trying to needle us a little, then. He said people always make a big thing out of despising something they know they can't have. He said it was the same thing used to make him go out and scratch brand-new cars."

"Did Cyrus know then that Rachel had access to the Spirit Box?"

"I think he'd got the plan already worked out in his head. For all I know he might have asked her out himself, once, and been turned down. He needed Rachel to get him what he wanted, and we were his way to her. Don took him up on it and the next thing I know is, I'm supposed to be part of a bet."

"So, what did you do about it?"

"Me, personally? Nothing." Bob shook his head emphatically, and raised a hand to underscore the point. "I never made a move," he said. "I'm not that type of person. For Don it was easy. Women seem to like him, even though I've never seen him treat any one of them all that well. It was no big problem for him to be pleasant to her and not mean it. Saying one thing. Thinking something else."

"Deceiving her."

"Exactly."

Freckly Don, a ladykiller? Well, you never knew. His was the species I'd been bracing myself to deal with in two or three years' time.

I said, "At what point did stealing the Spirit Box samples get introduced into it?"

"I didn't even hear about that until some time later," Bob said. "Cyrus never talked to me about it. I'm sure he always had it in mind, but he was playing a long game with us all. The first thing I knew was that it was something that he and Don had worked out. I was just assumed to be part of it. I wasn't. I never was. Please believe that."

"Go on," I said.

"Once they'd got Rachel on a hook, Cyrus convinced Don that he had a big-money buyer lined up for anything that Rachel could be persuaded to bring out of the Spirit Box. Anything at all. And because it's all that undocumented stuff, nobody could say what was missing or from where. So you can see how it developed. Cyrus throws down the challenge. Don targets the Ugly Duckling. Three weeks later he's sleeping with her and he's won the bet. Another three weeks and she's making all kinds of plans for the future they're going to have. That's the point where Cyrus tells Don he could get rich out of this. So Don goes to work on Rachel, and the next thing you know is, she's swallowing drugs in the Spirit Box to smuggle them out for him."

"So, how did he get her to do that? It sounds completely out of character."

"Believe me, it was. The first time he put it to her, she said no. So he dropped her like a rock and ignored her for a week. He told me that was all it took. By the time the week was over he reckoned he'd got her into a state where she'd have done anything he told her to."

"So how deep was your involvement at this stage, Bob?"

"I never *was* involved. I thought the whole thing was sick but I just kind of stood apart while they went ahead with it. But then as soon as

I found out about the stealing part, I made it clear that I was out. That's when Cyrus turned ugly and said I was as deep in as anyone. Which is a lie. It was Cyrus and Don. Cyrus and Don working on Rachel, and do you know why?"

I shook my head.

"Cyrus tried to convince me by showing me something he'd cut from a newspaper. He had it folded up in his wallet and he carried it around all the time. It was about how much it costs to develop every new drug and about how much money the successful ones can make. That was it. That was the entire basis of his strategy. Now, I don't know much about big business. But I quickly realized that I know a lot more about it than Cyrus and Don."

Bob went on and explained how Cyrus was so sure that finding a buyer would be no problem, he got Don Farrow to fall in with him by telling him that a deal was already in place. He convinced Don that the money was out there, waiting. Rachel was trapped by different means. For her the thought of money never even entered into it.

I said, "At what point did you walk away?"

"As soon as I realized they'd gone through with it," Bob Mechanic said. "It was obvious then that I couldn't hope to stand by and stay clean. I packed up my stuff at the Y and put in all the distance I could."

"But you didn't tell anyone."

"Not right away."

"Why not?"

"I reckoned they were going to get caught. I could be a snitch or I could walk away. It wouldn't make any difference in the end."

"Why didn't you talk to Rachel?"

"Yeah," he said, with a note of melancholy. "Why didn't I?"

I said, "I got a call on Don Farrow's phone. I don't know who was making it, but I believe it was Cyrus Behan. He said something like, "Get back here, she's got worse," and then he realized he was talking to the wrong person and hung up. Any idea what that could mean?"

"Sounds like something went wrong," Bob ventured, but it was obvious he knew nothing more definite about it than I did.

"None of them's been home since the weekend," I said. "Do you know where they might be now?"

Bob shook his head.

"Are you sure?"

"If I knew, I'd tell you."

Dan Mechanic leaned forward, intervening calmly. He said, "That sounds like you've got everything there is from Bobby, Mister Bishop."

"I'm almost done," I said, and then I returned my attention to his son. "You said Cyrus turned ugly. You've put quite a distance between you. Did he threaten you at all?"

Bob was silent and thoughtful for a while. I saw both of his parents exchange a glance across him. It looked as if this was something that he hadn't mentioned to them.

"Bobby?" his mother said. "Did he?"

"He talked about his uncles," Bob Mechanic said, looking uneasily down at the floor. "How he spent the summers with them and they taught him to hunt like they did. He kind of made the point that he didn't mind the sight of blood."

"Okay," I said, rising. "Thanks."

~

His parents offered me hospitality but I said I didn't want to be held up getting back, and I suspect that they were probably relieved. Their boy had veered dangerously close to trouble. Now he was doing the right thing, but it made for an uncomfortable time all around.

How did I feel about Bob Mechanic? It's impossible to say. Everything he'd told me should have made me dislike him, but I didn't have any strong feelings about him either way. I hadn't come out here to judge him and, besides, it's always too easy for us to say how others should have acted. We imagine ourselves in their place, doing exactly the right thing. Like we're so perfect. To his credit, he hadn't tried to rewrite his part in the affair to make himself look better.

His father walked out onto the deck with me. Down on the wet sand, beyond the dunes, there were the tyre tracks of some beach patrol that had gone by. Two long-billed birds were running along the water's edge, dodging the waves, checking for sand worms.

Dan Mechanic said to me, "I thought Bobby had told us everything, Mister Bishop, but I wasn't aware of that last part."

"The more I hear about Cyrus Behan," I said, "the less I like the sound of him."

"Will the police be involved?"

"The original plan was no. But that may have to change."

"I'll talk to our lawyer."

"Do that," I said. "If you need to worry, he'll tell you how and how much."

"Worry's a part of the job description for a parent," Dan Mechanic said as we moved to the top of the deck stairway. "Do you have children?"

"That's a difficult question," I said, and I left him to think about it as I started to descend.

Twenty-one

The boat that took me back to the mainland was the same one that I'd come out on. It was painted black and white, with a car deck of grey metal. I stood at the bumper rail and looked over the side. The water in the Sound was a deep, dull green. I turned from it, and leaned with my back on the rail. We were never quite out of sight of land, but the land was so low that it would be easy to mistake its presence for the horizon.

So.

My head was buzzing with Bob Mechanic's tale. I felt more twisted and turned about by it than ever. Rachel Young, an ugly duckling? I'd seen her picture. That wasn't fair. It wasn't so.

I had to tell myself to be calm.

We'd covered about half of the distance back to shore. I'd heard that for a long time there had been people out on the islands who were born there, lived there, and died there, and who'd hardly ever set foot on the mainland. They preferred to keep themselves as a separate community, and didn't care to mix much. It was a way of life that was dying out as people intermingled more, but I could understand its appeal. The world could be a rotten place. Not the kind of place you felt happy sending your kids out into.

The phone in my pocket started to ring.

Don Farrow's phone, remember.

I hadn't been expecting this. I took it out, and this time I remembered to look at it first. The little display screen was flashing a Charlotte area code for the incoming number. I pressed the green button and held the phone to my ear; because of the noise of the boat's engines I had to plug my other ear to make out what was being said.

"Yes?" I said.

"Hello?" I heard a male voice say. Not the same caller as the previous time. "Who's that?"

I said, "Who wants to know?"

"I believe you have my phone?"

Pow. I felt a surge of excitement. Don Farrow was calling his own number in an attempt to locate his misplaced phone.

"Yeah," I said, "that's right. Just give me one moment."

I moved from the rail to my car and got in. I needed quiet in order to hear him properly, and in order to concentrate. I closed the door, and the job got easier.

"You don't have to worry," I told him. "I'm keeping it safe for you."

"Where is it?"

"More to the point, where are you? I'll drop it by."

"No," he said, "that won't work."

I wondered if Behan had told him about calling his number and getting some stranger, or whether he was just taking a shot. I decided to try a shot of my own.

I said, "Is Cyrus with you, Don? Can he hear us?"

You could almost hear the thud as the boy's stomach dropped like a bowling ball at the other end of the line.

"Oh, *shit*," he said.

"Don't hang up on me," I said quickly. "I know you're in trouble. What's gone wrong?"

"Shit, shit, *shit*," he went on bitterly, and I don't know that he'd even heard what I was saying.

"Is it Rachel?" I persisted. "What's the matter with her? I'm not the police, Don. You can talk to me, I can help. What's happened?"

"Fuck you," Don Farrow said, and ended the call right there.

I knew that the handset had captured his number; I'd seen it on the screen and it would still be in the memory. If I could bring it up again, I could call him back. Even if he didn't answer, I'd have a handle on his location.

I did my best, but I had no idea what I was doing.

In the end I only succeeded in one thing, and that was to wipe the information.

Twenty-two

My first move when I got back into Charlotte that evening was to drive by Don Farrow's shared house again, where for ten minutes I sat across the street and watched the lighted windows as Bandanna Boy made trips between the TV in one room and the refrigerator in another. I guessed that he was alone because the only time he stopped scratching his nuts was to take his hand out of his pants and make a sandwich.

Then I went over to Rachel's. There was a light burning in the upstairs apartment and I took the stairs three at a time to get there, but no-one answered when I knocked on the door and when I looked in through the window, nothing appeared to have changed since my last visit. The light came from somewhere farther back and was leaking through all the open doorways inside.

I knocked again, harder, and the entrance door moved in about an inch.

I put my spread fingertips against the door and pushed, and after about a second of resistance it popped free and swung inward.

"Rachel?" I called out, stepping inside. "Rachel, are you there?"

Nothing. Not just silence, but no sense of anything behind the silence. I found the nearest light switch and turned it on. The lock on the door was intact, but the plate in the frame had been busted out. The broken wood was raw and yellow.

Somewhere outside and down below, I heard something clump. It was an odd sound, like someone had someone had picked up a chair and let it drop a few inches. About two seconds later, I heard it again.

When I moved to the open doorway and looked down, I saw that a woman was coming up the stairway to the apartment. She was in her sixties, wearing carpet slippers, and ascending with the aid of a tubular metal walking frame. As I watched, she lifted it to the next step, planted it with the clumping sound that I'd heard, and then slowly began raising herself to follow it up.

She wasn't looking my way, and I dodged back inside before she could see me.

I'm ashamed to say that I quickly calculated that I'd have a couple of minutes to look around before she made it to the top, longer if she were to stop for a rest. It would have been better form to go down and talk to her, and save her the climb. But if I did that and she told me to go, what then?

Clump. One foot up, then the next. Clump.

I gave the apartment the same kind of once-over that I'd given Cyrus' place, and with about the same level of success. Rachel Young wore pastel colors and owned more than one Bible. Her taste in calendar art favored flowers and puppies and her refrigerator door carried drawings from nephews and nieces. She was old-fashioned and unhip and as ordinary as could be. There was a framed picture of her with her parents, one of those professional studio jobs taken with a soft filter and printed with a canvas effect, and in that she didn't look geeky at all. Well, actually, she did a little. But pictures don't tell the whole story. The three of them were a happy-looking group. Sometimes that's all the story you need.

Clump.

The light that I'd seen had been coming from the bathroom, and had probably been on for ages. It wouldn't have shown up in the daytime. The toilet seat was down and there was an ugly, metallic smell in the air. I didn't get the chance to explore any further.

When the walking-frame woman finally arrived I was standing in the middle of the room with my hands in my pockets, looking thoughtfully around me. Not touching anything, not visibly interfering.

She stood in the doorway catching her breath, and said, "Excuse me?"

I affected to notice her. Like I'd been so absorbed in my thoughts that I hadn't heard her coming.

"I'm looking for Rachel," I said.

"Are you the father?"

"I'm with her employers. Do you know where she is?"

Frame-first, she came into the room.

"I haven't seen her since her boyfriend took her away," she said. "That would have been Wednesday night."

"Was that when the lock was broken?"

She didn't know about that. I showed her and I sympathized with her annoyance.

Her name was Ruby Crumb, she told me. She owned the house and lived downstairs. She'd let the top floor because...well, she asked me wryly, couldn't I see how much use it was to her these days?

Rachel had been a model tenant. Quiet, fastidious, trustworthy. In her opinion the boyfriend, as she called him, was the kind of trash that nice girls ought to have protection from.

She told me that Rachel had been unwell since the weekend.

"I got the clear impression they were trying to keep it a secret," Ruby Crumb told me. "It's not too hard to guess why."

"Can you tell me exactly what you saw?"

"If you were her father, it would be kind of hard for me to say it."

"I'm not her father," I said, and I pointed to the family photograph. "That's her father. Think of me as a friend she doesn't know she has yet."

"Well," Ruby Crumb said, "show me a scared-looking boyfriend and a girl doubled over with the stomach cramps, and I'd say the choice of conclusions is limited. I'm not a prude and I'm not a gossip. I just wish they hadn't treated me as if I was. I could hear her crying through the floor. It's not as if I could come running up those stairs every five minutes. But whenever I picked up the phone and asked to speak to her, he'd try to tell me that nothing was wrong. He was telling me that, and I could hear her yelling."

"Where would she have been?"

"In the bedroom," she said, pointing without taking her hand from the grey rubber grip on the frame.

I hadn't managed to get a look in the bedroom yet.

"Can I see?" I said.

We went through. I tried to stand back so that Ruby Crumb could lead the way, but she waved me on ahead. "Life's too short to be following a cripple," she told me, and I blushed and didn't know how to answer.

The bed wasn't unmade, but the covers were roughed up as if someone had been lying on them. I drew the covers back. The sheets underneath were clean.

I said, "If it was a botched abortion, wouldn't there be blood?"

"I didn't say I'd made a study," Ruby Crumb said.

I knew it hadn't been any abortion, anyway. I picked up one of the half-used bottles of medicine that stood on the bedside table. It was a drugstore constipation cure, non-prescription.

It was as I'd already suspected.

Whatever she'd swallowed had failed to come through. It was lodged somewhere in her system, blocking up the pipes. The longer it stayed in there with the gastric juices working on it, the more dangerous it would be for her. Much would depend upon what she'd used. Plastic would outlast latex. The usual form of such packaging was a knotted condom.

I said, "So when the boyfriend kept giving you these excuses, what did you say to him?"

"The longer he did nothing, the louder she got. So when it got to two in the morning I said that if he didn't get her to the hospital right away, I'd be calling in the police."

"Did he get her an ambulance?"

"I don't know what he called for, but it wasn't an ambulance that came. It was a friend of theirs who'd been around once or twice before. A big ugly boy in a van."

That sounded like Behan in his Dodge Ram. I said, "Did anybody mention his name?"

"If they did, I didn't hear it. They bundled her away like something out of witness protection gone wrong. I hope to hell they *did* take her to the hospital because a more furtive-looking pair you never did see."

"I'll check all the emergency rooms," I said. And I would, but I wasn't holding out much hope.

"You do that," Ruby Crumb said. "You do what's right by that girl and I'll pretend you didn't just walk in here without asking first."

I helped her down the stairs, me carrying the frame for her while she held onto my arm. She said that getting back down was always harder than climbing up. She knew she ought to find an easier place to live. But she loved her home.

I said, "The boy who came with the van. How was he? Calm? Jumpy?"

"I couldn't tell you his attitude," she said. "I can tell you I didn't like him."

I went into the ground floor kitchen with her and accepted her offer of coffee. I felt as if I owed her the company. We sat at her kitchen table and I glanced up at the ceiling. It was beamed, and between the beams I could see the underside of the boards belonging to the floor above.

I said, "How much of anything can you hear from down here?"

"Don't go trying to embarrass me," she said. "It's not as if I made a point of listening."

"But this is where you could hear she was in trouble."

"We're sitting right underneath the bedroom," she said. "And before you ask it, no, it's not every sound that carries."

"What did she say? I mean—"

"I know what you mean," she said. "I'm aware that some women have trouble keeping quiet in their moments of high passion. But it's a strange one that would cry out a thing like *Daddy, Daddy, I've done something stupid.*"

~

I was going to have to talk to the police. It was hard luck on Bill Nickles and his don't-compromise-the-company policy, but a life was at risk. An intestinal blockage alone was dangerous enough. But if just one of those packages opened up inside her, she'd take a system hit from its entire contents at once. There was no Poisondex on the planet for whatever those contents might be.

I couldn't let that happen. I was about to use Don Farrow's phone to make the call, when it came to life in my hand.

Same number as before. For the second time that day, Don Farrow was calling me. I opened the line and put the phone to my ear.

"Yes?" I said cautiously.

"Talking to you could be the most stupid thing I ever did in my life," he said.

"I don't think so, Don," I told him.

"Yeah, I know, the competition's too stiff. So who exactly are you?"

"My name's John Bishop. I'm with the British firm that helped to set up Macdonald-Stern. Nobody's looking for heads, here, Don. They just want to straighten everything out and keep it all very quiet."

I'd have been telling him this even if I'd already talked to the police. The last thing that I wanted to do right now was scare him off.

But by the sound of his voice it would probably have been difficult to make him any more scared than he already was.

He said, "I think Rachel's going to die on me."

"Stay calm, Don," I said. "Where are you now?"

"I'm outside this crummy motor court that Cyrus moved us to."

"Where?"

He told me the name and the road. I could picture it, vaguely, but I couldn't have said for certain where it was. If I was remembering right it was a faded, fifties-style place, with accommodation in bungalows stretching some way from the road. Get yourself set up in one of those at the very back, and you could scream and howl all you liked. The only people who might hear would be the ones least likely to give you any help.

I said, "And where's Cyrus?"

"He's gone to buy more medicines. He keeps pouring them down her, and they're only making her worse."

"She swallowed the drugs to get them out of the vault, right?"

"Yes. Now they won't come out."

"How were they packaged? How big were the samples?"

"I don't know." His voice was cracking and he was veering close to tears.

"Okay, Don," I said. "Do you have transportation?"

"No," he said. "Cyrus took the Dodge."

"We need to get paramedics to you and we need to get her to an emergency room as soon as possible."

"Cyrus said no hospital."

"I don't care what Cyrus said. I'll deal with Cyrus. Hang up, now, and I'll call 911."

"What if Cyrus comes back?"

"If we move fast," I said, "that won't happen."

Farrow hung up, as instructed, and I called 911 the moment I heard the dial tone. I didn't want to leave it to him. I needed to know that it had been done. I could too easily imagine him hovering around the phone and hugging himself, sniffing up tears of indecision until Cyrus' Dodge pulled up outside and it was all too late to act.

I did a perfect job of reporting. I could, after all, claim experience.

The emergency operator couldn't tell me for certain which hospital they'd be taking her to, but she gave me a number to call and find out. I gave it ten minutes, then I gave it another five, and then I called.

They'd picked her up and had intended to take her to Mercy South on the Pineville-Matthews road, but Mercy South was dealing with a five-way traffic accident from earlier in the evening and so the crew had diverted to Presbyterian. The ambulance was on its way there with her now.

Presbyterian Hospital was a place I could now find with ease. I'd been re-running the drive to it in my mind, over and over in unguarded moments throughout the past few days.

I started the Lexus and set out to do it again. Rachel's place wasn't so far from there.

She'd almost be coming home.

Twenty-three

I found Don Farrow in the phone corridor that ran between the Trauma area and the public waiting room. He'd ridden in with the ambulance and told them some version of what he knew, and I imagined they'd now sent him off to wait. He was wearing a parka jacket and jeans with Timberland boots. His hair looked as if it had been arranged by a bomb blast and he was walking slowly, wearily, with a dazed expression like someone who'd been snatched out of disaster and dumped in a movie version of heaven—one minute you're in darkness and raw terror, the next you're in a white place where they're taking your name.

"Don Farrow?" I called to him, and I saw his attention swing onto me and his eyes come into focus. I knew he was at least twenty-one, but apart from his eyes he looked about twelve years old.

He tried to say something, but it was as if his mouth wouldn't quite frame the words.

"I'm John Bishop," I said as I walked toward him. "We just talked."

He took a deep and shuddering breath, and nodded.

When he'd got control of himself he said, "I'm in a shitload of trouble, aren't I?"

Part of me wanted to say yes, and walk away.

But what I said was, "It doesn't have to be as bad as you think. At least you're doing the right thing now. What's happening with Rachel?"

"A whole team of them jumped on her as soon as we came in," he said, and he gestured vaguely back in the direction of the treatment area. "They took her through there."

I put my arm around his shoulder and walked him down the corridor and through the waiting area to where the vending machines were. He wasn't too steady and he didn't resist. I wanted to despise him, but I didn't have it in me. I was appalled at what he'd let happen but so, I sensed, was he.

I said, "How bad is she?"

"She just got worse and worse," Farrow said miserably. "She was bent over and screaming. She turned a color I've never seen a person go before."

"What did they say? Are the things just stuck inside her, or did the stuff begin to leak?"

"I don't know."

In the waiting area there were about a dozen couples and one or two loners. Nobody was talking and the only murmur was from the TV. Those waiting mostly sprawled in the low chairs looking slack and sad.

I said, "You were using her, Don."

"I'm not proud of it," he said.

"What were you thinking of?"

"Money!" he said, loudly enough and with sufficient exasperation to draw the attention of the black couple we were passing. They made no move but they tracked us with their eyes.

"What do you think?" he went on. "Cyrus said we could clear half a mill each and no-one would ever even know! Nobody was supposed to get hurt by it."

I squeezed his shoulder to calm him down, and we went on into the continuing corridor where the vendors were. The double-doors were pinned open but when we were out of earshot by the machines I said, "Cyrus is a loser. The drugs he had you stealing, nobody even knows what they are."

"It's the Russian stuff," Farrow said.

"I know it's the Russian stuff. Which is the equivalent of the dollar box of junk you buy at a farmers' auction because there's a slim chance you may turn up something worth having."

"I know that, now," he said. "I feel like an idiot."

I dug out some change to buy him a coffee. "You said it," I told him.

I saw the look he was giving to the snack boxes in the next vendor along, and it turned out that he hadn't eaten since the previous day apart from the motel's comped breakfast of watered orange juice and dinky muffins. Oh, and a large bag of tortilla chips that Cyrus had brought back from one of his trips to the drugstore. And some chicken nuggets he'd picked up at a drive-thru.

I let him select a heat-up cheeseburger and we put it in the microwave.

"Cyrus led you a dance," I told him. "This is where it brought you. What you made that girl steal has no market value. You'd better pray she doesn't die because of it."

He nodded. He knew it. Sometimes we screw up so badly that they only way to go forward with any dignity is to say so.

He said, "What do you want from me?"

"You want me to be honest, Don?" I said. "I want to see you punish yourself. Because if you don't, someone else will have to."

"You don't have to worry on that count," he said. "I feel like shit."

A handful of red dirt came out of his back, and the glass in the vendor behind him broke up into a million pieces. The sound of the shot came right after and was nothing like as spectacular.

It's a myth that a bullet hit throws a victim back against the wall. It goes straight through flesh like jelly, especially when it's from a high-velocity rifle at close range. Bone is no great obstacle either. In less time than it takes to snap your fingers, it's just pieces and powder in the wound.

Don Farrow began to topple sideways, away from me. In reflex, I reached to grab him. The surprised expression on his face suggested that he wasn't even aware he'd been shot yet. He put out an arm to stop his fall, and pushed the microwave off its shelf. He went down with it. The oven hit the floor with a crash and its door flew open. I was trying to get a hold on his clothes but all I could do was slow him and swing him off-course. I hadn't enough of a grip to keep him standing.

I got him lowered to the ground. There was broken safety-glass around us and all over us, and some of it was still dropping. I looked up through the doorway and saw, way across on the far side of the waiting area, a figure wearing a hooded coat and with a scarf across the lower half of his face. He looked like something out of news footage from some guerilla army. He was holding the rifle in his left hand and working the bolt on it with his right. He seemed to be moving in slow motion, but that was just my impression. Someone in the waiting area was screaming and I could see people scrambling away. I saw him turning, pivoting his weight on his left foot, my slowed-down perception giving him an unexpected grace. He was satisfied with his shot and now he had business elsewhere.

There was a tamper alarm whining on the vendor, adding to the overall sense of confusion. I leaned over Farrow, feeling powerless and gripping his hand in my own.

"Don?" I said. "Can you hear me? Squeeze my hand if you can hear me."

He was staring at the floor ahead of him with its litter of glass and busted oven and broken-up cheeseburger.

"Fuck," he said dazedly.

The folds in his clothing were such that it was hard to see what his injuries were. Maybe it was a clean shot and they weren't so bad. As I was reaching with my free hand to take a look, I heard two more shots from somewhere deeper within the building. I could hear someone wailing and I could hear another voice calling on Jesus for help.

Farrow was bleeding heavily, front and back. As I drew back a part of his jacket, a thin jet of blood shot forward before his eyes in an arterial squirt.

"Oh Christ," he said. "Is that me? Oh, Jesus."

I used his own jacket to staunch it as quickly as I could. Behind me I could hear someone running toward us in the corridor, running flat out, and then seconds later two hospital security guards came around and all but jumped over us as they headed for the source of the gunshots. The second guard skidded on the glass underfoot, but quickly recovered his balance. You don't often see them armed; these were.

I could hear more shouting, now, but I couldn't tell where it was coming from. I saw a couple of people from the waiting area making a run for it into the parking lot, crouching low as if to make themselves a smaller target. Not thinking, just taking flight. Some doors flew open and a nurse burst out at a run and disappeared off somewhere.

I called out, "Medic! Anybody! Got a man losing blood!" but there was nobody on hand to respond. I looked down at Don Farrow.

"Oh, God," he murmured weakly. The blood was pooling underneath him now and the pool was growing visibly bigger with frightening speed. It was a deep red, like ruby wine.

We couldn't just wait here for help to arrive. He had minutes, or less.

"Come on, Don," I said. "Walk with me."

I started to pull him up. He was no use at all. He was just hugging himself and staring ahead, pale and scared. I had to lean right over and yell *Come on!* in his ear, and then he flinched and made an effort. It wasn't much, but it was enough to make it easier to manage him.

I got him to his feet, I got his arm over my shoulder.

"Ow," he said.

"Hold this," I said, and I put his free hand on his coat and made him press his own wound shut so that I could concentrate on getting him to some attention. I urged him to walk. He tried a couple of staggering steps but then his legs just gave out and I had to all but carry him forward, the toes of his boots trailing as I did my best to keep him clear of the ground.

"It hurts," he said.

"That's good," I lied.

Most people in the waiting area were down on the floor. There was no-one behind the triage desk and the phone corridor beyond it was empty. One of the payphone receivers was swinging off its hook. I could hear what sounded like somebody shouting instructions deep in the building and I could hear sirens outside. I heard a door behind me open for about as long as it would take for one swift look through the crack, and then slam shut again.

"I want to lie down," Farrow said tearfully.

"Hang on, Don," I said. "Don't fall asleep on me."

This was the way the gunman had gone. But it was also where the doctors were. Two armed guards had gone ahead of us and I reckoned that if I fell over their bodies, that would be a signal to go no further. Otherwise I'd have to press on.

Don Farrow was in pain, but the only sounds that he could make were odd, little ones. My guess was that he was rapidly going into shock. When I saw the spare stretcher that they kept by the emergency room doors, I got him over and swung him around onto it.

The automatic doors of the treatment area were banging open and shut like a serving hatch as people ran back and forth inside, triggering the sensors. They stayed open as I manoeuvred the trolley through and entered into the melee.

Most of those I could see were guards and medical people. I was half-expecting to see bodies or the gunman pinned down on the floor, but there were none. Wherever the gunman was, he wasn't here. A man in scrubs had opened the sliding door on one of the treatment cubicles and was yelling the same question over and over, and like everyone else I couldn't make out what it was. People were using the phones at the desk and one of the guards was on his radio.

For a moment I felt as if I was invisible. I added my voice to all the others and no-one noticed as it blended right in with all the other racket. "Need some help, here," I called out. "This boy needs a doctor." Then I felt a touch on my arm.

"Is he hit?" the doctor said, sliding past me to get a look at Farrow. He was one I'd seen before, the bearded one.

"I saw him take a bullet," I said, and the doctor looked back over his shoulder at me.

"What about you?" he said, and I looked at myself and realized that I had enough of Farrow's blood down me to pass for a slaughterhouse worker.

"This is all from him," I said. "I'm fine. There was a girl with him, do you know what happened to her?"

"Nobody knows anything," he said, and I was immediately forgotten as he signalled to one of the others to help him get Farrow into one of the cubicles.

The police started arriving then. I knew that it would only be a matter of minutes before everything was brought under tight control, and I tried to get a look into each of the acute rooms to see if I could locate Rachel Young.

I had a bad feeling. In one there was a battered-looking teenaged boy whose treatment had been interrupted by the incident. His mother was in there with him and he appeared to be scared but stable. Don Farrow had been taken into the next, and he was getting the works. It was a bloodbath in there and I realized that his chances probably weren't good.

The third room was set up ready for use and the last was in a state of disarray, as if it had been used and not cleaned up. I looked around, saw a blue-gowned nurse, and caught her attention.

"Where's the girl who was in here?" I said.

She looked at the state of me and said, "Are you shot?"

"No," I said, at which she looked past me and went on.

Damn. I looked around. Two more of the staff went shouldering through the growing crowd and into the room where they were working on Don Farrow. One of the police officers was trying to get some attention from everyone. I could hear a woman crying.

I pushed my way through to the cubicles on the other side but these were the non-acute rooms, the ones they'd taken me to so that I could sit with Gillian, and all but one were empty; in the exception there were half a dozen people and in the middle of the half-dozen I caught a familiar glimpse of flame-red hair, a shock of autumn color tied up at the back. I saw her through glass. She was surrounded by concerned bodies, all talking to her; she was shaking her head, holding up her hands, protesting that she was okay…none of those around her seemed to believe her and she didn't look it, either.

I entered, squeezing in behind the rest of them. She looked scared but unhurt. Her hands were on her stomach, the way you'd hold a fragile ball of glass. She glanced up at the movement, and our eyes met.

"Where is she, Kate?" I tried to call through them. Nobody else was aware of me yet, apart from her.

I said, "He took her, didn't he? Did he take her away?"

She put one hand up to her mouth, and that hand was shaking. Suddenly I wished I hadn't spoken. The others noticed me then.

"Hey," someone said. "Mister. Wait outside please."

They closed ranks around her and someone guided me out of the door. I believed I'd had my answer.

Out in the middle of the treatment area they'd cleared a way through and I saw Don Farrow being sped out, probably to surgery. They were getting blood plasma into him by the litre and it looked as if most of it was coming straight out again. A uniformed cop was following the trolley, speaking into his radio; I moved after him and caught him by the sleeve.

The officer turned on me and was about to say something, but when he caught sight of the blood on my clothes he faltered.

"I'm not hurt," I said. "I can tell you what happened."

"You'll get your chance," he told me, and looked past my shoulder to summon someone over.

Order was gradually being restored. I reckon it couldn't have been much more than ten, twelve minutes since Behan had shot Don Farrow and then walked into the ER and taken Rachel. How had he known where she'd be? It could only be that he'd returned to the motel in time to see her being driven away, and had followed the ambulance. He must have had the rifle with him all the time.

I was taken to join a crowd of other witnesses, all of us seated side-by-side to await questioning. Next to me was an elderly man with glasses so thick that the lenses were like tiles.

I wondered if he'd been anywhere close when Behan had come for Rachel.

"Did you see anything?" I said to him.

"I saw Satan," he said confidently.

"I'm talking about the boy with the hunting rifle."

"I seen all his disguises," the man said.

Twenty-four

After a while, individual policemen and women came over and started matching up with witnesses. They sat down and started taking statements from us, one-to-one. The uniformed woman who talked to me listened for a couple of minutes and then took me out of the crowd and stood me by the main ER desk.

"Don't move from there," she said, and went off to look for someone.

I waited as I'd been told to. Order had mostly been restored but there was some kind of an argument going on about an incoming case. The trauma center had been declared closed until the police lab people released the crime scene, but no-one had told the paramedics on the road. As half a dozen people thrashed it out, the case was stretchered in and past me. He was a man of about my own age, conscious and scared-looking and wearing an oxygen mask.

From behind me I heard, "Hey. Sir?"

I turned. It was my policewoman.

"John Bishop," I reminded her.

"Come this way, please."

She took me just out of the treatment area and she put me into the first empty room that we found. It was another one of those windowless internal offices and when she closed the door, I felt the level of disquiet rise within me and had to go over and open it again, just a crack, so that I could hear the noise of activity outside.

When I settled back onto the chair, all the excitement and the energy seemed to drop out of me and I sat there feeling wasted and spent. For the moment it was as if I'd fought my way to the center of a tornado. I could look up and see an eye of stillness in the sky above me, even though everything around me was in chaos. I also knew that the moment couldn't last. I'd have to move forward just to stay in place, or the chaos would suck me in.

I looked down at the blood on my shirt. No wonder everyone had thought I was injured. I picked at the material and felt it peel away from my skin. The moment I let go, it stuck itself back down again. I hadn't really noticed it before, but it made me feel squirmy and uncomfortable now.

Three people came into the room then, plus the policewoman who'd put me in here. The others were in plain clothes and I didn't need to be told that one of them was a senior investigator. He pulled out a chair and sat in front of me. There were no chairs for the others and so they stood around.

The investigator said, "What can you tell us?"

"How's Kate O'Brien doing?" I said.

"Kate who?"

"The red-haired one. The patient rep. The pregnant one."

"She wasn't hurt," he said. "But no pregnant woman wants to see a gun being pointed at her. It's given her a scare and it'll take her a while to get over it. What happened to you?"

"I was talking to Don Farrow when Cyrus shot him."

He glanced approvingly at one of the others, and I heard a click which might have meant that someone was recording me.

"Right," he said. "Cyrus who?"

"Cyrus Behan."

"How do you spell that?"

I spelled it for him, and he nodded and shot another glance at one of the others. I heard somebody sliding out of the door behind me, probably to run a check on the name. I could hear him making a call just outside.

I said, "Is Don Farrow going to die?"

"Nobody can say that, yet. Tell me what you know."

Now that I had the invitation, the words seemed to desert me. "Oh, shit," I said, and I ran my fingers through my hair. "Where to start?"

"Why would Cyrus Behan kidnap a sick girl out of a treatment room?" the investigator said.

"Because he thinks he's protecting his investment."

I went on from there.

He gazed at me steadily as I told him the story, and I didn't need to read his expression to know that I was losing him fast. My performance was lousy. I was too tired, and my head was in a mess. I was throwing in all kinds of details and I kept getting sidetracked by my own train of thought. When I heard myself wandering I'd drag myself back on track, only to find that I'd missed out something vital and had to go back. I got this phonecall. No, wait, I didn't tell you about how I came to have Farrow's phone.

I could sense their patience running out and I hadn't even got to the crux of it yet. After a while the investigator cut in and said, "Slow down, here. I thought you said her name was Rachel Young."

"That's right," I said.

"So who's Gillian?"

"Gillian's my daughter," I said.

"What's she got to do with it?"

"She died on Sunday," I said, wondering what he was talking about and unaware of any lapse. "She died right here."

"Mister Bishop," he said then, leaning forward. "Even the names in this tale you're telling us keep changing. Are you entirely certain of whose story this is supposed to be? Do you actually know what happened here?"

My head suddenly cleared. I don't know whether it cleared for real, or whether that was just an illusion. It was like an acidhead's certain perception of a reality he can't begin to express. In that moment I saw myself through their eyes, and realized that if I couldn't convince them otherwise, I'd be just another unreliable would-be witness in a world of satan-spotters and fantasists and losers off the street.

"Yes, I do," I said. "I'm sorry if I'm rambling. Whatever you see is not the impression I set out to make. But call Bill Nickles at Macdonald-Stern and he'll confirm everything I've told you. I *am* John Bishop. I *did* receive a call that I couldn't explain. I *have* been pursuing a theft from the company's vault because of it. Everything I'm saying is the truth."

A voice behind me, belonging to the officer who'd slipped out to use the phone and who'd since returned, said, "I called his company and spoke to...Rose Macready?"

I nodded vigorously, in confirmation.

"I know Rose," I said.

"She says he's been suspended from his job since last weekend. She says we have to treat anything he says with a lot of caution."

I was still nodding as this sank in. Then I felt my stomach do a flip as I realized what he'd said. Although in that moment I hadn't even begun to think it through, I reckon that at some deep-down level I suddenly grasped where all of this was now going.

"She's lying about that," I said. "None of that's true."

The Investigator didn't take his eyes off mine. But something in them had changed.

"Why would she lie?" he said.

The voice behind me added, "This Rose Macready also says that he's been refusing psychiatric help and that he won't even speak to his wife about their daughter's death."

The investigator looked to me for comment, but his body language had altered now. He wasn't encouraging me to speak. It was more like he was daring me to persist.

He said, "Is she lying about that, too?"

"And," the man behind me went on, still banging those nails into the coffin of my credibility, "she insists that there's been no theft of drugs or of any other substance. And they'll set lawyers on anyone who publicly suggests otherwise."

They all waited.

"Well?"

"I'm not inventing all this," I said with desperation. "Why would I? They've got to back me up."

"Looks like they don't," the investigator said with a show of sorrow, and I heard another one of those clicks which meant that if they'd been taping me, they'd stopped.

I put my face in my hands.

"Oh, shit," I said, "tell me they can't do this."

The senior investigator started to rise. The others were beginning to move as well. They'd come in here looking for a star witness and I'd failed to measure up. I was just a disappointing lead and it was time for them to move on.

The senior man said, "I'll tell you what will help me. Write it all down."

"Don't walk away from me," I said.

"I'm not walking away," he said. "I'm doing my job."

"Please," I said, and I got a handful of his shirt as he tried to pass me. Everything happened very quickly right then. The others jumped forward and grabbed me and put me back in my seat. They don't like it when you touch them, but they can be awfully fast when they want to get their hands onto you.

They pinned me there as he said, "Listen to me, you. I'm sorry about your daughter. I've got an idea of what you're going through. But you've got to understand that I can't waste time while you punch around in the dark."

"I'm not insane," I said.

"I didn't say you were. But you're not being consistent either. I don't blame you, and don't blame yourself. It's how these things are. Now let me get out there and let me do what I do."

The other two cops held me in place until he'd gone. Then one of them said to me, "Okay, now?"

"Yes," I said, and they cautiously let me go.

I straightened myself in the chair as they stepped back. They looked at their hands and their clothes and saw that some of Farrow's blood had transferred itself to them.

"Ah, no," one of them said. "I got it on me."

"Someone better tell us if the kid got tested," the other one said.

They left the policewoman to get my details, and I could see that she was subdued now and less than pleased with me. There was no further mention of me writing down my story. Presumably that was something I was supposed to go home and do with crayons, as therapy.

I had to find a washbasin in another part of the hospital, where I cleaned myself up as best I could. My clothes were ruined and I couldn't get any of the rest of me clean as long as I still had them on. I could hardly look at myself in the mirror over the basin. I'd thought that I had some measure of control, but the walking wreck that I saw seemed to have none.

Washed in the blood of a sinner. All that I succeeded in doing now was to make a mess of the men's room. I wondered how Farrow was, but I didn't try to go back and find out. At least if he lived, he'd be able to back me up. They'd take me more seriously then. But I tried to wish him life regardless of any advantage to me. He'd behaved like a shit toward Rachel but he didn't deserve to die.

Out in the parking lot, I saw Kate O'Brien being helped into a car by a man that I assumed to be her husband. I couldn't see much of him from a distance. When he'd got her safely installed, he headed back to the main building. I knew from last time that when the barrier was unmanned, you had to go and ask for a four-digit exit code to get you out.

I walked over to her car. She saw me coming, and lowered the electric window.

"I'm going home," she said. "You should do the same."

"I'm sorry," I said.

"For what?"

"I don't know."

"Don't apologize to me," she said. "I'm going home and I won't be coming back. I've got to think of myself from now on, so I won't be able to help you any more. I don't really feel that I've helped you as it is. Please, John, do something to straighten yourself out. The worst thing in the world that can happen to anyone has happened to you.

You'll never get over it and life will never be the same as it was. You have to go to some new place."

"Did he scare you?"

"What do you think? I never had anyone point a gun at me before. I was terrified."

"What are the police saying about it?"

"Just your basic junkies and weapons incident. We've taken knives off them before. This has been a first."

"I don't suppose you know whether the boy was able to tell them anything."

"Last I heard, he was still in surgery. Apparently the bullet that hit him was a Black Talon. They open up like a claw as they go through. The doctors hate them. They leave tiny blades behind in the wound and cut their fingers through the gloves. Will you do what I've asked you, John?"

"I don't know," I said. "I don't know what I'll do."

I could see her husband returning. I told her good night and good luck, and I backed off from the car. He was giving me a wary look as he came around to the driver's door, but I gave her a wave and walked away. They left the parking lot ahead of me. Her head was bowed and she didn't look back.

I'd heard of Black Talons.

Winchester made them. Hunters used them.

~

Just your basic junkies and weapons incident.

God, I hoped Don Farrow lived to tell them different. Because it was clear that nobody was going to listen to me. As I drove back to my motel I found myself looking at every vehicle on the road, half-expecting to catch sight of Cyrus' Dodge with Rachel in the passenger seat. But if I'd been Cyrus, right then I'd be heading for anywhere that wasn't this city. Even if no-one acted on my information, the chances were they'd have picked up his vehicle and maybe even his license plate on the parking lot's security cameras.

I didn't think that Cyrus was particularly bright. But I certainly didn't think he lacked cunning. I thought of his face in the file picture with its straggly beard and deadpool eyes. There had been a boy just like him in Gillian's class when she'd been about six years old. I remembered him from the school nativity play. He'd just stood there and wouldn't speak, staring flatly out at the audience while the rest of it was staged around him. I couldn't have told you what he was thinking. I don't believe anybody could. I don't know what became of him.

My motel room had been made over, the carpet vacuumed and the bedcovers straightened. There was a red message light blinking on the room phone, but I ignored it. I undressed under a pounding shower and left my bloodied clothes in the stall. Even when the water ran clean I continued to feel sullied, as if I'd participated in a sacrifice.

Wrapped in motel towels, walking barefoot on thick motel carpet, I plodded to the bed and sat heavily. I'd thrown out my wallet, my keys, my change, everything onto the bed as I'd headed for the bathroom. Now I gathered them together and moved them to the bedside table along with all my papers, the printouts, and the Macdonald-Stern files on the agents of the great Spirit Box heist.

Once I'd cleared myself space I flopped onto my back, thinking that in a minute or so I'd crawl under the covers but first I'd work out what I was going to do in the morning.

However, all I could see when I closed my eyes was Cyrus Behan, turning on his heel. Cyrus Behan, swinging his rifle around as he worked the bolt in slow motion. I could see now that he wasn't just turning away; he was acting the turn, throwing in a little flamboyance, living out the movie that was playing in his head.

That's almost the last thought I can remember. I didn't check what time it was then but I must have slept for two or three hours, at least, with the lights on and my hair still damp and the shower still dripping. In my disturbed sleep I saw Rose Macready bending over me. She was naked and she was heavily pregnant. I felt her warm breath upon me and I felt myself responding, and I was shocked and ashamed but I'm not sure of why.

The phone woke me.

I sat upright and before I'd even thought what I was doing, I had it to my ear and was saying my name.

Bill Nickles didn't have to identify himself. I knew his voice straight away.

Which was just as well, because without any preamble he went straight in with, "You did the one thing I told you not to."

"Sorry, Bill..." I said, rubbing my eyes and yawning. "Bring me up to speed."

"Get this clear," he said. "Nothing's missing. Nothing's happened. Nobody ever gave you the authority to do a damn thing."

"What about Rachel Young?"

"Rachel Young is a former employee with a private life that has no connection with the affairs or the internal security of this company."

"What's inside her could kill her."

"That's one possible result out of many. It isn't in my hands and it isn't in yours. You've got all the troubles a man could ask for, John. You don't need more."

With that, he hung up.

I sat there with my head in my hands. It felt like a dead weight and I could barely hold it up. It was only then that I noticed something. On the bedside table were the keys and the wallet that I'd placed there, but there were no longer any files or papers of any kind. I looked all around me, stupidly, but I couldn't see them anywhere.

I got to my feet and checked the entire room in case I'd moved them again without thinking. But even as I was going through the motions, I knew that I hadn't. There was only one conclusion I could draw. Someone had actually been into the room and removed them as I'd slept.

I was half-convinced that I could detect someone's perfume in the air.

I could almost go further, and convince myself that it was the same as that which still lingered on my pillow.

Twenty-five

I didn't go back to sleep. I called the hospital and they told me that Don Farrow was out of surgery, but they wouldn't tell me his condition. I knew at least that he'd survived, but I also knew better than to think that this was the end of it. You can get your children into the hands of the miracle workers, but your children can suffer every miracle in their repertoire and still die. They can fix and patch them for you, they can irradiate, they can operate. But they can't make time run backwards.

I combed my hair, cleaned my teeth, got some fresh clothes out of my suitcase, and drove over.

It was still the evening, now sometime after ten. I saw that it had rained again while I'd slept. Two guards looked me over as I went in through the hospital's main entrance, but that was all the extra security that I saw. I took an elevator up to the fifth floor, where a nurse on the Surgical Unit desk told me that Farrow was being held in post-anaesthesia care. Immediate family were being allowed in to see him at the doctor's discretion.

Normal visiting had ended at nine and the Unit's waiting area was all but deserted at this hour. Not only did I spot Don Farrow's parents immediately, but I recognized his father and his father knew me. Clayton Farrow was one of our site safety officers. If I remembered right, he was an ex-fireman. His hair was iron-grey and wiry, his handshake was firm. His wife had a stunned and not-quite-there look, like someone recovering from a taser hit.

I said, "How is he?"

"A lot better than he has any right to be," Clayton Farrow said. "They told us he bled out twice over while they had him on the table. You're John Bishop, aren't you?"

"Yes, I am."

"He told us he would have died if it wasn't for you."

"Does that mean he's talking?"

"Oh, he's talking," the mother put in, and seemed about to say something more before she lost her way and dried.

"He woke up with so much to say that the doctor gave him a sedative to put him back under," Clayton Farrow said. "Even that hasn't worked. We owe you a big debt of thanks, Mister Bishop."

"All I did was walk him around the corner," I said. "How come you're out here? Won't they let you sit with him?"

"Rose Macready's there. She asked if we'd mind leaving them for a few minutes. To be honest with you, I think we needed to catch our breath. I never want another night like this one."

I said, "Where's the room?"

I didn't run, but only because I didn't want to draw attention. She was gone when I got there.

Post anaesthesia care was like a field hospital in space. One big clean-environment room, sectioned off with drapes so that the nurses could see all the beds but the patients had some privacy from each other. Only three of the bays were in use and so the rest of it was open floor. Two nurses were keeping everything ticking over and neither seemed worried by my presence.

Don Farrow's eyes were on me as I went over to his bedside. The bed was a major work of technology on its own, wheeled-in and locked-off to put him in a half-sitting position. Don looked frail and in less than great shape. A lightweight collar braced his head and there was a tube in his neck. The part of his torso that wasn't covered by dressings was stained a yellowish-brown by some paint that they'd slapped around the wound site. His eyes were dark and sunken but they were one hundred and ten per cent alive.

"Hi," I said.

"I can't talk to you." His voice was a whisper and he spoke with his teeth clamped together, but I had no problem understanding him.

"How long's she been gone?" I said.

"Couple of minutes."

"What did she say?"

"Among other things? She said I can't talk to you."

"Let me guess," I suggested. "You stay quiet, you've got a future. You say what really happened, then you're fired."

He shook his head, as far as the brace would allow. It was only an inch from side to side but the intention was clear.

"What, then?"

"My dad," he said.

Realization hit me then. I'd been stupid not to see it. Where the company was concerned, Don Farrow had little to lose. Their leverage on his career and his future was negligible. He'd go elsewhere, he'd find another ladder to climb. But with a man in his fifties it would be a different story.

I drew up a chair and sat beside him.

He said, "If it was just me, it wouldn't matter."

"Don't misunderstand me, Don," I said, "but your father's not a young man. Getting retired now may be no big deal for him. Why don't you talk it over with him before you decide what you do?"

"If that's all it was," he said.

"What do you mean?"

"She told me they'll pull everything he's entitled to. No benefits, no medical insurance. And they call in the company loans. That's not retirement. I don't know what you call it, but it ain't golf and sunshine."

"Oh," I said.

And then I said, "Are you going to tell him?"

"No way," he said.

We sat in gloomy silence for a while, and finally I said, "So what do we do, Don?"

"I'm sorry."

"No," I said, wondering if I could somehow pressure him for Rachel's sake, knowing that I couldn't. Not now. Not when he was like this. I'd been hoping that he'd get what he deserved, but this was way beyond it. "Don't be sorry," I said. "You're not in the wrong."

I thought for a while longer and came up with nothing.

"Shit," I said.

Don Farrow took a rattling breath that was deeper than most of those that had gone before it and said, "What's gonna happen to Rachel?"

"Looks like that's for Cyrus Behan to decide," I said. "How's his conscience?"

"I don't believe he has one."

One of the nurses came by then, and cast a critical eye over Don.

"Still fightin that sedative?" she said, and then, to me, "You ain't his daddy."

"Nope," I said. "Just a friend."

"Well, say your goodnights and let the boy sleep," she said, and after she'd noted something on his chart she moved on.

Don said, "I'd better tell you this fast. Cyrus started making new plans this morning. He reckoned that if the medicines didn't work then he'd have to try something else."

"Like what?"

"He said if Rachel's going to die anyway, he might as well salvage his investment and cut the drugs out of her before they get a chance to break up and disperse. Can you imagine that? It's what made me call you."

"Cut them out of her?"

"That's what he said."

"Saying it's one thing. Doing it's something else."

"He says his uncles taught him how to butcher a deer. He doesn't see this as anything much different."

I suddenly felt sick.

I said, "You really think he could carry that through?"

Don tried to smile, weakly, but only one side of his face made a proper job of it.

He said, "You're asking a guy with a hole in his chest and a tube in his throat, all thanks to Cyrus. What do *you* think? I know what I believe. Either she shits him a fortune in the next twenty-four hours, or he goes in and gets it."

On the other side of the room the nurse said a pointed, "Hel-*lo?*" and so I got to my feet and put the chair back where I'd reached it from.

"She's no ugly duckling, Don," I said. "She didn't deserve that."

"I know it," he said.

"Any idea where they might be now?"

"No," he said. "You could try those uncles. It's hard to picture anyone else who'd take him in."

Twenty-six

I might have had a fighting chance at finding Behan's relatives if Behan's file hadn't been taken from my room as part of the damage limitation exercise that seemed to be going on. By morning I guessed it would be complete, if it wasn't already. I'd been thoroughly discredited, Don Farrow had been silenced, and as for Rachel Young—well, I couldn't clear my mind of a picture of Rachel hanging by her heel tendons like a butchered carcase, strung up on a couple of hooks in a dark shed somewhere. If not already, then sometime soon.

Would Cyrus have the nerve? Could he go that far?

To my mind, the answer to that one had to be yes. Didn't it? This was a man who could stand there and shoot his confederate at close range with a razor-blade round. Masked or not, from the moment he'd walked into Presbyterian with a loaded rifle he'd had nothing to lose. He'd abandoned his past in the anticipation of riches; any vision he might have of the future depended on the fortune he thought he was taking away. The laugh would be on him in the end, when it eventually dawned on him that his treasure really was no more than ashes. But long before that happened, Rachel Young would be another tragic casualty of his misconception.

I drove across town, out toward the plant. Macdonald-Stern operated throughout the night, although after regular hours all the offices stood empty and the night shift was a small force concerning itself with rush jobs and anything that needed round-the-clock monitoring.

The country roads that led me down to the science park were all but deserted at this hour. I saw the occasional light through the trees, but no other traffic. At one point I saw a deer crossing the road in front of me, walking with an easy stride at first, breaking into a lope as it became aware of my headlights; in three quick bounds it was across the immaculately-kept verge and into the roadside foliage.

The security hut at the main drive-in entrance was closed-up and unmanned. This time I put my card through the reader the right way around. The barrier jerked into life and lifted and I was through.

My headlights made an over-arching tunnel out of the trees on the driveway as I followed it up to the parking area. There were very few cars in either of the two lots, and those present were all at the end closest to the footpaths. I left the Lexus with them and walked with my head down, thinking it might make me unrecognisable to the cameras.

At the locked doors to the admin block I used my card again, and heard the buzz as the automatic bolts sprang open. The entrance hall was silent and the day desk was unattended, and my footsteps echoed as I headed across for the elevators.

I'd worked a lot of late nights here, and I could never quite get used to that after-hours feeling. Most of the lights had been left on for the office cleaning staff to find their way around. This gave the entire building a strange atmosphere, as if a nuclear wind had ripped through it and sterilized the place of all life.

Up in my corner office, I switched on my monitor and logged on. That was where I hit my first problem. Although my swipe card still worked, my system password had already been cancelled.

But then I tried it with Rose Macready's, hoping that her password for the main server would be the same as the one she'd given me for her powerbook. It was. After a tense couple of seconds, I was in.

This was potentially a better move than I'd imagined, because as Rose I had access to even more in-depth personnel information than before. I ran a search with 'Cyrus Behan' as my keywords and immediately found myself faced with far more detail than I could ever use. I didn't want his stats or a breakdown of all his overtime for the past two years, and I didn't want to know how many times he'd parked his truck in the disabled drivers' spaces.

When I found his personal profile I went into that, but the results I came up with were disappointing. The 'next of kin' field had been left blank and the record showed no past addresses other than the one I already knew.

From behind me I heard, "Stand up and step away from the desk, please, Mister Bishop," and I'll swear that I lifted about six inches out of the seat.

The night security crew were a different set of people to the daytime ones. Sometimes they swapped back and forth but mostly they stuck to their own hours. This man was only slightly familiar to me, although he clearly knew who I was.

I reached to do something with the screen but he said, "We'll just leave that as it is."

So I just stood up and showed my empty hands. The younger man who'd come in behind him now stepped forward.

"I'm afraid we'll have to search you, sir," he said.

"I know," I said, and I stepped away from the desk and submitted to the kind of pat-down they give you at airport security. He found my wallet, and they took out my company ID and the card I'd used to get in. He found Don Farrow's phone and, after examining it, kept that as well.

"Thank you," he said as he stepped back.

He'd also kept my car keys.

They didn't do anything with my terminal, other than turn the monitor so that it couldn't be seen from any of the windows. Then they moved me out of the office and locked the door after us.

"Looks like I won't be coming back," I said.

"Our orders are to escort you from the property," the older man said.

"What about the personal stuff in my desk?"

"I'm sure all of that will be returned to you, but I don't have the authority to do it."

I knew there was no point in arguing.

"Did they tell you why I'm getting this treatment?"

"That's really none of our concern, sir."

They walked me out and I just went along with it. There was nothing else I could do. They made no conversation and I didn't try to get one started.

When we were out in the parking lot, one of them waited with me as the other opened up the Lexus and gave it the once-over. He found the Gap bags with the new clothes that I'd put in the trunk and done nothing with. He glanced through them and then lifted up the trunk carpet and checked the well underneath it.

"Where's the disk?" he said when he'd done with the car.

"What disk?"

"The disk of files that Ms Macready's assistant made for you."

"Try the CD tray on my office machine," I said. "It's been there for a couple of days."

They exchanged a glance. I could see that they probably believed me.

I shivered a little in the night chill. In the darkness of the driveway I saw headlights approaching. After a few moments I could see that they belonged to a dark Cherokee Jeep which made a big arc around the parking lot and pulled up alongside us. I was surprised because I'd heard that Bill Nickles usually drove some kind of a special-edition roadster, the kind of young man's car that only rich old men can afford. Maybe this was his wife's vehicle.

He wasn't dressed for business, either. One side of his sport shirt collar was up, as if he'd thrown it on in a hurry. He looked at the car and then he looked at me. He wasn't angry, he wasn't smiling. The problem I presented him with no longer called for any of that pack animal social give-and-take.

The security guard closed the trunk of the Lexus. When he met Bill Nickles' eyes briefly, he gave a slight shrug and a shake of the head. Nothing found. Nothing to get excited about.

I said, "Don't do this, Bill."

"Don't do what, John?" he said, coolly, turning to look at me again.

"Let me carry on and find her. Otherwise you might as well go out there and kill her yourself."

"That's a very twisted way of looking at it."

"That's good, coming from you," I said. I was trying to keep emotion out of it, but I could hear it creeping in all the same. "Say what you like about me," I said. "The way I feel right now, my life's over anyway. But don't write that girl off."

Bill Nickles stuck his hands in his pockets and slowly walked around behind me, looking thoughtfully at the ground. The two guards just stood there, nameless presences with the gift of professional amnesia.

Nickles said, "We do what we can with the things in our grasp. But there are things out there we don't control. You have to know when to stop trying and this is one of those times. If you think you can make a difference, you're like a dog chasing a bus. This is something that ran away from us. All we can do now is take care of business and limit the damage."

He stopped right in front of me and looked me in the face.

"John," he said, "I'll say this to you one last time. Go home."

And there, in a nutshell, was my underlying problem.

"To what?" I said.

"This may or may not be of interest to you," he said. "But your wife's at the Days Inn by the airport. I offered her somewhere a little more upscale, but it's the first place she saw and it's the place that she chose. I spent two hours with her this afternoon, trying to explain something. I was trying to explain *you*. It wasn't easy, trying to make sense out of something I don't even begin to understand."

I looked past him.

"Do I still keep the car?" I said.

"Give things a chance to work themselves out," he said, ignoring my bid to divert him. "You may feel as if you're all alone, but that's not true. Look to your own concerns, now. Those kids are seeing out something they should never have started. All I can say about that is, whatever happens is what happens. Even the worst can sometimes be for the best. Do you honestly think that God doesn't watch over us?"

I looked at him then. I thought he was being ironic but he was absolutely sincere. None of us needed to look out for Rachel, because God would take care of her future. And if Rachel should come to some serious grief, then God had clearly had that in mind for her all along.

It was an awfully convenient credo. I couldn't help noting that in the time since he'd joined us, Nickles had never yet chosen to head off to the golf course while the Almighty got on with the day-to-day running of the business.

Did I honestly think that God didn't watch over us?

I knew for sure that he didn't watch over me. I had the proof.

They put me in the passenger seat of the Lexus, and the younger one drove me to the gate. The other man followed in one of the security cars, a white GMC Jimmy truck with an orange lightbar on its roof. Nickles didn't come with us.

Once we were outside the barriers, the young guard who'd been driving me got out and left the engine running.

"You can take it from here, sir," he said. "Please don't try to re-enter the site. You won't be admitted."

"I can imagine," I said.

The other one joined us. He gave me back my wallet, minus the ID and other stuff.

"Your phone," he said.

He was assuming it was mine. Of course he was. Why shouldn't he? "Someone's been trying to call you," he observed as he glanced at the display.

"When?"

He gave a little shrug as he handed me the phone. The display read 1 CALL MISSED.

"I didn't hear it ring," he said.

They both got into the Jimmy truck, and they waited and watched as I drove off with the phone lying on the seat beside me. As soon as I was away from the site and reached a stretch of the road where it was safe to stop, I pulled in.

I was on the dirt shoulder of a country lane and when I switched off the engine, I could hear woodland sounds all around me. There's nothing tranquil about a forest at night. The moment it gets dark, everything dives screaming onto everything else and it's mayhem out there. The food chain in action.

I waited. I knew from previous experience that if someone had called, received no reply, and then left a message on the system, I'd be getting another call soon as the system tried to deliver it.

I didn't dare to fiddle around with the handset. I might delete something vital again. I noticed that the phone's battery level was getting low. I looked at the charger lead from my own phone, but it was a different kind of plug.

Sure enough, it rang.

What I heard then had no solid existence, not even as a recording on a tape. They don't use tape. It was like a held thought, somewhere in the system. It existed until it was forgotten. And then it would be as if it had never existed at all.

I heard a sob.

And then, as if from space, I heard her speak.

Hello? she said. *Don? Is there anybody there? Anyone? Help me. Please.*

She went on, sobbing and pleading in much the same vein. It was almost unbearable but I had to listen. I waited on edge for some hint of where she was calling from, feeling as if I was going to burst, but there was none.

It lasted for one precise minute. Then it stopped, and I realized that I hadn't taken a single breath since it had begun. A voice like a robot schoolteacher told me what button to press to replay the message. Part of me didn't want to, but I did.

Strange to say, there was nothing new in it the second time around.

Nor did it get any easier to hear.

Twenty-seven

Driving up Plaza I saw signs for tattooists, for spiritualists, for places where checks could be cashed and Western Union money orders wired. I saw billboards and pawnshops and Seafood you-buy-we-frys and a bingo barn with space before it for a thousand cars, if you could find a thousand people who weren't too choosy about where they liked to park.

I saw plenty of light and color but what I didn't see was much sign of life at this hour. It was almost midnight and I was running out of options fast.

Then I thought I'd got lucky. I pulled into the parking lot of a Giant Penny food discount store because I'd seen a banner across its marquee that read BEEPERS in big, red letters. The store was an all-nighter and so I got out of the car and went inside.

Normally I wouldn't even have risked being on the streets so late, let alone go wandering unprotected in a district I didn't know. Most of what I usually saw of the city's nightlife, I saw on the local news. Mostly that consisted of dazed-looking people being bent over police cars and handcuffed.

I didn't actually want a beeper. I was just hoping that the sign would lead me to what I *did* want. I stood just inside the doors and looked around. Nobody was shopping but there were a couple of people stacking the shelves. Over to my left was an indoor ATM machine by a magazine stand, screen all aglow like some communication device dumped among us by aliens. Right in front of me was a display of torn greetings cards being sold off at seventy-five cents each.

Beyond the greetings cards stood disappointment in the form of a booth for the sale and service of pagers and cellular phones. The booth was a wooden enclosure like a rough stockade, the display under its glass counter crowded with used cellular phones and empty pager bodies. The disappointment came because it was closed. On the lockdown roller screen was a home-made sign that read, *Ask about our layaway plan.*

I went to the pay phones at the front of the store and found one with a hanging phonebook that had most of its pages intact. I looked in the Yellow Pages section and then a couple of minutes later I was back on the road with an address followed by the words *24hr Service* still fresh in my mind. I was hoping that it was accurate and that it wasn't out of date.

I couldn't stop thinking of that voice. It was Rachel. It was Gillian. That investigator had been right, I couldn't tell any more. I knew that it came out of the body of Rachel Young but in my heart was the conviction that there was some deeper dimension to it that would ever resist any ultimate explanation.

The place I was looking for stood in an old strip mall along with a 60 Minute Cleaners' and a True Value hardware store. It took up two thirds of a long, low building, old brick painted grey with three satellite dishes on its roof and a wooden overhang at the front. All of the windows had been blanked out with some sort of gold reflecting foil, apart from the entrance door which had wire reinforced see-through glass.

I saw lights. Through the door I saw movement inside.

The entrance door was locked. It was controlled by a buzzer with an intercom and an overhead video camera. I pressed the bell and waited.

There was a sound from the intercom that could have been anything.

"I need some help with a phone," I said.

I stood there looking up at the camera, trying to appear innocent and certain that I must be looking increasingly shifty. After an eternity, the buzzer sounded and I was able to push the door open and go inside.

He was an Asian Indian with a Carolina accent. He was in shirtsleeves and a dark tie. According to the tag on his shirt his name was Nick Patel.

"I'm looking for a specific model of cellular phone," I said, and I showed him a piece of paper on which I'd written the make and model number of Don Farrow's in block capitals. "Do you have it?"

"I've got a better one that'll cost you less," he said, and he started to move down the counter to get a box from those he'd got stacked all the way up the wall behind it.

"No," I said quickly. "It's got to be this one."

He looked surprised. "Why?"

"The insurance company say they won't pay out for anything else," I said, but to my dismay he pulled the box he'd been going for anyway and brought it back down the counter to me.

"You won't get that one anywhere," he said, opening the box and taking out packaging inserts and leaflets to get to the instrument in the middle of it all. "They stopped making it. They change all the models every six months or so. This is almost the same thing. It's the same basic design. They just improved it. They're always improving them."

"That's all very well," I said. "But will it work the same?"

"What do you mean?"

"I mean, are the functions the same?"

He shrugged.

"Sure," he said.

He slipped the phone out of the plastic sheath it was packed in and handed it to me, but of course it wasn't the phone itself that I needed to see. I was looking at the instruction book on the countertop. It was in a sealed polythene packet with some other paperwork.

He said, "I can give you a paper says the old one's been deleted and what the newest equivalent is. That's how they always do it. I've never known it be a problem."

I turned it over in my hands.

"Can I go back through the memory and check on the numbers of all the people who've called?" I said.

"They can all do that."

"I need to see how."

He put out his hand. "Give me the phone," he said, and I handed it back to him. "Now get the fuck out of my store," he said.

I felt wrong-footed. His sudden change of attitude took me completely by surprise.

"I asked a simple question," I said.

"You can ask all the questions you like," he said. "You can look at every phone in the store and if at the end of it you still don't buy, I'll just say thank you and good night. That's business. What you don't do, is come in here and lie to me and waste my time. Now get the fuck out. The Goodnight's free. I'm gonna count to ten and call the cops."

~

I stood outside in a daze. I'd been too damned clever for my own good and now I was stuck. Over the past few days I'd got so into the habit of deviousness that I'd forgotten it was sometimes possible simply to ask for the help that you need. When I looked back in through the wire-reinforced glass, I could see a pissed-off looking Nick Patel throwing the repacked box back onto the stack with the others.

I'd nowhere else I could go. I was desperate. If I couldn't get the number that Rachel had tried to call me from, I had nothing. If I got the number and it turned out to be another cellular phone, I'd still have nothing.

If I tried for it myself and managed to wipe it like I had the last time, I think I'd have gone looking for the nearest WRONG WAY sign on the interstate and carried on past it until the big bright oncoming lights put an end to the way I'd be feeling. There's only so much holding yourself together you can do, and I'd passed my imagined limit long ago.

I went back to the door, and I pressed on the bell again. Nick Patel had seated himself in a niche that served him as a work area behind the counter, inspecting the motherboard out of a disassembled phone through a big magnifying lens on a swivel arm. He looked over and angrily waved me away. I pressed again, and he opened the intercom.

"Get lost," he said.

"I'm sorry," I said. "I need your help. I want to explain."

"Go home and take your medication."

"Listen," I said, and I held Don Farrow's phone up so that the earpiece was right against the intercom's pickup. As I'd been speaking, I'd been dialling the message repeat code and now it played back into the mike.

I'd no idea how clearly it was getting through. I'm not sure whether I could actually hear it at my end, or whether I was replaying it in my head. It would have been just as vivid either way.

Nothing happened for a while. I saw him disappear into a room at the back.

When he returned and saw that I was still waiting there, he buzzed me in resignedly.

We stood looking at each other across the counter.

"Was that your kid?" he said.

"No," I said. "It isn't my phone, either."

"What exactly are you trying to do?"

"Find out what number she called me from."

He held out his hand, and I gave him the phone. I gave it to him with the kind of nervous trust you have to place in anyone who can do something for you that you can't do for yourself. He played around with it for a while, sucking in his cheek. It was clear to me that he didn't know exactly what he was doing, but he'd handled so many devices like it that he hardly needed to. My heart lurched when the phone beeped and he made a small sound of annoyance, but then he did something else and turned the phone toward me to show me the display.

"That look like the one?" he said.

I got pen and paper out and wrote it down. Just in case. As I was copying it I said, "When I tried to do that before, I wiped the number off."

"I doubt it," he said. "They'll stay in the memory until the power goes down."

"This number," I said. "It's just a regular land line?"

"That's a North Carolina number with an area code."

"Would you know for where?"

"The 704 means it's somewhere in the mountains. Asheville or Boone, one of those places up there. If you're in luck, then the next three digits could help you narrow it down to a town or a county. What's the story?"

"I wish I had all night then I could tell you," I said. "Forgive me. And thanks."

He sighed and made a face, like he knew he could have and should have been tougher.

"Yeah, okay," he said. "Next time…don't try to get tricky. Just ask."

~

I knew that I'd find a different manager handling night duties at the Thrift Efficiencies, but he wasn't in the office when I got there. I waited, and when he came back from whatever he'd been sorting out I took one look at his face and thought, Don't try to ask. Just get tricky.

I said, "Cyrus Behan."

And he said, "What now?"

"Couple of things we missed earlier," I said, counting on the police having been here before me. "I need you to let me in."

He didn't look happy but he didn't challenge me or argue, either. He led me up the stairway at the side of the building. The night man's back was broad and his neck was short, with bristles. I'd noticed he had that pop-eyed, chameleon look that sometimes comes with a thyroid condition. But he also looked as if he could bench-press around three hundred pounds, and I suppose that would be enough to make anyone's eyes bulge a little.

There was a scrap of police tape still fluttering on the balcony rail opposite Behan's door. Once we were inside, the night man switched on the lights and I looked around. On the kitchen counter, Felony Investigations had left a copy of their search warrant and an inventory list of the property they'd taken away. Behan's computer was listed; I looked, and it was missing. Not the keyboard or the monitor, just the box.

From behind me the night man said, "Will this take long?"

"Not too long," I said.

"I'll wait and close up after you," he said, which made me wish I'd given him a different answer.

I went over to the wall where Behan had his snapshots on display. There I started taking them down, beginning at the top left-hand corner. They were just the regular size, the way they come in the envelope from the Quick-Foto processor. Each was held up by a blob of white-tack that left a greasy mark on the paper.

The night man watched me for a while and then ventured, "That boy sure can take a lousy photo."

"He surely can," I agreed.

"That an Australian accent?"

"Police exchange program."

I was just collecting all the pictures together into a stack without looking at them. I'd give them closer study later. When I had the wall cleared, I started looking through the drawers to see if I could find any more.

The night man said, "The guys who came around earlier? They had a little dog. Dog had a little coat on. Jumped all over everything."

I had nothing I could say to that.

"That's something you don't see every day," he concluded.

I found about half a dozen more packets in the drawers and I took them all. I was thinking. If the police had brought a sniffer dog to check out Behan's apartment and had taken away his computer to check its hard disk for contacts or records, that probably meant they'd formed a picture of him as a small-time dealer in street drugs.

For now.

They'd dismissed my version, but they surely weren't stupid. If, on searching through his hard disk, they found the computer file with the text of that pharmaceuticals-for-sale note, someone would have to see how it tied in with my story. All of the corporate manoeuvring and tracks-covering might yet go for nothing. Give it a few days or weeks, and I might even be vindicated.

Rachel would be long dead if I did nothing until then, but you can't have it all.

"I think I'm done here," I said to the night man. I had what I'd come for. I only hoped that I had what I wanted.

The night man turned to let us both out. The unit's door was of pressed metal, and it wasn't an exact fit. Where the metal had chipped bare along the edge, it had rusted.

I gave one last glance back before he switched off the light and followed me onto the balcony. Behan had lived here, but it wasn't the kind of place that took on a person's mark. I wondered if he was any more useful a hunter than he was a photographer. Probably not. He'd dropped Farrow but even with a Black Talon he hadn't killed him, and the distance hadn't been all that great.

I hadn't had a good look at Behan's rifle, but I could picture it being some big-ticket precision weapon that was way out of his class. Yes, I could well imagine that. He was like a lousy guitarist thinking that owning a Fender would put him up there with the best. For all he might love the hardware, it would never love him back.

That was his tragedy. Nothing he could do would ever bring him closer to his dreams. And yet he'd do everything he could possibly think of to get him there. At the end of it, knowing himself no better than he had in the beginning, he'd arrive at the conclusion that his failure had to be something personal between him and the rest of the world.

Why? Because nothing else could explain it. Such people can end up carrying a terrific weight of anger. They're like mad dogs or jilted lovers, ready to strike at whatever they can reach. They don't have to be bright to be dangerous.

I thanked the night manager and left him up there, picking at the knot of police tape to get it off the rail. He was like a big side of middle-aged beef but he picked at it delicately, like a gorilla taking fleas out of a daisy. He was so distracted by it that he was barely able to raise a grunt of acknowledgement when I told him good night.

Behan had run for the hills, taking Rachel Young with him. The picture I had in my head was of a bear dragging some woozy herbivore off into the darkness of its cave, where unspeakable things would happen with the victim's full awareness.

I seemed to be the only hope that she had.

And I could only think, God help her. For my track record in this area was not among the best.

Twenty-eight

Saturday, March 19

-

I f I'd been paying any attention to the news or the weather reports over the past few days, I'd have known that while we were getting cold rains in the south of the state, the mountains in the north were getting it even colder. Snow doesn't fall every year in North Carolina, but when it comes you can get anywhere up to fifteen inches of it in a matter of hours. The first I knew about it was the rain turning to sleet around the time that I was getting into Asheville, so early in the morning that the street lights were still on and the dawn was only just brewing somewhere deep in the clouds. I turned the wipers on the sleet, and they plowed it into a sludge at the edges of my windshield. I turned on my radio and it warned me of worse ahead.

Asheville. A big town, already stirring. I stopped the car on a street of old buildings just off Biltmore Avenue and, with the engine running and the heater on, I went through Cyrus Behan's photographs by the glow of the interior light. Most I could safely discard. The ones that I was interested in were the hunting pictures. Some showed his uncles, or at least two men that I guessed to be his uncles. They weren't especially strange-looking but they were no great prizes either. They looked as if maybe someone had been peeing in the gene pool. There were a number of after-the-hunt shots where they crouched by their kills, holding up the dead animals' heads. I'd seen others like them when I'd flicked through Behan's magazines. Fat men in camouflage, posing like heroes. *I may be ugly but I shot this elk.*

The best ones showed the cabin. This was obviously their base. While the hunting pictures showed forest and landscape that had a generic, could-be-anywhere look, I was hoping that the house would be somewhere that I might be able to identify.

My guess was that they owned it. There was too much personal crap and debris around it for a rental, and the shots seemed to cover more than one season so I could tell that the mess was ongoing. The cabin itself looked like an ageing self-build job by someone with basic carpentry skills but no eye for overall design. I doubted there could be another like it. Its proportions were all wrong, as if sections from two frame houses had been reassembled into one. It was on a brick footing, and the walls had been finished off with plywood that still had the maker's marks on it.

Of course, I might find it, and find it empty. Maybe he'd run with some other hideaway in mind. Just because I found it difficult to imagine where, that didn't mean it wasn't so.

But I had a feeling. If I was reading the pictures right, the cabin had a regular power supply and a telephone line. So it couldn't be *that* far out of the way.

I got my area pinned down with a well-spent hour in the Appalachian Diner on the northern side of town. It was very much a working man's place where the one waitress knew all the customers, and the customers were mostly drivers and early-starting manual workers. The front door was open, but most of them seemed to appear from somewhere at the back, as if there was another entrance that only the well-briefed knew about.

The unlikely hero of that hour was a man whose age was impossible to guess but who came in wearing a pair of jeans so grubby, and a t-shirt so holed, that they looked as if he'd put them up on a washing-line and blasted at them with a shotgun. Having said that, neither looked as if they'd actually been near a washing-line in ages. He was pretty much a stranger to soap and a razor himself. He slid into the booth in the smoking section where the waitress was sitting on her break, and squeezed her up against the wall and gave her a hug. She knew him by name but I didn't get what it was.

She was blonde, young, and plump. When she came over to take my order, I showed her the phone number and explained that I was trying to get some idea of where in the area the call could have been made from. She puzzled over it for a few moments and then the next thing I knew, she'd called the question back over her shoulder and everyone in the diner was getting involved. For a minute or two they all argued with each other and then they were all pulling cellular phones out of their pockets and looking through their relatives' numbers to see if they could find a match for the area code.

Raggedy Man's was the most spectacular. His was a mobile phone and palmtop PC combined; it opened up like a glasses case with the phone functions on one side and the keypad on the other. He logged onto the internet and ran my number through a search engine. There was no exact match but there were a number of part-matches from the Church of God Ministers' Address List. Five numbers all had the same local code. All the addresses were in the same part of Madison County.

Rachel had to have been calling me from somewhere in the area around River Springs, was the verdict. It had taken about five minutes with the cellular network's slow transfer rate, and it really was as simple as that. He tried for a phone company database to see if he could get an exact address for me, but there the luck ran out.

It was pretty good going, all the same. I paid his check and tipped the waitress and got back on the road without even ordering.

I'd been strongly tempted to call the number back, but so far I'd managed to resist. What would I achieve? Chances were that I'd simply alert Cyrus to the fact that someone was on his trail. He wouldn't know that, yet. Better to let him go on thinking that he was safe and out of sight.

Don Farrow's phone had been beeping a low-battery warning at me for the last half hour of my drive. At some time while I'd been in the diner it had stopped beeping and shut down. Now it lay on the seat like a dead thing.

Well, that was that. No more messages from beyond.

~

Daylight had broken and the sleet had turned to snow. They were big, wet flakes that hit the windshield like bugs. Beyond Asheville I could now see the real mountain country, layer after layer of tree-lined heights; no cliffs, no rocks, just a carpet of heavily-frosted green rising into the sky and getting lost in the clouds.

The drive into Madison County took me up on winding roads and along valley floors. To either side of me stood flat, snow-covered tobacco fields; above me were the rollercoaster curves of the mountains. The roads weren't so bad. They'd been cleared and salted during the night, and every vehicle that went through ahead of me cut a set of glistening black tracks through snow that wasn't quite cold enough to stick.

That changed as I climbed, though. I could see it in the trees. Where at first the snow on them had been like a sprayed-on glaze, it now began to take on a weight and a presence. Out there in the fields, the ancient, weathered tobacco-drying sheds made Christmas-card Bethlehem scenes. The road grew more difficult and I sensed a general silence descending. The Lexus coped, although just about everyone else I saw out on the road was coping better in a truck.

I descended into River Springs on a wide and serpentine approach road, switchbacking its way down to where the little spa town stood in a hollow surrounded by hills. I took it slowly and I felt myself losing it once or twice on the curves. When I finally came in over the bridge at the end of town, I was all but spent. My knuckles were white on the wheel and my sphincter was like a knotted shirt. I saw some civic buildings to the left, a laundry and a cafe to my right.

I swung right and stopped outside the cafe. A red Toyota pickup that had been patiently dogging me for the last half-mile put on a burst of speed and headed on down the main street, its wheels spraying a heavy grey slush.

There was fifteen minutes of the daily breakfast buffet still to go. The place was almost empty but there was enough food out to feed a small army. I'd skipped from the last place without ordering but now I was feeling lightheaded and shaky, and I knew I'd better eat.

At the counter I thought I'd chance a long shot, and I said to the woman folding napkins there, "Did you ever hear of Cyrus Behan?"

She said, "The only country singer I ever had time for was Patsy Cline," and that was more or less that.

I eavesdropped while I ate, and learned nothing of value. I borrowed a phone book and looked for Behans, but I found none in the River Springs area. Either the number was unlisted or they were his maternal uncles, and didn't share his name.

Outside again, I felt underdressed and overwhelmed. After only a few strides in the compacted mush of the cafe parking area my shoes were letting in water, and I shivered in the cold. What had seemed feasible in its broad strokes from a hundred miles away now seemed more daunting when I got down to the fine detail.

I got back into the Lexus and ran the engine for a while, waiting for the heat to kick back in. I needed to pick up a cold-weather jacket from somewhere if I was going to last out the day. The Carolina I knew best was a place of much higher temperatures than these. My last experience of the mountains had been of rafting on the French Broad River where the water had been sluggish and clay-brown and somewhere close to blood heat. I don't think I'd ever seen snow in the three years we'd been living here.

More than anything, I needed to work out what best to do next. I held my head in my hands and tried to think it through. But instead of thinking, I found myself imagining the skull beneath my fingertips,

picturing it from touch as a blind man might, aware of its fine structure
and frailty; appreciating the workmanship of it, in a morbid way.

Too little food, too little sleep. I'd been neglecting my instrument. I
was a wreck and now my neglect was beginning to tell. I sat back and
tried to haul myself together. I didn't count. I didn't matter. Nowhere
near as much as the task in hand, anyway.

I looked out of the car window. The town was still going about its
business despite the unexpected drop in temperature. The white
blanketing had brought along with it certain changes in perception.
All faces were pinched and red, all colors were pastel. The sounds had
no sharp edges.

Opposite the cafe was a building which had once been a row of
shops and now combined the local police headquarters, the City Hall,
and the Water Department. They probably had one person answering
the phone for all of them. In the same row stood a branch of the
Wachovia Bank and, on the end of the block, an old-fashioned store of
the kind that sells hardware and work clothes. When I saw that, I shut
off the engine and got out of the car.

Then I crossed the street and went inside.

The interior was so deep and vast that I could barely make out the
ill-lit back of it. It had a dusty upper gallery and a big fan propeller to
move the air around in summer. The fan wasn't working now.

What artificial light there was came from a fluorescent fitting with
a wire strung up to it. Before me I saw rope, fan belts, dog collars,
hurricane lamps, and a rack of heavy work coats that looked as if it
had been dusted off and dragged forward at the onset of the weather.
I was aware of someone rising in the gloom at the back of the store; I
grabbed the first coat I saw in my size and took it down toward him.

The display counters looked like museum pieces and there seemed
to be no particular layout or order to any of them. It looked more like
a salvage sale in a derelict building than a going concern.

"Hi," he said pleasantly. "How're you today?"

"Fine," I said. "I think I need this."

"From the look of how it's going out there," he said, "you probably
do."

He had one of those faces that's all cheekbone and forehead, and
he'd scraped his thinning hair across the part where he'd gone bald.
He was tall and slightly stooped in a way that made me think of an
undertaker. Behind him at the back of the store there was a
woodburning stove with an assortment of old easy chairs around it.
On the wall behind, where the stove chimney disappeared into a sooty
plate, there hung fading pictures of all the Democratic Presidents of

the US. Pride of place and the best frame went to Kennedy. Second in prominence was a dried-out wasps' nest, and the others came somewhere after that.

I said, "Have you got some bad-weather boots of any kind? Lined, waterproof?"

"Ohhhkay."

He got out some steps to reach one of the shelves, and as he was positioning them I was trying on the coat. Thinking I'd get the same kind of response that I'd had at the cafe across the street, I said, "Does Cyrus Behan ever come in here?"

"Cyrus Behan," he said as he started to ascend, and then there was a pause and all I could hear was the creaking of the ladder. I couldn't tell whether he was thinking it over, or searching his memory, or whether he was just one of those people who makes you wait for an age as he processes one patient task at a time. The coat was a good enough fit.

He said, "Is he the boy with the uncles?"

My heart did a dangerous-feeling skip.

"That's him," I said. "Do you know him?"

"Can't say I know him," the man said, and then I had to wait again as he descended with a selection of lined rubber boots in one hand like a brace of game birds. "But if we're talking about the same boy, he came in here this morning to see about a knife."

"How long ago was this?"

"No more than an hour. Picked out the best one in the place and then wanted me to let him have it on credit. Does that sound like him?"

"I'd say it does."

"He tried to tell me he was good for it because his uncles buy their stuff here. Told me his name like he expected me to recognize it. I didn't know him and I can't say that I can picture them, either."

I showed him their photographs. He looked, and shrugged; maybe he'd seen them before, maybe he hadn't. Owning a cabin for use in the hunting season didn't make them local.

He said, "Either way it wouldn't matter. I always say you want credit, use a credit card."

"So what happened?" I said. "Did he get a knife, or not?"

"After he'd done drooling over the most expensive one in the case, he only had the money for the cheapest in the shop," he said. "See this."

He turned to one of the dusty counters where a display of knives sat under glass. They were arranged on a deerskin that reminded me of the hide in Behan's apartment, the one he'd put on the floor and used as a rug. The biggest knife in the display was a ten-inch hunter with a stag's horn handle. He raised the glass cover and lifted it out to show me how it balanced.

"This is your classic big game field dressing tool," he said. "File work on the blade spine, solid butt cap, spacers on the handle. What you're looking at here is a five hundred dollar work of knife art. It had to be this one, he told me. He was real disappointed when he couldn't have it. Tried to tell me he was coming into some big money soon."

"What's that extra piece on the end of the blade?" I said.

"That's called a gut hook," he said. "I gather you're not a hunting man yourself."

"I really need to find him," I said. "Did you get any idea of where he went from here?"

~

He didn't know, but he did tell me that there was a realtor with an office down the street who knew just about every property in the area and might be able to help me identify the cabin from a photograph. I threw my wet shoes and my old unsuitable jacket into the back of the car, got back behind the wheel, and set off to look.

Slowly, my wheels cutting up slush like a shallow flood, I began to cruise down the one short main street of River Springs. It was called Bridge Street and it was like one of those little toytown streets where there's one of everything. I passed a motel with a flagpole in its court, a canoe rental yard with the snow-covered boats all up on metal frame storage, and the bohemian-looking Bridge Street Cafe and Inn with its open-air verandah on the side. The River Springs Post Office was a low, square and comparatively modern building.

The Realtor's was a white frame house that looked like somebody's residence, with a front porch and a stiff-frozen Stars and Stripes hanging over it. The giveaway was a lawn sign out by the shovel-cleared sidewalk that read *River Springs Real Estate* and then below that *James R Faust, Broker* followed by a couple of phone numbers.

I was on the wrong side of the street, but it was wide enough for me to make a U turn and there was parking space in front of the building. I was thinking that if I had no luck here, I might try the drugstore. Back in Charlotte he'd been pouring medicines down Rachel in a last attempt to move the packages through her, and he might still be trying.

As I swung out, my head was so full of Cyrus Behan that I had a vision of him standing on the sidewalk. He drifted past my window like something in a dream; the kind where you're on a river, and people that you thought were lost are passing by you on the bank. He was just standing there, looking ahead. He was wearing the same hooded coat that I'd seen at the hospital, but now the hood was off and he wore a dark woollen cap. His face was as pale as the blue of his eyes.

Then when I looked in my rearview mirror and saw the shape of him crossing the street behind me, I realized that it had been no vision; he was there in the flesh and I'd seen him, and I'd done no more than to drive on by.

I was almost overcome by the rush of adrenaline that came with the realization. I braked hard and slid for at least twenty-five yards, feeling the Lexus start to turn in the road and unable to act to stop it. The skid control cut in but the wheels had no traction. My back end fetched up against the curb with a gentle bump. A big delivery truck swung out to pass around me, horn blaring like a freight train's.

Oblivious, I jumped out of the car and ran to look for Behan; a white panel truck had to swerve to avoid hitting me.

When it cleared my field of view, Cyrus was nowhere in sight.

Twenty-nine

I spent about ten frantic minutes looking for him on foot and then about as long again driving around all the backs of the buildings, but I saw nothing. It was as if he'd vanished. The truth was probably that he'd climbed into his Dodge and driven away, right behind my back. I felt like an unusually stupid dog in the park, missing all the squirrels. By now my breath was coming in ragged gasps and my lungs felt like open wounds packed with salt. I could taste the pain they were giving me.

I'd seen him and lost him. By seconds! I could almost weep.

Then suddenly my head cleared and I knew what I needed to do, and quickly.

Further down the street stood Campbell's Deli, a low building with an ill-fitting roof. From what I could see of the inside it was half general store goods, half video rental tapes. Outside there was a big grey ice chest, two Coke machines, and a couple of public phones.

I fed quarters into one of the phones and I dialled the number that I hadn't dared to dial earlier. I could see my breath in the air before me.

If Behan was here in town, then Rachel was in the cabin alone. He couldn't be in two places at once. I knew he hadn't cut her open yet, because he'd come into town to buy the knife to do it with. She'd managed to reach the phone once before and I was hoping she might have some way of getting to it now.

After four rings I thought that she'd picked it up and I started to say her name, but then I realized that I was listening to a machine.

A twangy, stringy voice that I'd never heard before said, *"Here's the beep, you know what you can do."*

The uncles! I hadn't even given a thought to them. I hadn't been expecting this, either, and I hadn't got anything prepared. The simplest thing to do would be to hang up.

But instead I had a sudden impulse and heard myself saying, "Got a message for a Mister Cyrus Behan. I'm calling from the Post Office. Your money's here waiting."

And *then* I hung up.

After that I went back to the Real Estate Broker's house. There was a little brass bell with a pull cord by the door. I rang it, and an elderly woman came to the door and let me in.

Over in the hardware store I'd been told that her name was Bettina Faust and she'd been River Springs' realtor for almost forty years, handling the business alone since the death of James R. over a decade before. She was small and shrunken and pale, so pale that it was as if there wasn't an atom of pigment in her apart from a few coffee-grain spots along the edges of her lips. But her hair was pink-rinsed and set and she was immaculately dressed for business, with a pale chiffon scarf knotted at her throat.

In her office, I explained what I was looking for and showed her the best of the cabin photographs. I think she sensed my desperation even though I didn't try to explain it.

"Oh, my," she said, giving it a professional eye, and she all but winced. "Now there's a place you'd need all your charm to get sold."

"Do you know it?"

"I believe I might," she said. "Let me see some of those other pictures."

I waited as she spread them out and studied them.

"I can see you're anxious," she murmured without looking up, "but if you'll stop drumming your heels on the floor I can concentrate better."

"Sorry," I said.

Finally, she sat back and said, "It's not a property I've ever handled. But if it's where I'm thinking of then I did sell a couple of twenty-five acre lots for building on the same mountain. The two men who owned that place kept trying to hold up the sale with some frivolous litigation until we worked out a deal where they got their utilities put in for no charge. Which was what they'd been after all along. They are in my sincere opinion a couple of assholes. It's a nice location but the house does it no justice."

"Can you show me how to find it?" I said.

"I can," she said, "but you'll need a four-by-four to get up that road in these conditions. There was another severe weather warning this morning and I heard they're trying to get everyone down from the hills. We don't often see it as bad as this but when it hits, it hits hard."

She took out one of a number of well-used maps, and I sneaked a look at my watch as she was doing it. Tracing with a finger that was bent like a hook, she followed one of the roads out of town and then pointed out an almost invisible track up along the side of a ridge. It wasn't even shown as a solid line; just dashes.

"What does that mean?" I said. "Is that a dirt road?"

"Dirt or gravel," she said. "I can't remember which."

She was right. In these conditions there was little chance that I'd make it in the Lexus. And Cyrus had a head-start on me already.

"Who's the local law?" I said.

"That'll be Ben Steed."

"Where will I find him?"

"Try the Police Department at the end of Bridge Street. It's part of City Hall. Don't blink as you go by, or you'll miss it."

~

All of those civic buildings were in the same row of storefronts and had been linked together behind the scenes. The part that was River Springs City Hall had two rooms and one phone. They had one person to answer it and to run the police radio, and she was having quite a morning. Some hikers had gone missing and been out of contact since before the snowfall, and now the National Guard were being called in to provide backup and equipment for the search.

When I asked to see Ben Steed, I had to insist that it was over a matter of no less urgency. A life was in danger, I told her. She called him on the radio, and I took a seat to wait.

As I waited, I rehearsed my story.

A big all-terrain vehicle in police livery went by the window, and Ben Steed came striding in from the cold a short time later. He was big and broad-shouldered, and he looked the way that some sports figures do when they get middle-aged and turn to doing TV commentary. Like they raced the rest of us up the hill, but all that happened was that they got over it first.

I was the only person in the reception area and he looked straight at me.

"Are you Mister Bishop?" he said.

"I am," I said. "Thanks for coming in."

"You can see I don't have a lot of time. I don't mean to be discourteous, but tell me as quickly as you can how I can help you."

We went through into the Police Department, which was just one of the rooms in the City Hall's makeshift warren. The glass door was marked with a big silver vinyl self-stick police badge, and for some reason the room beyond it made me think of a really crummy barbershop. There were venetian blinds at the windows, cheap wood panelling on the walls, and a coat rack with a broom propped alongside it. There was a blue desk facing the room for the chief and two other desks facing the walls for his absent staff. An old sofa and a couple of filing cabinets pretty well filled up the rest of the space.

He sat behind his desk, and indicated for me to pull up a chair. On the wall behind him were various framed certificates and citations, and above them was a shelf with a line of model cars on it.

I said, "Let me get straight to it. You've got a twenty-two year old girl hidden in a cabin about seven miles out of town. She was kidnapped out of the emergency room at the Presbyterian Hospital in Charlotte at about six o'clock last night. She's got five packets of unknown substances in her gut that she swallowed and she can't expel. The boy who took her mistakenly thinks they have a value. He's preparing to cut her open to get to them."

Now, here's the thing about talking to policemen. You can't shock or surprise them. If you did, it would probably kill them to show it.

Ben Steed said, "And how do you know this?"

"I've been tracking the drugs for the company they were stolen from," I said. "They're all experimental. I can't tell you what will happen if any of the packages bursts or leaks. Chances are it won't be good."

"Do these kids have names?"

"Rachel Young. Cyrus Behan."

"Cyrus?" he said, and I felt my heart sink a little.

"So you know him," I said.

"I know his uncles. They're the Bellamy brothers. They practically live up here for half of the year. Heywood Bellamy must be the worst driver in the world. You don't have to wonder why he's never had kids, once you've seen him try to park his truck. Cyrus I've just seen around."

"I was in the hardware store," I said. "He bought a knife this morning. The kind you use for dressing deer."

"Don't think I'm doubting what you're telling me. But if it's true it's quite a story. Who can I speak to for confirmation?"

"Probably no-one."

He gave me a look, polite-incredulous, inviting me to go on.

So I said, "My employers won't admit to any theft. They think it'll damage business. The moment the police got involved, they slammed down all the hatches. You ask them about me, they'll tell you I'm a mental case living out some kind of a personal fantasy. As far as the Charlotte police are concerned, this is some junkies' squabble that blew up in public. But even if that's what you choose to believe…you've still got a kid who's in danger."

"And you reckon she's up in Heywood Bellamy's cabin."

"I had a call from her there."

He sucked at a tooth and made a face of mild pain. Every now and again I could hear clipped, incomprehensible bursts of speech from the shortwave radio in the reception area outside, and the woman's voice as she answered.

He said, "I got my manpower stretched tighter than a tick's foreskin. If I'm going to act on this, I need a second opinion."

"Look," I said. "I can tell you this before you even pick up the phone. They're not short of ammunition for shooting me down. I know how I look. I know how I probably sound. But I'm not deluded. If I'm obsessed, it's with good reason. All I'm trying to do, Ben, is preserve a life."

He nodded, as if that sounded entirely reasonable. I tried to make out whether he was simply humoring me. Could I have presented myself any better? If I could, I didn't see how.

He said, "Let me explain the difficulty I have with what you're telling me."

"Just tell me this, first," I said. "What's it going to cost you to check it out? An hour of your time."

"Don't imagine that's something I can write off lightly. I've got a party of hikers missing since before the snowfall and the oldest of them's not a day over nineteen. You're on their time right now."

"Then give me a gun and a truck that's big enough to get me up there. You see to your kids and I'll see to mine. Can't you deputize me or something?"

He held up a hand. "Just…slow down, Mister Bishop," he said, and started to rise from his chair. "Stay right where you are and give me a name."

"What kind of a name?"

"Someone I can talk to about you."

I was lost for a moment.

Then, with sudden inspiration, I said, "Kate O'Brien. She's with the Presbyterian hospital. She works in the emergency room but you'll probably have to get them to call her at home. She was with me when they admitted my daughter."

"Your daughter?"

"Make the call," I said. "There's no point in you hearing it all twice over."

Steed went out into the common area and asked the woman on the desk to find the necessary numbers and place some calls. I heard her explode and I heard him calm her down. I didn't stay in my seat as instructed, but went over to the window and looked out through the slats in the blind. Ben Steed's all-terrain vehicle was standing outside. It looked like one of those monsters from a touring truck-o-rama show and it had a gun rack at the back of its cab.

From behind me, Ben Steed said, "Don't even think it."

"I'm only looking," I said.

"That's okay," he said. "Looking's free."

The call came through, and Steed went into another room to take it. A couple of minutes later I heard the outer door slam and when I moved to the office doorway and looked out, I could see the all-purpose do-everything woman heading out across the street.

I could hear Ben Steed. He hadn't quite closed the door behind him. I heard him say, *Yeah? So what does this Farrow kid say about it?* and then there was silence as he listened for a while and then he said, *Well, what do you think I should do with him?*

Nothing was going to happen.

I knew it then, although I couldn't have told you how.

So while Ben Steed was still on the phone listening to my story being destroyed, I slipped out through the Water Department and was on the street before he knew.

Thirty

I'll be honest with you, I'd have taken Ben Steed's truck if he'd been sloppy enough to have left the keys in it, but he hadn't. I looked.

As I was walking away from the building, two of his uniformed officers passed me walking toward it. Behind them at the curb was their cruiser, a blue-grey Chevrolet with a gold stripe. It was so filthy with road dirt and salt that it looked like a dog that had been rolling in muck; brown snow hung from its bodywork like concrete, and dropped from its wheelarches into the gutter like a slow card shuffle. The men themselves looked serious and tense. They disappeared in through the doors and I went back to where I'd left the Lexus, and got in.

I was expecting to hear someone call out and stop me at any moment, but nobody emerged from the building. I don't know whether that was because Ben Steed was still tied up on the phone, or whether my walking out had meant the welcome removal of a complication from his day.

Then when I was driving back up the street I saw the woman crossing back from the cafe, a paper bag in one hand and a tall cup in the other. The cup was trailing steam like a ghost. I slowed as she passed before me, then picked up as much speed as I dared once the street was clear.

The road that took me out of town followed the river, past the overgrown estate where a big spa hotel had once stood. The spa had been the reason for the town, and now it was gone. If I'd read the map right I'd have to follow this route for about four miles and then turn off it onto a gravelled track for another three. That was where the real climbing would begin, and I wasn't looking forward to it. The Lexus was a heavy car and it had the biggest available engine option, but it was no off-roader.

All the same, I tried to tell myself, a dirt road was still a road. Behan's truck had managed it and so would I. The way I felt right then, I'd keep the car on track with the sheer force of my determination. I could feel it seeping out of my bones and through the steering column, sucking me down to the pavement. I was like a bug, single-minded, hugging the earth. The world could flip over and I wouldn't fall off.

Behan had his huntsman's armory but I'd no weapons or protection of any kind, I now realized.

Well, I'd have to do without.

The road by the river took me past farms and through logging land. Every half-mile or so there'd be a mailbox or three at the roadside. Across the fields I'd see the buildings they belonged to. The same surname kept turning up on at least half of the boxes. I could imagine one family settling the valley all those years ago, with this modern share-out of the land reflecting the fortunes of all the later generations. The near-mansion of the great-granddaughter, elegant and snowbound like a pocket wedding cake. The low trailer home of the black sheep cousin, dodged-up with a fake roof and side-skirts that fooled nobody into thinking it was anything better than it was.

My job got easier after a while, because there was only one set of fresh tire marks leaving the road in the place where I'd expected to find the turnoff. I didn't have to be Tonto to guess that they were Behan's.

I felt the difference under my wheels as the pavement ended and the surface changed to stones. After a hundred yards or so the trees closed in and the track ran onward into the darkness of the woods, and the only hint of anything ahead came from a KEEP OUT sign that had been tacked to a post at the side. The car was doing fine but I was remembering the contour lines on the realtor's map, so many and so close that they looked as if they'd been dragged on with a comb.

The dirt road splashed through a ford, and something with big dark wings flapped out of one of the trees as I went by.

It was a well-made road of its kind, but it wound up through the forest like a snake. It made for the kind of drive where you look forward to how you'll feel when it's over. Every now and again, on one of the sharper turns, the tires would lose their bite and then spin and the car would start to lurch around. I'd think that I'd lost it completely before it somehow found the road again and I was able to carry on.

As I got higher, the air inside the car seemed to get thinner and colder. The woodland was denser here, as well. Downslope, the mountain fell steeply away. If the car should leave the track, I'd career down the hill like a pinball. After a dozen or so tree hits I could forget about seat belts and safety cages. They'd find me unmarked but whiplashed, all broken up on the inside like a sack of crackers.

Every now and again I'd see a new-looking utility pole planted close to the road, while above me crossed those power lines that the asshole uncles had held out for. I was encouraged whenever I saw them. This wasn't wilderness, and for a dirt road in winter it wasn't so bad. Under normal conditions there'd probably be lumber trucks and Rangers' vehicles up and down here all the time.

Here was one now, coming around the bend ahead of me. But it was no Forest Ranger.

This was Cyrus Behan's black Dodge Ram truck, and I could see Cyrus at the wheel of it.

It's difficult to say how I felt right then. I felt elation and apprehension, both at the same time. He must have got back, heard my message, and turned right around and started out for town again.

We came to a stop almost bumper to bumper. He got out of his cab, and I got out of the car.

~

I hadn't been sure what to expect. Before this I'd only seen him in bad photographs and in life with his face covered, rifle in hand, turning away from me in the hospital corridor. I was caught out by how young he was. Twenty-seven by his file, but he looked younger. He was bright, dishevelled, and hollow-eyed, and I realized that he'd had no more sleep or respite than I had.

He was plainly in an upbeat mood, though. I'd thought that my message might perplex or intrigue him at best, but he had the look of someone who genuinely believed there was a fortune waiting for him at the bottom of the hill.

He looked at my Lexus and he said, "Pardon me for asking you, Mister, but where do you think you'll be going in *that?*"

He didn't know me. Of course he didn't. When he'd fired on Don Farrow in the hospital, I'd been some anonymous nobody with my back toward him. I'd been slowly getting into Cyrus Behan's skin over the past few days, but from his point of view I was a ghost of whom he'd had no cause to be aware.

I said, "I've got some friends up here. They've got a house on twenty-five acres. Would you know of them at all?" and I prayed that he wouldn't ask me for a name.

He was shaking his head.

"You'll never make it," he said.

"I reckon I'll try."

"Your funeral," he said, and he slapped the Dodge. It stood there beside him, vibrating gently with its motor ticking over like a big ugly dog. "Anything less than one of these, and you wouldn't even catch me leaving town on a day like today."

"Does the road get worse?" I was glancing at the cab of the Dodge without trying to be obvious about it.

"You can bet it does," he said. "The only things you'll see moving around up here are bears and me."

"Maybe I need something more like that truck of yours."

"You'd need the skill to handle it as well," he said. "You're looking at the Dodge Ram Sport fifteen-hundred with the V8 engine. Me, I can get to anywhere I want to go. That's because I'm riding on a set of Sport King A/T steel radials in your premiere state-of-the-art American rough country vehicle. Where'd they make that car of yours?"

"Japan, I think," I said.

"The prosecution rests," he said.

Through the windshield and framed against the back window I could see a gun rack just like the one I'd seen in Ben Steed's truck. The rifle on it made a perfect silhouette, and it was within easy reach of where he was standing.

Strangely enough, I felt no fear for myself. But I did feel every apprehension that if I put a foot wrong now, I might be prevented from getting to Rachel in time. Or at all.

"So how do we get out of this?" I said, indicating the two vehicles. Each of us was blocking the other's way.

"Prepare to be amazed," he said, and he swung himself back into the Dodge's cab and closed the door.

He backed up the Dodge a few yards and then came for me, swinging off the track so that the tires on one side went right over the shoulder of the road. The entire truck went over almost to a forty-five degree angle, but it didn't roll. I scooted back around the car to give him room to pass.

The Dodge eased by me like a ship leaving harbor, clearing the Lexus by about a foot. Cyrus was steering one-handed, looking down from on high and into the big sticking-out mirrors to check on his positioning. The one-handed business I think was a pose. He had just his fingertips at a fancy angle on the top of the wheel, letting the power steering do all the work. There was something of the little boy in it...*Watch me. Dad? Just watch this.*

Once he was clear, he came back up onto the dirt road with a scrambling burst of acceleration. The big tires kicked up a spray of snow and gravel that peppered the back of the Lexus like buckshot.

"Good luck," he shouted out of his open side-window. "You'll need it."

A minute or so later I saw and heard him passing below me on his descent as the road hairpinned back and forth. The Dodge flickered in and out of sight through the trees and I saw a glint from the chromed roll bar behind the cab.

I wondered what his disposition would be like when he got down there and found that there was nothing waiting for him after all.

Better if I didn't stick around to find out.

The back wheels spun when I tried to get going again. I had to find some rotten wood to put under them, and I had to dig around in the snow to find that. There was ice in the ruts under the snow and I had to break it to get the wood out. Behan had been right about one thing. Under normal circumstances I'd have been mad even to attempt this.

It took me another ten minutes to reach the place where the forest road divided. I saw a board nailed to a tree and on the board was the hand-painted word PRIVATE, and that was the way all the wheel tracks went.

The cabin was instantly recognisable from Cyrus' photographs. It stood in a wide clearing on a levelled piece of land. There was a weight of snow on the rusty tin roof, but there was no mistaking those bending walls that made it look as if the entire building had been ever-so-gently mushed out of shape. A big drift had piled up against one side of it, but the other walls and the ground before it were more or less clear.

I drove into the churned-up circle that the Dodge had left. Within minutes or less, I'd know if I was too late. My heart was beating hard and I could barely get my breath. I was scared of what I might find. I got out and I went over and tried the door, but Cyrus had locked it on leaving.

I banged on it and I called Rachel's name. When I listened out for a reply, all I could hear was a soft patter of dislodged snow coming down from the eaves.

The door was good and solid. It didn't even give when I drove the Lexus into it.

The frame gave, though, and when I was out of the car I was able to rip the entire door structure out of the wall like a cardboard pop-out. While I was doing this, more snow was falling with the shock of the impact, an entire avalanche off the roof.

With my apprehension growing, I stepped into the gloom of the Bellamy brothers' cabin.

I couldn't see or hear any immediate sign of anyone, but the first thing that hit me was a foul stink in the air. It was like that burning smell you sometimes get in a train when it brakes and I realized that I'd last come across something like it in Rachel's apartment. Some heat was on in the cabin's main room, coming from an old-fashioned electric fire. It wasn't making much difference. And even with that orange glow and the snowlight from the window, the room was depressingly dark. The walls were lined in a mahogany veneer and there was a brown looped nylon carpet on the floor.

Before the fire stood a squashed-looking couch in imitation leather, worn right through at all corners. By the couch were a blanket, a bucket, and a pair of kicked-off women's shoes.

"Rachel?" I called again, and I heard my voice echoing through all the empty rooms of the house.

I found her in the bathroom.

The odor got stronger as I moved closer. The door was slightly open. I pushed at it, and it hit something.

"Rachel?" I called out again, but there was no reply.

Whatever was blocking the door, it was something soft. I didn't want to cause any damage and so I pushed again with care until I could get my head inside. I was holding my breath.

She was lying on the bathroom floor and the mess around and under her was indescribable.

I was too late. He'd gutted her and left her to lie in her own offal.

Thirty-one

I couldn't believe it. I reached out and pulled on the cord to switch on the overhead light. It was one of those high-wattage sun bulbs and its glare was so bright and so sudden that, dead as she was, she winced and turned from it.

I realized then that all the mess was hers, but she was still intact. She was lying hunched up in a wallow of vomit, liquid faeces and strange, jelly-like stools. There was some blood in them, but mostly it was other stuff. She'd tried to make it to the toilet bowl but it was like she'd exploded at both ends before she reached it. There were bodily fluids here of a kind whose existence I'd never even imagined.

I had to breathe then, and the air nearly choked me. No matter. I stepped over so that I could crouch down before her, and I nearly slipped and fell in the process.

"Rachel?" I said. "Rachel, don't be scared, I'm here to help."

Poor kid. She made a sound, so I knew she was conscious. The mess was on her clothes and in her hair and everywhere. I took her by the shoulders and tried to get her to sit up.

"Come on," I said, "let's get you..." I'd intended to say *Let's get you out of here,* but one good look at her and the idea was defeated before it had even formed. She was loose and floppy and miserable. Her pants were down around her knees and everything that she was wearing was soiled. I couldn't imagine doing anything with her in this state.

"Ah, Jesus," I said, "we'll have to get you cleaned up."

There wouldn't be much time. I didn't want to stay around here for a confrontation.

I took her under the arms and I hauled her over and into the shower stall. That was the only option, there was no bath. The floor of the stall was of tiny hexagonal tiles sloping down to a central drain, and it was all contained by a deep rim of black tiles. There was a lime-green vinyl curtain and the shower head was one of those big adjustable monsters.

The hot water, if you could call it hot, came from a wall box with an electric thermal coil in it. I held the shower head and ran the spray against the tiles until it came warm. The pressure was low and it barely got above blood heat.

Rachel sat doubled over, hugging herself. I kept on talking to her, doing my best to reassure her.

"How do you feel now?" I said.

"It still hurts," she said.

"Better or worse than before?"

"It hurts just the same. I'm all messy."

"See if you can wash yourself down," I said, and I turned the shower onto her. She made a yelp of protest as the water hit her and soaked into her clothes.

"I'm sorry, Rachel," I said. "It's on you everywhere. I'll have to find something clean for you to wear. Can you take over?"

She didn't answer, but I handed her the shower head anyway. I had to take her fingers and wrap them around the handle part before she could even grip it. With her other hand she was trying to tug the hem of her ruined dress down to cover herself, but it was all snagged around her hips. I had to lift her so she could manage it.

I leaned her against the tiles so she wouldn't slide down, and then I gingerly stepped through all the diarrhea and clotted matter to get to the door. The stink was fetid, but it was hardly her fault. When I looked back she was just sitting there, head against the wall, the nozzle clutched against her chest, the water streaming out from under her and draining away.

"Rachel?" I said, worrying that she'd passed out.

But she grunted, so I thought it was safe to leave her for a while.

It wasn't just that I didn't want us to be here when Cyrus got back. I didn't want us to meet that big truck on the road coming back up, either. I went all the way through the cabin, looking for any kind of clothing.

It truly was a dismal place. The ceiling tiles had the texture of pressed cardboard. There was a table with fancy wrought iron legs and cigarette burns on its wooden top. The biggest piece of furniture was a huge dark wooden cabinet with drawers underneath and a space at the top for a TV to sit in. There was an antenna plug but there was no TV. I reckoned they probably took it away with them whenever they went home.

The phone was on the top of the cabinet but it was just the base without the cordless handset, so I couldn't call out for help. He must have hidden the handset, or taken it with him. There were no closets in any of the bedrooms, just open rails with clothes hangers. By one of the beds there was a Westclox alarm with a red digital display that was blinking on and off. I imagine that Cyrus hadn't bothered to reset it when he'd switched on the cabin's power.

The only usable thing that I found, apart from some threadbare towels, was a heavy jacket hanging on the back of a door. It was so soiled that it looked as if it had been worn to get around in the crawlspace under a building.

Then I had a blinding thought, and went out to the Lexus and got the Gap bags out of the trunk. I left the bags on the sofa and took the towels through into the bathroom.

She didn't look as if she'd moved since I'd left her. After I'd put the lid down on the toilet seat to make a clean place to put the towels, I disengaged the shower nozzle from her hand and turned it onto her hair.

That revived her a little, in a way that she made clear she didn't find welcome. But even as she winced and moaned, she knew what I was doing and she put up with it.

"Who are you?" she said, her voice almost breaking up as she shivered.

"My name's John Bishop," I told her. "I came here to find you. Did Cyrus say where he was going?"

"He got a phone message. I didn't hear it, but it made him dance around and punch the air."

I bet it did. Gullible bastard. And I could imagine his reaction when he got down there.

I said, "Come on, Rachel. We need to be out of here before he gets back."

"I'm not clean yet."

"You'll be clean enough. I'm going to close my eyes and pull your dress over your head while you give yourself a final rinse-down. Nobody's looking at you. You're not much older than my daughter. You don't have to worry about me."

I kept my eyes mostly averted as I tugged on the dress until it came off her like a wet skin. I couldn't look away completely or we'd have been there all day. She was pale, and she looked unbelievably vulnerable. She made a few moves but she couldn't do much to help.

I threw the dress over onto the washbasin, which was of cream-colored plastic with glittery gold streaks in it for a marble effect. Those

Bellamy brothers, they lived like kings. My throw nearly missed but the dress caught and hung there like a shitty wet curtain.

We discarded her underwear in a corner of the shower stall and then I turned off the water and wrapped the towels around her.

"Do you think you can stand up?" I said.

"Yes," she said, but again the effort she was making got her nowhere. Once I'd got her to her feet, I reached under her knees and swept her right up.

Once again, I picked my way through the mess. Rachel's head rested heavily on me, right against the bony point of my shoulder. It hurt, but I let it stay there.

She said, "He told me that if I didn't have them out of me when he got back, I'd be sorry."

I could imagine. I turned us sideways to get along the short passageway to the main room. You always think that women will weigh nothing, until you try to lift one of them up. Even the slight ones can make your legs buckle.

"You know what he meant by that?" I said.

"He showed me his new knife."

I put her on the couch. The heat in here might not have been much, but it was better than the unheated bathroom. Compared to how she'd been when I'd found her, the cleanup seemed to have revived her a little. She was coherent enough for me to see how scared she was.

"I know everything," I said. "I know what you took from the Spirit Box, and I know why you took it. I even know how. You're not in trouble, Rachel. I'm on your side."

She said, "I got rid of *something*. I feel like I'm losing all my insides."

"Dry yourself off," I said, and I put a corner of one of the towels into her hand. She made a vague attempt to rub at her hair and her face with it.

"Keep at that," I said, and went back to the bathroom.

The bright light was still on and the smell hadn't got any better. But it no longer bothered me. There are worse things in the world. I crouched down and began to poke through the mess. After a few moments I found a little sliver of rubber like a discarded monkey condom, and then another.

I could see what they were. They were the fingers from a disposable latex lab glove.

Five fingers, five stolen substances.

I found four.

Of the four, three were intact like little knotted sausages. The fourth was just an empty skin. I checked and double-checked to be sure there was no fifth. There wasn't.

I washed my hands and then I went back to Rachel. She was lying there, still with the corner of the towel squeezed in her fist, although she didn't appear to have done much with it. She opened her eyes when she heard me.

"Where did you go?" she said.

"I had to check on something. Don't worry, I won't leave you. Let's get you dressed before you freeze."

This wasn't what I'd had in mind when I'd bought the clothes, but no matter. Again, I had to do most of the work while she made a game effort to join in. Gillian had been tall for a teenager, but Rachel had a slim and almost childlike frame for a grown woman. Enough of the things fit to make it worth doing. I hadn't brought shoes, but Rachel's own were lying on the floor close to hand and were still wearable.

"Let me look at your eyes," I said.

I wasn't too sure what I was looking for.

I can say it now. After the way I'd been drawn here, I think that in spite of myself I was looking for some sign of Gillian.

The whites were a touch yellow, but her pupils seemed normal in size. It was impossible for me to say what her temperature was. The air in the cabin was cold, but I could see a velvet sheen of sweat on her brow.

Smoothing back her wet hair from her face, I said, "How are you feeling now?"

"Sorry I ever got into this," she said. If it was a joke it was a rueful one, but I took it as a good sign.

I said, "I've spoken to Don."

"Cyrus said he shot him."

"He's in the hospital now. He's not feeling good about this either."

"I hope he fucking dies," she said. "Then I'll be happy for him to feel better."

"We've got some ground to cover," I said. "I want to walk you out to the car. Can you try that for me?"

She nodded.

"It's either that or face Cyrus," I said. "I don't want to risk that because I don't know what he might do."

"I can take a wild and flying guess," she said.

Her voice had an unsteady energy in it. That ought to have been a good sign, but I was concerned about where the energy might be coming from.

"Rachel," I said, "I think you have at least one of the drugs in you."

"I know I do," she said. "Don made me put them there."

"I mean, in *you*," I said, and I explained about the glove fingers that I'd found. Three accounted for, one emptied, one still missing.

"Nobody knows what those substances are," I said. "I can't tell you what they're for and I can't say what they'll do to you. If you're feeling strange, will you tell me?"

She gave a little snort.

"Like I'll know the difference," she said.

I was about to raise her to her feet when the empty phone base began to ring.

We stopped.

I said, "Do you know where he hid the handset?"

"No," she said, as the answering machine cut in and took the call. "He said he caught me trying to use it last night. I don't remember."

At that point, the caller's voice came out of the machine. The volume was right up at the limit and it made the speaker rattle.

"Rachel?" he said. "Can you hear me?" There was a pause. "I know you can hear me. Listen to this. It's important. If anyone comes to the house before I get back, you hide. I'll make you sorry if you don't. You got that?"

The sound was so poor that I moved across the room to hear it better. I found myself stepping silently, almost as if I was scared that he'd hear me. I could see that the answering machine had been dropped or broken at some time, and fixed with an all-around binding of silver duct tape.

I froze when I heard Cyrus say, "Is there someone else with you?"

Of course, he couldn't hear me. But it was a well-aimed shot in the dark. In the background on the line, I heard something noisy drive by. I realized that he was probably calling from outside the convenience store. If not from the same phone that I'd used, then from the one next to it.

"You're fucking dead, whoever you are," he said.

I was waiting for him to end the call. I could still hear traffic. Then I heard a car door slam and an engine starting up, and I realized that Cyrus had walked away without hanging up the phone.

At the end of a full minute, the machine switched itself off. We couldn't wait any longer than that.

I got Rachel to sit up. I put her in the jacket I'd found. On her it was like a midlength coat, and the sleeves would be long enough to keep her hands warm as well.

As I walked her out into the cold open air she said, "That stuff I swallowed. Will it kill me?"

"I don't think so," I said, but she saw right through me.

"You don't know," she said.

"I won't let it happen," I told her.

We got into the Lexus. I'd done more than half of the walking for her. I made her as comfortable as I could in the passenger seat and then I started the engine.

I followed my own tire tracks out, heading back toward the dirt road that would take us off the mountain. I felt as if we were all but home and dry.

A dangerous feeling, as I well knew.

Here's what happened then.

I braked as we got to the dirt road, but the car just kept on going. Nothing helped. Not the ABS system, not the brake assist, not the skid control system, nothing. We were sliding toward the edge of the track and for a few moments the car was turning about its own center in a lazy ice ballet.

Then we hit one of the utility poles and bounced off it, and the airbags triggered and I saw nothing for the next few seconds.

Thirty-two

I'd never been in a car with an exploding airbag before, and for a moment I had no idea what was happening. By reflex alone I fought the deflating bag down and saw that the car was still in motion and the forest was spinning around us outside. An instant later there was a loud bang and a jarring stop that rocked the vehicle and snapped me forward so that my belt locked and my chin hit my chest like a blow from a fist.

I was still reeling when, moments after that, there was a thudding flurry as enough snow came slamming down onto the windshield to cover it to within an inch of the roof.

I was hanging forward against my tautened belt. The engine was still running, racing, even, but the car wasn't moving. I was seeing stars and I could taste blood. As I straightened up, I could almost feel my neck do a ratchet-click like the hammer on a revolver. I looked around me, bewildered and disoriented.

"Ow," Rachel said, and she was raising her hands toward her head in slow motion.

"Are you all right?" I said.

She didn't answer, but sat there gripping her head.

I undid my belt and reached to open the door. It swung out a few inches and then jammed up against the fallen snow. I had to work it open before I could squeeze out of the gap and see how we were.

We weren't good.

We were partly blocking the track. We'd have gone right over the edge if we hadn't hit the pole first. It was a tree that had stopped us, and our impact had shaken the snow down out of its branches. The engine was still running but I couldn't do anything with the transmission. The bodywork was in no great shape either. Cars look so solid until you crash one. Then you realize they're just metal balloons, all skin and guts, and you can never quite believe in them again.

Shit. Behan was already on his way back from town. It had already been touch-and-go whether I'd get Rachel off the mountain before he reached it. What was I going to do now?

Various plans ran through my mind. Wait for Behan to return and then somehow get the drop on him and take his truck. Hide Rachel in the trunk and get Behan to pull the car out for me, all unawares.

These were fantasies. None of them had any chance of working, and I knew it even then.

I reached in and turned off the engine. Then I went around and began to kick the fallen snow away from Rachel's door.

When I'd got it open I said, "Rachel, I'm sorry. We've got to walk again."

"My head hurts," she said.

"Come on," I said, and I undid her belt and started to pull her out of the car. First she protested, then she resisted.

"Where?" she said.

"There's another house. We'll call help from there."

"I can't."

"We can't stay here. Look, Rachel," I said, "I talked to the local law this morning. They've got the National Guard coming into the area. They'll have half-tracks, helicopters...come on, Rachel. Believe me. I know you've had a rough time but it's nearly over. The one thing we can't do is stop moving."

I got her out of the car and onto her feet. I'd dressed her for the ride down, but I hadn't dressed her for this. These were Gillian's funeral clothes. Warmth had never been an issue.

Her shoes were no good, either, and within a minute of starting to climb she was telling me.

"Cold," she said.

"Keep going," I told her.

I unzipped my coat and tried to put it around the two of us by enfolding her in it, but it wasn't big enough. So I gave it to her as an extra layer, and she lumbered along in it like a dazed bear while I hung on like her keeper alongside. I thought I'd get chilled myself, but with the effort of getting both of us up the hill it wasn't too long before I started to sweat.

The warmer the exertion made me, the colder the air that cut into my sinuses. The pain of it made tears in my eyes. With every step, Rachel lurched heavily against my side. The snow underfoot was making that satisfying, crunching sound like fine packed cornflour, and in the stillness it was the only noise to be heard apart from my ragged breathing and the occasional sniff or sob from her.

I've never been any great lover of forests. I've always liked the hills, but forest paths have never appealed. Especially commercial forests and logging roads. I don't care how they dress them up with nature trails and chainsaw sculptures. You can walk for hours and whenever you stop and look at the view, all you ever see is the same endless thicket that you've been walking in since the beginning. This was no different, until it opened out.

The way that led to the second house on the mountain was an unspoiled sweep of sculpted white. No marks of passage, just drifts and shadows. The snow was knee-deep in places, and when I glanced back I saw our own tracks behind us like hoofprints up a beach.

I could see the building now. No tracks in the snow, no smoke from the chimney. If anyone was home, they were hiding themselves well.

"How are you feeling?" I said.

"I feel strange," she said.

We covered the last couple of hundred yards. This place was quite unlike the cabin and, had they been any closer together, they'd have made an odd-looking pair of neighbors. This was a real architect-designed country home with laid-out grounds and a barn-sized garage with more accommodation above it. There was a basketball hoop in the yard and a snow-filled, snow-topped tire swing on one of the trees. The lower story of the house was faced with decorative stone and there was a soaring pitched roof whose gable end was all glass, giving it a cathedral effect. When I went around the side and broke a window to get us in, an alarm bell sounded.

That was no problem. If it was one of those boxes plugged into a phone line that would automatically call in the law, that was even better.

I got Rachel into the main room. This was on two levels, the lower part of it dominated by a big stone fireplace at one end. The walls were panelled in knotty pine and the lounging area was immense, with views right out across the rolling hills. Up on the dining level there was an enormous table that had been made from a single cross-section cut out of a redwood tree.

It didn't feel any warmer in here than it had out in the open. Our breath fogged in the room air as we limped across the rugs. The bell that was ringing on the outside was complemented by a deafening howler somewhere inside the building.

When we reached a couch, I guided her onto it. She sat, and then pitched over onto her side and drew up her knees as if to make herself as small as possible.

I stood there looking down at her. For how long, I can't remember. Long enough for her to become aware of it, at least.

"What?" she said foggily.

"Nothing," I said.

"It's making my head hurt more," she said, and I assumed that she meant the siren.

"I'd stop it if I knew how," I said.

I found their phone and tried it, but it was dead. For all I knew, the car might have brought the line down when it hit the pole. After that I went upstairs in the hope of finding some more layers of clothing for Rachel to wear.

From what I could see, this was the seasonal home of a well-to-do family of five. The youngest I guessed to be a girl with a taste for soft toys and plastic Disney figures, and there was also evidence for two grown-up boys who shared a bedroom and whose poster fantasies revolved around Nascar racing and swimwear models. All of the bedlinen had been taken out for the winter, but I found a couple of unwashed sweaters under one of the beds in the Church of Testosterone and a pair of moon boots at the back of a cupboard in the master bedroom. The master bedroom, I have to tell you, was a nightmare in pink.

As I was carrying my haul down the stairs, the howler alarm finally cut out and left my head ringing like an empty pail.

I took the sweaters and the boots to Rachel, and I sat on the sofa alongside her.

"Change of plan," I said. "Calling the law won't work. There's no phone."

"Okay," she said.

"How are you doing now?"

"I feel great," she said.

I found that worrying. She looked anything but. She looked pale and terrible.

I said, "They'll have search planes up there looking for some lost hikers. I want to see if I can get their attention."

"Okay."

I held the sweaters up where she could see them. "I need to leave you again," I said. "Can you get into these? You'll be warmer when you do."

"Okay."

She said it, but I didn't really believe that she'd be able to do it. She was just lying there agreeing to anything. So I draped the knitwear over her for the moment, thinking that I'd sort her out properly when I came back inside.

From the kitchen I got a bread knife and one of those little butane wands for lighting barbecues and bonfires, and then I went outside into the yard and made for the tire swing.

I cut the tire down with the knife before rolling it into the open and trying to set light to it. The smoke from a burning Pirelli would be visible for miles, I thought, and it seemed like as good a distress signal as anything I could think of.

But I quickly found out that it's no easy matter to set light to a car tire, especially when you're trying to heat up the rubber with a flame so mild that you can run your finger through it. I crouched there trying to get a hot spot started, and the slightest breeze kept blowing the wand out.

So then I went over to the garage block in search of some gasoline or anything flammable that would get some scary black rubber smoke pumping up into the sky with a minimum of delay. This being a garage, the doors were big and the windows were tiny and set high-up to discourage snoopers like me. I had to stand the tire against the wall and climb up onto it to see inside.

It was pretty dim in there, but what I saw through the window excited me so much that I jumped down and ran all around the building looking for a rock or a piece of railing or anything that I could use to get me inside.

I even forgot myself and put tracks across the part of the yard where I'd planned to scratch out HELP in the snow with a stick.

But if this worked out, I wouldn't need it anyway.

Thirty-three

What I'd glimpsed was more workshop than garage. When I got the big doors open I could see it better. Maybe this was the result of a father-and-sons obsession or maybe it was just the two boys working on their own, but what they had here was a complete facility for the service and maintenance of a home-built racing car. The car stood on a towing trailer that took up about a third of the interior space.

Nascar, it wasn't. This one was strictly for the amateur circuits. The car looked as if it had been pieced together out of wrecks and was mainly held together by its bright yellow paint. It had no glass in its side windows and its doors were welded shut.

It was also without wheels or an engine. The hood was up and there was nothing to see under it apart from the floor. But it wasn't the non-functioning Demolition Derby vehicle that interested me anywhere near so much as the one alongside it.

That was customized Land Rover with a tow hitch, a big Cinderella of a truck for getting team and trailer to and from the races. It had been knocked-about and neglected but there was never any danger of mistaking that boxy shape, the flat fold-down windshield with its useless little wipers, the classic aluminum body shell. It was like coming face-to-face with some old friend from home. The surge of nostalgic feeling it gave me was almost sentimental in its intensity.

It was at least a thirty-year-old model, perhaps even older. As well as the tow hook at the back it had a front-mounted power winch. It was the long-wheelbase version, but with an adaptation of a kind that I'd never seen before. At the back someone had added another axle, making it into a six-wheeler.

A stretch Land Rover, no less. Only in America. They'd set out to turn it into a home-made tow truck but the effect was like some kind of a desert assault vehicle.

If I could only get it going.

I climbed into the cab and got behind the wheel. I've sat on brick walls more comfortable. There was no need to look for keys because it didn't seem to need them. What it had was a screwdriver thrust into the ignition like a knife in a zombie's neck. This appeared to be the permanent starting arrangement.

When I switched on, I saw the needles on the dash leap and so I knew that something was happening. But the engine made one brief dinosaur moan and then fell silent. It hadn't even managed a complete turn.

But I knew that sound well. Until I was almost thirty it had been the sound of every car I'd ever owned. As a student I'd always been generous with rides, knowing that a carload of passengers was the best insurance for those times when a push was needed. And those times were legion.

There was no chance of a rolling start here. I needed to get some power into the dead battery. I couldn't believe they wouldn't have a charging unit, and I wasn't wrong.

The unit was a big pitstop model on a two-wheeled trolley, and getting it around and into place was like trying to maneuver a safe on a wheelbarrow. I lifted the Land Rover's hood, scraped all the white fur off the cell terminals to get a contact for the crocodile clips, and hooked in the unit on a fast-charge setting. I threw what looked like the right switches and then got in to try the starter again.

Suck on this, Cyrus, I thought. You, and the premiere state-of-the-art American rough country vehicle you rode in on.

This time the engine managed to turn over twice.

I'd tried it too soon, that was all. It needed some time to build up a charge. The engine was cold, the oil was thick, and the spark was weak. The monster needed just a little more lightning to kick it into life.

Patience and timing.

Not the easiest qualities to come by in a life-or-death situation, but there you go. I left the charger doing its job, and went back to the house.

Just as I'd expected, Rachel hadn't made any move to get into the extra clothing. I felt her cheek, and it was cold.

Her eyes flickered open and she looked at me.

"I think God just gave us a break," I said, trying to sound encouraging.

"It's about time that fucker stepped in," she said.

That surprised me, a little.

I slipped her out of the coat and then helped her to sit upright, and then I worked the sweaters down over her head before getting her arms into them one at a time. The extra layers added to her bulk, but if anything they emphasized her smallness. As I was straightening the sleeves and generally trying to get her neatened up, I explained about the Land Rover.

"If I can get it running," I said, "we can drive it straight down the mountain."

"And Cyrus can pick through my shit for his money," she said with bitter satisfaction.

This, from the girl with three bibles in her apartment.

She winced then and hugged herself around the middle so hard that I couldn't persuade her into the sleeves of the coat, but when I asked her where it hurt she said it didn't. So for the moment I just put the coat around her shoulders, and I said, "You need to walk some more. Can you do that for me?"

"Yes," she said, and she let me help her to her feet.

I couldn't work out whether she was improving or getting worse. The signals were so mixed. I suppose I could pick out what I wanted to believe, and go with that; but instead I probably latched onto what I most feared.

As I was steadying her, she said, "How old's your daughter?"

"Let's not get into that," I said.

"You started it."

"Nearly fifteen."

"She's dead, isn't she?" Rachel said.

That one went into me like a big, long needle.

"How do you know that?" I said.

I knew I hadn't told her. I couldn't even think of anything I might have said that could have implied it.

She didn't answer that.

Instead she said, "I don't ever want to see Cyrus Behan again. Although I'd make an exception for an open coffin."

"He's your basic sickboy, all right," I said, not sure whether I welcomed the change of subject. By now I was walking her up the steps from the lounge area and toward the hallway.

At the top of the steps, she shrugged me off and tried to do it alone. She kept one hand pressed against her middle while with the other she reached out for the wall or any handy piece of furniture. This was as fast as she could go. I had to make a real effort not to attempt to hurry her along.

She said, "How did I get into this? They ought to have Olympics for stupid. I'd win all the gold."

"We're going to come through it, Rachel," I told her. "I won't let anything happen to you."

"Yeah," she said. "With *your* record."

We were about halfway down the hallway now. She stopped, drew a breath, and seemed to gain a little in strength.

As we moved forward she said, "How are we going to get past Cyrus?"

"The road carries on," I said. "We'll follow it down the other side of the mountain."

"Are you going to use the map?"

"I don't have one."

"I mean the one in the frame over the fireplace. You walked past it about three dozen times."

I looked back.

I could all but feel the egg on my face.

"Can you manage without me for a minute?" I said.

She made a face that I took to mean yes, and so I went back into the lounge area and, sure enough, there it was. What I'd glimpsed out of the corner of my eye and subconsciously taken to be a washy art print was actually the Department of the Interior map for the area, mounted in a clip frame.

Thank God at least one of us had been paying some attention. I took the frame down off the wall and levered off the edge clips with my thumbs. The clips flew off somewhere and I didn't notice where they fell.

I'm not saying that I gave no thought to the people whose house I was using like a common burglar. I'd seen enough to be sure that they were an ordinary family whose property ought to be respected. But there were two different worlds, here, momentarily occupying the same space. Theirs had everything going for it; health, happiness, a resilient normality. Mine was an angry mess. It would pass through theirs like a freak storm and leave a little damage in its wake, but it was nothing they wouldn't get over.

The map was dated 1940. I didn't know whether that meant the map itself, or the survey it was based on. I found the town, I found the river, and from that I found the dirt road I'd come up on.

There it was, sidewinding up the mountain. The broken line representing it was like the way a cartoonist draws something that's supposed to be invisible. These buildings weren't shown, but I'd a rough idea of where on the map we were.

If anything, it looked like we'd have a much straighter run down the other side. Although I was a little wary of the words 'LOCATION APPROXIMATE' printed alongside a part of the track.

Doing my best to refold the map as I moved, I hurried to rejoin Rachel. She wasn't in the hallway; she'd carried on outside and was almost all the way across the yard, plodding doggedly in my tracks with her shoulders hunched and her arms around herself. She was a tiny dark figure in an otherwise silent and snow-covered landscape.

Just seeing her like that made my heart turn over.

I pulled the house door shut behind me, and I caught up with her before she reached the garage.

She said, "I could hear something."

I stopped and listened. I couldn't hear any sound that wasn't being made by us. Not even a wind. It was as if the snow had laid a blanket of silence over the entire mountain.

"I don't think so," I said.

"It's him," she said. "It's Cyrus. He's coming for us. A stupid car in the way won't stop him."

"We'll be gone before he finds us," I said.

Thirty-four

I couldn't do much to make her comfortable on the vinyl bench in the Land Rover's cab. I'd looked in the back, but the load space was no place for riding. It was oiled-up and grimy, and most of it was taken up by the racing car's partly-dismantled engine sitting on old sacks to prevent it from sliding around. I didn't try to move it.

I'd have been happier if the battery had been trickle-charged for hours rather than blitzed for a few minutes. But what else could I do? The only hand you can play is the hand that you get.

After the Lexus, the Land Rover's instrument panel was like something you'd find in an old biplane. I pulled out the Bakelite stalk of the choke and set it about halfway. Then I took hold of the screwdriver in the ignition and gave it a half-turn.

The first couple of tries ended in misfires but on the third, with the brief charge waning fast, the engine actually caught. For a few seconds it was like a number of people all beating on trays with hammers and no common rhythm, but then everything suddenly seemed to fall into place and instead of struggling, it was running. It wasn't what you'd call smooth, but it was loud and it was more or less even.

I jumped out and pulled off the clips and dropped the hood, and while I was doing that the engine began to jerk and falter, so I quickly scrambled back in and trimmed the choke. Setting it about half an inch out gave me the healthiest sound. The entire cab rattled with the noise and vibration, and when I climbed back in it was as if we were seated on the back of some glorious brute.

I sat there, revving the accelerator but hardly daring to do more, until Rachel started to cough on the exhaust smoke that was building up in the garage. The pipe ran up the side of the cab and vented above the roof, so the place was getting fume-filled from the ceiling down.

So then I engaged the long stick shift, gave it far more pedal than it needed, and eased off on the clutch to start us out with a graceless lurch.

The contrast with a vehicle like Behan's couldn't have been greater. Whereas the Dodge was like the best-bred beast on the farm, the Land Rover was an old bull elephant out of the wild. No power-assisted steering here. It was a two-handed job to swing the wheel as we rolled out into the yard, and my first gear change was a panic snatch because I was trying to do it and keep turning the wheel at the same time.

But there was none of that queasy sense of skidding around that I'd had when I'd been struggling to drive the sedan on the icy mountain road. Not with six big wheels and a ton of weight holding them down.

"Okay," I told her, "we're rolling now," and I got some kind of an indefinite sound by way of a reply.

I don't think we got much above twenty miles per hour but compared to the time it had taken us to walk here, we were flying along. I grew less anxious as the engine warmed up and my handling of the Land Rover became more certain. This time I picked up the old logging road with no problem at all. The last I saw of my trashed company car was in the Land Rover's side mirror as we left it behind and headed onward, breaking new ground, plowing our way into untouched snow.

We were cutting a trail for Cyrus to follow, but I couldn't help that. As long as we were ahead of him, I'd maintain a lead. Cyrus wasn't even the biggest of my worries.

Rachel said, "You wanted me to tell you if I felt strange."

I risked taking my eyes off the track for a second or so to look at her.

"And?" I said.

"I feel strange. What was in all that stuff I stole?"

"Nobody knows for certain."

"I feel like I'm floating outside the car. If I close my eyes I can see the ground going past underneath me."

She went silent then, and I said, "Keep talking to me."

"I'm spreading out my fingers and I'm flying."

I took another quick look at her. She was still hunched up sideways on the seat, her arms wrapped around her body as if to hold herself together. Her eyes were closed and her eyelids were so bloodless they were almost translucent. I could see the faint blue veins under her skin. She looked like one of those blind fish they sometimes bring up from incredible depths.

She was worrying me, now. I needed her to stay awake. Saying almost the first thing that came into my head, I asked her, "What do you want to do when this is over?"

"See my dog," she said.

"Yeah?" I said, keeping it going. "What's his name?"

"It doesn't matter. He got old and died."

"How old was he?"

"They bought him just after I was born. It wasn't fair. We were supposed to grow up together. He wasn't supposed to leave me."

I tried to keep her talking, but it was hard work. I asked her any stupid question I could think of, so I shouldn't have been too surprised when some of her answers made no sense. It didn't matter. As long as she stayed conscious.

I even asked her who the President was, and she made a face and said, "Who cares?"

We'd gone less than half a mile and this old logging road was beginning to worry me. We'd barely covered any distance and already the standard of it was falling. Where before it had been properly built-up and graded, here it was little more than a wide trail scraped out of the ground. It was nothing the Land Rover couldn't cope with, but it made me worry about what might lie ahead.

But even if I could have found a place to turn us around, I couldn't consider going back. Meeting Cyrus would be a certainly, now, and that was the last thing I wanted. I won't say that I was personally scared of him, but I was certainly worried about the harm he might do. He wasn't just armed and dangerous. He was armed, dangerous, stupid, and thwarted. And his stupidity was the complicated kind, not the straightforward naive-and-dysfunctional kind that meant you could dismiss him.

All in all, he'd be better avoided.

This road was getting even harder to follow. Some effort had been made to keep it open, but it hadn't been much effort and it certainly wasn't recent. In one place an enormous tree had fallen right across the track, looking as if it had died and rotted and fallen apart under its own weight. Instead of moving it, someone had chainsawed the middle out, leaving the trunk in ragged section with just enough space for a vehicle to get through.

The next fallen tree that we came to had simply been left to lie there. It was too big to drive over, so I had to leave the trail and navigate a way through the woodland around it.

The entire bodywork of the Land Rover juddered as the wheels passed over root systems buried just under the snow, and all the pitching and jolting around made Rachel stir and open her eyes. The heater was working now. It sent out a blistering jet of hot air and its overall effect in the cab was nil. You could get burned by it, but you couldn't get warmed. My leg felt as if it was being blowtorched while my knuckles were cold and dead on the wheel.

"I bit my tongue," she said.

"Try to stay awake," I told her. "It could get rougher."

The further on we travelled, the more neglected-looking the road and the forest became. I could see more fallen trees through the woodland to either side, leaning at impossible angles like dead soldiers caught and held up by their comrades. The tallest and oldest ones had been stripped bare, like fishbones.

We went into a shallow descent. One deep v-shaped valley after another cut into the hillside and the trail snaked in and out, high up on each of them. Into the deep shadows, out around the next headland. The further along we went, the more thoroughly convinced I became that this was now an abandoned trail and there was no guarantee that it would get us anywhere at all.

It doesn't necessarily take long for a trail to fall out of use. Woodlands like these can swallow up railway lines, mansions, even entire settlements in a matter of fifty years or so. There are helicopter landing pads out there that can feel like relics on a par with dinosaur footprints when you come across them. One lost road was nothing. There are thousands of them.

I took a chance, and stopped the Land Rover for a while. With the engine idling and the useless heater still blowing, I reached for the map.

"Why have we stopped?" Rachel said.

"I just need to check something," I told her, and I was studying the symbols on the mountain even as I said it.

We were bang in the middle of *location approximate*. It was approximate, all right. I couldn't work out any relationship between the landscape we'd been passing over, and anything I saw before me. I could find no obvious landmarks, no points of reference.

"Are we lost?" she said.

"Of course not," I said, refolding the map crudely and stuffing it into the gap between the seats so that I could get us rolling again.

The next valley in the sequence was the deepest and the darkest yet. The long, straight trunks of the trees dropped into it like fishing lines, way down into the depths. We crawled around its upper slopes, hugging the side of the mountain, toward a point where the head of the valley narrowed to a rocky gorge.

Now, here was a sight.

At the narrowest part of the gorge there was a wide wooden bridge, braced on trestles that were like railway sleepers. I'm talking about a serious span, and it didn't even have any side rails. The bridge and all the trestles were coated with snow. The trail picked up on the other side and continued off around the next hill.

I stopped the Land Rover a few yards short of the bridge, and I got out. Rachel didn't say anything, but I could see that she was conscious and looking out of the window.

I went to where the bridge started, and looked over. The bridge itself was a substantial platform, built to take the weight of logging vehicles. The sides of the gorge beneath it were of a brown rock so rugged that it looked as if someone had abandoned an attempt to carve it into chunky, Easter Island faces.

It was a deep one. Somewhere way down below was the valley floor, but from here all I could see was winter foliage and darkness.

The bridge looked sturdy enough under its cake-icing of snow, and the trestles supporting it looked even more enormous close-to. However long ago it had been built, they'd built it to last. And it was good and wide.

I walked out onto it for a few yards. The going was firm. Snow was powdering off the edges as the wind blew, making a fine cloud in midair. The bridge felt solid. Nothing creaked. I walked out further, and stopped. No planks rocked underfoot, nothing moved at all. I might as well have been standing on concrete.

I took a deep breath of the cold forest air, walked back to the Land Rover, and climbed in. I slammed the door once, and then slammed it again to make it catch.

"I hope we don't get too many of these," I said. It took me a couple of tries to get the gears engaged, but then I managed a reasonably shudder-free start to get us rolling. I reckoned I was improving. I lined up with the center of the wide bridge, and drove onto it.

Everything was fine at first. Everything was fine until the last set of wheels was off solid ground, and then suddenly it wasn't so fine at all.

It's hard to explain, but something in the handling of the vehicle changed. We were still moving but there was something freer and less controlled about it, more like the movement of a boat across water.

Don't get me wrong. We were going exactly where I wanted us to go. It's just that I wasn't entirely confident that I was responsible for our progress.

I was worried, but I didn't panic. We'll be okay, I thought. It would take just a little more care than I'd expected. All I had to do was steer straight and keep moving and in a minute or less it would all be over.

I changed up a gear, and that was a mistake. We started to lose traction and I felt the wheels begin to spin. I hurriedly changed down again, and mistimed it, and without meaning to I let the clutch out at the wrong moment and stalled the engine with a violent jerk.

We kept going for a short distance. Only I knew it, but in those few yards I had no steering control at all and I felt the vehicle sashay a little, weaving in its tracks before running out of momentum and sliding to a halt. I sat there in the silence, gripping the wheel. I looked at Rachel and I managed what I thought was a confident smile.

"Brief technical hitch," I said.

I pushed the choke all the way in. The engine was running hot by now. I ran a little mental prayer and then I gripped the ignition screwdriver and turned it.

The starter moaned like a Jonah but the engine caught straight off, no problem at all. I revved it, engaged first gear, and opened up the accelerator.

Nothing for a moment as I let out the clutch. And then a wild spinning and I felt the back end begin to drift sideways, although we were barely moving forward. I immediately floored the clutch and let off the pedal, and the drift stopped along with everything else.

My heart was hammering. I could taste bile. It's not pleasant and it's never a sign of things going well.

I tried again, keeping the engine revs at a minimum. Once more we started to move, but not in any controlled way and I quickly laid off the pedal again. The Land Rover felt like a big dog on an iced-over pond, scrabbling comically to get to its feet.

Cold as it was, I was starting to sweat.

I checked that we had drive to all four wheels engaged. According to the set of the handle we had, plus there was all the extra weight of that engine in the back. Snow or no snow, we ought to be sucking onto the bridge like a leech.

Then I had a thought, and I opened the door and hung out of it to take a look at the front wheel.

Well, that explained it.

Sure enough, there at the center of the wheel was an extension like a tin can. It was a freewheeling hub with a manual unlock. They saved on fuel and transmission wear, but for offroad use they had to be locked down again. Ours weren't.

They were simple enough to operate, just push and twist to lock them. I stepped down out of the cab, and in an instant my feet shot out from under me.

Reaching out in panic, I grabbed the door just as my knee hit the ground. The knee jarred badly and I almost bit through my lip.

Recovering my balance and clinging to my vehicle like a drunk, I spat out some of the bitter taste and saw my blood and spit pepper the snow.

Still holding on with one hand, I reached down and brushed some of the snow aside.

Under the snow, the bridge was glass. Pure slippery ice. Where my heels had skidded, I could see more of the slick stuff underneath. Shadow-shapes of the timbers were visible through it, but the ice was inches thick.

No wonder the entire deck had felt like concrete. It was one long frozen slab. Worse still, out here it seemed to slope away to either side, giving the entire iced-up platform a cross-section like a convex lens.

Oh, great.

We were at least one-third of the way over. The only thought that scared me more than that of moving forward was that of trying to back up. The only prospect scarier than either was that of staying put.

If it had just been a matter of my own survival, I might never have been able to unstick myself from the safety of my handhold on the door. But it's easier to be brave when you're doing it for someone else.

As I made for the wheel, I hung on hard and tried not to imagine sliding helplessly to the edge and right off into the void. I'd go like a bungee-jumper off a dam. Without the eventual benefit of the bungee.

I felt the hub engage when I pushed it in, and I felt it lock when I twisted it. One down, one more to go.

As I made my way around the front of the vehicle, I hung on to whatever I could reach. I was like an inexperienced skater dragging himself around the outside of the rink. I had one more bad moment but mostly, where the snow was thick and undisturbed, my footing was deceptively firm. All the same, I took no chances. Not now I knew that a glacier lay underneath.

I was on my way back to the driver's side of the cab when Cyrus Behan's Dodge Ram came into sight behind us, emerging around that last headland.

He stopped it just short of the bridge, and got out.

Thirty-five

He had the rifle in his hand.

From by the door of the idling pickup he looked the situation over and then called out, "I always wondered if that old bridge could still take a truck's weight. You wouldn't get me driving on it to find out, though. That takes a special kind of stupid."

With that he stooped down and, with the hand that didn't have the rifle in it, pulled up a big piece of ply from the ground. The snow dropped from it in a breaking-up sheet.

"See what you miss when you don't pay attention?" he said.

He held up the ply and I saw that it was an ancient painted board that read DANGER! BRIDGE CLOSED. The surface was all weathered and blistered and the nails that had held it had rusted right through. There was still some fencewire attached to it, but the fence must have fallen long ago and been covered-over in the snowfall. He held it there for long enough for me to read it, and then he let it drop back to the ground.

"I've seen you before," he said.

"Yep," I said. "Couple of hours ago."

"I mean, before today."

"I don't think so," I said, and I glanced toward the cab to see if any part of Rachel might be visible to him.

It was the rifle that bothered me most. That, and its load of Black Talons or whatever else he had in the magazine right now. I was partway across the bridge and I was out of his reach, but whatever the load, it made for rather more than an equalizer.

He said, "I definitely know you."

"I don't see how," I said. "We never met before."

"You think so?" he said. "Try the hospital. You were talking to Don Farrow."

"You've got me there," I conceded, changing my handhold on the Land Rover and managing to move just a little more within scramble-in distance of the cab.

"Now I believe you've taken something that's mine," he said, and he worked the bolt on the rifle. The sound of it carried clearly from where he was standing and I think it was the most purposeful noise I'd ever heard.

"Cyrus," I said quickly, "listen to me. I don't care what you read in a newspaper. You've been misinformed. The stuff in Rachel's body has no commercial value."

"Don't treat me like I'm stupid," he said. "Any one of those drugs could be worth a billion."

"Any ticket could win you the lottery, but it's still only worth a dollar."

"Oh, yeah?" he said. "Save your breath. People like you make me sick."

"Who are the people like me, Cyrus?" I said, and I was looking from him to the cab and thinking that the moment I saw him raise the rifle to his shoulder, I'd have to go for it and hope that he'd find a moving target more difficult to hit. Part of my mind was making a dispassionate calculation. How wounded could I get and still be able to drive?

He said, "You people in charge. You think you can tell the rest of us anything and we'll just swallow it. If she's worth nothing, why'd you come all this way just to take her?"

"It's got nothing to do with money, Cyrus. I'm trying to save her life."

"You don't even know her," he said.

"That doesn't matter."

"I'll tell you what, Mister whoever-you-are. Bring her back to me here and then I won't have to shoot you."

"I'm not bringing her back," I said.

It may not have been the wisest thing to say because all he did was shrug and say, "It's all the same to me," and then he swung the rifle up to his shoulder and fired one off so quickly that I had no time to react, other than to flinch and quickly press myself in against the Land Rover.

I'll swear I heard it whizz by me, although I may have imagined that. If he'd taken the least care to aim I'd probably have been dead, but he was so concerned with making a showoff gesture out of it that the shot went seriously wide.

"Are you mad?" I shouted at him. "Never mind me. One stray bullet and there goes your so-called meal ticket."

Now, that was *definitely* the wrong thing to say.

"There's a point," he conceded. "I've got to kill her anyway."

And at that he sighted the scope onto the Rover and started rapid-firing into the back of it, blowing out the rear windows first and then puckering the metal with bullet-punch after bullet-punch. I shouted, "Get down, Rachel! Get down!" but I wasn't even sure if she'd be able to hear me over the gunfire. I dived for the cab while his attention was off me.

Whether she'd heard me or not didn't matter. She'd slid down onto the floor of the cab and was safe. I could hear the bullets spanging off the engine block in the load area behind us, but none of them was coming through.

"Well," Rachel said drily, "you really handled him." Her head was down against the floor.

"He's demented," I said.

"Welcome to Cyrus' world. I've had a week of it."

It all went quiet, then. I took a risk and hooked the door with my foot so that I could swing the mirror in and get a look behind us with relative safety. I was just in time to catch a glimpse of Cyrus' back as he returned to his Dodge. My guess was that he was going back to reload.

If he had a choice of ammunition in the truck, the results of the next salvo might be different.

"Let's go for it," I said, and I scrambled up to get behind the wheel.

I engaged the gears, and started us moving forward. There was a quick spin before the tires got a grip. With the front hubs locked and all four drive wheels pulling, the entire feel of the vehicle was different. The going was still kind of greasy, but I felt as if our progress was under control.

I flinched as one half of the windshield blew out in front of me and put a fan of shattered glass across the Land Rover's hood. I hunkered right down then to make as small a target as I could. I kept myself so low that I could have steered with my teeth.

These shots were rocking the bodywork in a way the others hadn't. He'd switched to a different kind of ammunition. Then I saw a few bullet hits on the bridge sending up sprays of ice all around us, and I realized that he'd altered his tactics, as well.

I said, "He's trying to hit the tires."

"I hope he shoots like he takes pictures," Rachel said from her place down in the footwell. "He did one of me. He's the worst."

I flinched again as the next shot took out the door mirror. There were no more after that.

The Land Rover crawled onward. We were about two-thirds of the way across, now. I didn't dare speed. I didn't dare slip. We kept on moving toward the end of the decking, which drew tantalisingly closer.

"He's coming after us," Rachel said. She'd raised herself and she was looking back over the seats, out through the shattered rear windows.

"Stay down," I said, but when I looked across to the unbroken door mirror I could see that she was right. I could see the Dodge moving.

He was following us onto the bridge.

The timbers started to creak with the extra weight. He was being a lot less cautious than I had, and he was moving faster. I felt the entire bridge vibrate. There was no more than a second or so of this and then there was the most tremendous, splintering bang.

"What the hell was that?" I said.

But Rachel was back up in her seat now, and looking down out of the side window.

"The ice is cracking," she said. "All the extra weight's bending the bridge."

Just what I needed.

I risked increasing our speed, but by now we were almost there. We got to the end of the deck, and as we rolled off it I felt a fierce kind of elation as I sensed dirt and snow beneath our wheels. Behan's Dodge was already halfway across behind us, but when I looked back I could see that he was in trouble.

Most of the bridge's strength had been illusory. It was the ice. The ice had been bracing it like a cast. Without its frozen cladding, the deck itself was weak and rotten. The heavy supporting beams still looked dependable enough, but that deceptively solid-feeling planking was actually so spoiled and decayed that it was like shipwreck timber.

Rachel was right. Just a couple of inches of flexing movement had stressed the ice enough to break it up into big sheets like the ice floes on a river. We'd got off it in time, but now Cyrus was struggling.

There must have been a particularly lousy plank under the wheels on one side of the Dodge. There was a loud crack, and the plank gave way completely. One end flew up in front of the wheels, the other sprang up behind. One side of the Dodge dropped as the wheels went through. Almost the entire weight of its underside came down onto the deck.

I stopped the Land Rover, and we watched. I couldn't do otherwise. Even if I'd wanted to help him, I couldn't.

His wheels were down through the broken planks, spinning uselessly in space. He was stuck there like a misplaced slot racer.

But Cyrus was fighting back, revving the engine hard and trying to climb his way out. With two of his Sport King radials still up on the deck, he was making the truck scream as he urged it forward.

All that happened then was that when the trapped wheels met timber, they started to eat up the bridge like a buzzsaw. Rotten wood sprayed up from underneath.

Then his front wheel hit one of the supporting crossbeams, and it looked for a moment as if he was going to do it; here was something solid to work against, and as the tire spun against the beam it seemed possible that the Dodge might get purchase to climb out of its midair rut and make it to safety.

Tire rubber squealed, the Dodge rocked up almost out of its hole.

Then it lost it and fell back with a bang that shook the entire structure of the bridge. Immediately it bounced back and rocked higher. Sheet ice was breaking loose and falling from the sides of the bridge now in great, translucent guillotine blades.

Despite everything, there was a part of me that was rooting for him. It was like watching a giant reptile trying to climb out of a mud pit. You're caught up in the drama of it even though you know you'll have to run for your life if he succeeds.

I couldn't exactly see what happened then, but I think the forward pressure of the truck must have taken out the cross-member like a rotten stair. Whereas before he'd been on bad wood, now he was on bad wood with nothing underneath it.

It went all at once. The wheels screamed and the tires smoked for a second as Cyrus tried to drive up the falling deck, but the deck was disintegrating under him and all that happened was that his spinning tires made it disintegrate faster.

He dropped right through the middle of the bridge. The Dodge fell as if a hangman's trap had opened underneath it. Looking down, I couldn't see Cyrus. Just the truck, dropping through space in a way that you never expect to see such a big piece of human technology fall.

I could see the wheels spinning freely as it plummeted, and I could hear the engine racing in a banshee scream. It was like some cartoon character, out in mid-air with its legs still running.

I saw it hit the lower slopes and roll. Then it was gone.

Nothing after that.

I sat there staring. Rachel sat back and closed her eyes. Neither of us spoke.

After a while, I got out and looked into the ravine. There was nothing to see. Just branches, and more branches, and darkness beyond.

The back of the Land Rover's body was thoroughly punctured with bullet-holes. The metal around each hole was bent inward and wherever there'd been a hit a corona of paint had been lost, exposing a circle of bare aluminum. Both windows had been smashed and the interior now glittered with a carpet of diamonds. The spare was ruined and one of the tires on the rearmost axle was out, but the six-wheel arrangement meant that we could still be mobile.

I moved slowly, with care. I felt the way I imagined I might if I'd taken a week-long beating.

When I climbed back in behind the wheel, Rachel was sitting with her eyes closed exactly as I'd left her.

Without opening her eyes, she said, "He isn't dead."

"Well," I said, "I wouldn't rate his chances."

She looked at me then. Her eyes were like scary little lizard slits.

"If he was dead, I'd be able to see him," she said.

I faced forward, and we drove on.

Thirty-six

A memory.

It was in our first year in the state, the summer when we'd done most of our touring around. We'd landed for one night at a riverside motel attached to a campground somewhere. I can't even tell you exactly where it was. I remember we ate in a seafood restaurant where they made a fuss of Gillian and her accent, and then afterwards went on to a small amusement park which in places was ankle deep in water from the recent tropical storms, and whose machinery creaked as if threatening to expire in some disastrous accident at any moment.

When we got back to the campground, Gillian spotted a raccoon. It was scavenging under the cars, and allowed us to get within about ten feet of it as it picked at a piece of a discarded sandwich. I know they're not uncommon, but I'd never really seen one before. Certainly not from this close. It looked like a cross between a cat and a fox, with delicate, prehensile hands. I'd imagine it as the kind of life form that would emerge and adapt in the aftermath of a nuclear holocaust.

I didn't sleep well. There was no particular reason for that. I often don't. Sometime before seven the next morning I got up alone and went out, leaving the others undisturbed. There was a dense mist clinging to everything that only the neon of the roadside sign seemed to penetrate. It deadened sound, and it sucked all the color out of light.

I'd picked up a towel and I had an idea about going in the river. A swim before breakfast is one of those lifestyle things that I can always picture myself going in for, but which I rarely do anything about. It's an achievable fantasy that I never quite stir myself to achieve. It's like driving out to watch a sunset or slow-dancing in an empty restaurant, the kind of thing they do in those impossibly perfect lives they lead in

TV ads…the life I'd be leading too, if mine had a better budget and more flattering photography.

Moving through the weekenders' trailers on their permanent sites, I felt as if I was walking through a spectral fairground. They looked like closed-up sideshow booths that had been standing for years under the overhanging branches of the riverside trees. The grass had grown up around them and most of them were streaked with moss, like ancient rock faces.

I couldn't get to the river. When I reached the path that went down to the riverbank, I found the way barred by the woman we'd seen in the office the evening before. She was in her work clothes of shorts and baggy T-shirt and sneakers, and she had her arms folded across her chest against the morning's chill. She told me that there was a rabid raccoon further down the path, and she was there to keep people away from it until her husband returned with his gun. I looked past her, and I could just about see it. It was a long way off. It seemed to be circling drunkenly and trying to bite at its own hindquarters. I couldn't say whether it was the one we'd seen the night before, or not.

They were still asleep when I got back to the room. I sat outside on one of the plastic chairs, listening to the racket of all the air conditioners in the block being almost drowned out by the racket of the insects in the foliage all around us. After a few minutes I heard a gunshot in the mid-distance, closely followed by another. Less than a minute after that I heard the sounds of the Cartoon Network from the room behind me.

We moved on that same morning. I suppose that the raccoon went into a plastic bag and was taken off somewhere for testing. I told Gillian about it, and she wasn't upset. She complained because I hadn't woken her to see it being dealt with. Gillian's notions of herself as non-squeamish and an early riser were on a par with mine as a dawn athlete. She sincerely believed it was her style. It was just that there was always a good reason why today had to be an exception.

We all agreed that it was a shame. What I think I'm saying is that you can fear a thing, but that doesn't mean you have to hate it as well. I was sorry the creature had to die, but if it was so diseased then I was glad that it was dead.

By the same token, the loss of Cyrus Behan was not something to be celebrated. Someone had lost a son. Two overweight and squinty-eyed brothers had lost a nephew that they thought enough of to instruct in their ways.

He was a dangerous piece of shit, but it was still a tragedy. That's all I'm trying to say.

~

When the abandoned road finally became an impassable one, I stopped and got out the map again and searched it for answers. Desperately. As if it had secrets that only the power of my concentration could bring to the surface.

Rachel's deterioration was happening in steps and jerks. It was quite unlike Gillian's which, now I looked back on it, had been a single, hours-long, gradual decline. It had been like having someone slide away from you to just beyond fingertip reach, so that you can't help believing that with a little extra stretch, a little extra effort, you might still somehow bridge that trivial distance and bring them back.

Even now.

With Rachel it was if there was an entire factory of diverse reactions going on inside her. She'd go from a miserable kind of hibernation to a startled, perplexed awareness, half-sitting up at a particularly bad jolt and looking around as if her entire history and surroundings were something new that had been sprung upon her in this very moment.

"We've stopped," I heard her say.

"Well spotted," I told her.

This seemed to be one of her more lucid moments. She said to me, "So why *are* you doing this?"

I didn't look up from the map. "What do you mean?" I said.

"Cyrus was right. You don't even know me."

"That doesn't matter, Rachel."

"It doesn't explain it, either."

"What's to explain?" I said. "I came when you called. I wouldn't like to think a stranger would turn away from a child of mine in your situation."

There was a silence for a while, and then when I started to put the map away Rachel said, "What was her name?"

"Whose?"

"You know who I mean."

"Gillian," I said.

"Now, her I can see."

I know she wasn't saying it to taunt me or to cause pain. I knew she was in delirium. But this was difficult for me to hear.

I said, "What are you talking about, Rachel?"

"I don't know," she admitted.

In appearance she was no less far-gone that before. Her eyes were half-open, but they were glassy. Her skin was sallow. She looked very sick indeed.

"I don't think I'm going to make it," she said.

"Yes, you are," I told her. "There are people out there who love you. Don't make them feel the way I do."

"Gillian says you haven't really felt it yet."

I kept on watching her for a while, but she didn't look at me.

"Rachel," I said. "Why are you doing this to me?"

"I don't know," she said.

And as I was putting the Land Rover into gear she added, apropos of nothing, "My dog died."

According to the map, there was a lookout tower on the next ridge. It meant climbing again, but I was getting nowhere trying to descend. The forest had closed up ahead of me like something living, the kind of thing you might get in a fairy tale. It was probably too much to hope that the lookout post would be manned, but with any luck there could be a phone or a radio or even a decent road out.

It wasn't a hard decision to make. The bridge was down, and there was no way back.

So onward and upward we went.

~

I was worried about Rachel.

Even if she were to survive the physical effects of whatever was inside her, I dreaded to consider what it might be doing to her head. My fear was that it could be vandalising her mind, like kids let loose in a computer store with baseball bats. She was seeing things. She was hearing voices. At one point she'd believed that she was flying alongside the Land Rover, even though on one level she was fully aware that she was inside it and talking to me.

She saw her dead dog. She even said she saw my dead daughter.

What was inside there? What was it doing to her? She'd be the last one to give me a reliable analysis. There was no way of knowing, no way at all.

Nothing can taunt you more than infinite possibility.

I was watching her for any sign of a convulsion. I knew now that they'd signal the beginning of the end. In Gillian I'd taken them for a sign of continuing life, when in fact they'd been the last collapsing function of the body. They came when life was already standing just outside and closing the door.

I desperately, *desperately* wanted her to live. More, I reckon, than even her own father would have if he'd been there in my place.

How can I say that? It's simple. Think about it. He'd be sitting there and telling himself that somehow it would all be fine, and that it was inconceivable that she might die.

I'd been there. I'd done that.

I knew better now.

There was a moment, as the thinning-out trees and the sight of the winter sky were telling me that we'd climbed almost to the top of the ridge, where I sensed her beginning to shake. I felt it, a quite different sensation to the vibrations of the engine and the constant jarring of the terrain. Without stopping, I reached over and put my hand on her and shook her once, hard, and shouted her name.

Except that I'm not sure now whose name I called out. It might have been Rachel's, it might have been Gillian's. It was part of my own private fugue of disorder that I'd been running the two of them together in my mind for so long that it's impossible to say.

She opened her eyes and looked at me with a kind of puzzled uncertainty, the way you'd look at a stranger who grabs your arm and seems to know you. I realized then that what I'd taken for shuddering was actually shivering, and I thought what a bitter irony it would be to deliver her from Cyrus and to save her from the drugs, only to lose her to exposure.

I took my hand from her, and she closed her eyes and turned away.

There was another bad moment shortly after that, when the Land Rover's engine started to splutter and I felt it losing power. It was going exactly the way that engines do when they're running out of fuel.

I looked at the gauges on the dash and realized for the first time that there were two of them. What I mean is, that there were two of them that apparently served the same purpose. One needle seemed to be showing that I had about three-quarters of a tank of gasoline, while the other was resting right over on the pin where it said 'empty.'

Underneath them was a Bakelite arrow with no markings of any kind. I tried moving it, and found it would make a quarter-turn before it stopped. It had been pointing at one gauge, and now it was pointing at the other. A few seconds after I'd done this, the engine note picked up again.

Two tanks, and a valve to switch between them. I'd come across that before. A lot of ex-Forces vehicles had found their way onto the market at home, re-registered and with quick paint jobs and no way of determining their age or past use. Many had been adapted for one purpose or another, and very few of the adaptations were what you could call standard. They went all around the world and they wound up in the strangest places.

Few stranger than this, though.

When I first saw the lookout tower through the tops of the trees, I could hardly believe it. It was almost as if this journey had become a life in itself, in the way you can get so wrapped up in the process of moving forward that any new development catches you out.

The tower was a cabin in the air with an observation platform all around it, the entire thing raised high above the forest on cranefly legs. It had a pitched roof, with above it an antenna so slender that it was almost invisible against the sky. On the pylon structure below the platform were two enormous lightweight satellite dishes.

When we got closer to its base, I saw that it stood on the wider end of a teardrop-shaped hump of ground with a clearing below it. I drove the Land Rover up into the clearing and stopped there.

I squinted up at the tower. We'd been so long in the shadows that the raw light of the sky hurt my eyes. I couldn't see any sign of it being occupied. Not only were there no tracks or marks in the snow around the base, but each step on its iron stairway carried a thick, untouched of crust of white. Up at the top, the cabin's wraparound windows were all shuttered.

"Can you hear me, Rachel?" I said. "I'm going to see if I can get into the tower."

"Can't walk," she mumbled.

"You don't have to walk. Just wait here."

"Cold," she said.

I took my coat off and covered her with it. I left the Land Rover's engine running and the heater on, although it made even less of a difference now with no windows front or back. I took a useful-looking piece of iron from among the engine parts in the load space, shook the broken glass off it, and with that in my hand I plowed my way across the knee-deep snow in the clearing and began to ascend the outside stairway.

The whole thing was a four-legged lightweight metal structure held together by bolts. Lightweight for its size, I mean. It shook and rattled underfoot as I climbed up the side. All along the handrail people had scratched graffiti into the paint with keys, sometimes with dates and full names.

When I got to the top of the stairway, I found it barred by a heavy trapdoor grille above my head. I tried to lift it, but there was a padlock holding it down. Around the edge of the deck there was a triple layer of barbed wire, to discourage anyone from attempting to monkey-climb up the outside.

I went for the hasp and staple, attacking the spot where it was fixed to the underside of the deck. It took me a while and it was a fierce and ugly process costing me a lot of effort, but in the end I had the bolts prized out of the timber.

My hands were cut and my knuckles were skinned and I'd no clear memory of how that had happened. But I was finally able to throw back the metal trap and clamber up onto the observation platform.

Then I had to do it all over again to break into the cabin. The observation deck was about four feet wide and I was some way above all the treetops here. I took a look out, but there was too much haze to see very far. Most of what I could see was just bare trees and wind-whirling snow.

Between attacks on the padlocked door I'd look down over the rail, to see if everything was all right with Rachel. I couldn't see much other than the roof of the Land Rover, and I couldn't see anything of Rachel at all. I could hear that the engine was still running. It seemed to miss a beat every now and again but whenever I checked, nothing seemed to have changed.

In the end, having ignored all the trespass warnings and the penalty notices, I finally succeeded in busting my way into government property.

I had to leave the door open because there was no light from the boarded-up windows. You could see that people worked here but it was cramped and spartan, like a tollbooth in the sky. I went straight for the radio set and threw every switch that I could see. I reckoned I had a good chance of it working because underneath the table was a bank of power cells about the size of a steamer trunk.

The cells were in good order. My reward was a glow of red and amber working lights. It was as if I'd awakened some kind of secret life that had been hibernating there.

I pulled over a chair and picked up the handset. I had no idea of what to do, but there was a paper with some names and numbers on it scotch-taped to the casing of the machine. Some kind of an aide-memoire for the regular Ranger staff, I imagined. Once I'd worked out how to set a frequency I started going through the numbers and Maydaying away until somebody answered.

The somebody wasn't the right person, but when I'd explained my situation they told me the right frequency to call.

Finally.

"My name is John Bishop," I said. "I need medical assistance for a seriously ill young woman."

I explained where I was, and what I'd had to do to get us there.

The voice at the other end said, "Can you get her into town from where you are?"

"If I could do that, I'd be on my way right now," I said. "We're stuck on the mountain and she needs immediate attention. It's going to take a half-track or a helicopter to get us down from here. It's a long story. Ben Steed knows the details."

"Okay," the voice said. I heard some off-mike talk then, and I was able to pick out the word *paramedic*. The voice came back on-mike and said, "Describe her condition to me."

"She's delirious and hallucinating," I said. "Her breathing's shallow and her color's bad. She's got two different drug samples in her gut. At least one of them's been released into her bloodstream already. Maybe both. I don't know."

"Is this woman a user of narcotics?"

"No!" I said. "Talk to Ben Steed. I already explained the situation to him. Tell him the proof of my story's right here."

"Okay," the voice said. "Please keep your radio on this frequency and wait beside it. Don't worry, Mister Bishop. Everything's going to be fine."

"Don't tell me that," I said. "You don't know."

I didn't stay. I went down to Rachel.

I opened the Land Rover's passenger door. She was sitting there with her eyes closed, her head nodding slightly with the vibration of the engine.

"Rachel," I said. "Can you hear me?"

"You don't need to shout," she said without opening her eyes. Her voice surprised me. It wasn't loud, but it was clear and unexpectedly strong. Almost as if she'd been playing a scene, and she was still in all her sick-girl makeup, but she'd momentarily let herself slip out of character.

"I have to wait by the radio," I told her. "I've spoken to the rangers. Everything's going to be fine."

"Uh-huh," she said, her eyes still closed.

"Do you know where you are? Do you know who I am?"

"Uh-huh," she said.

I went back up the tower. I could hear them calling for me before I was even halfway up the stairs.

I grabbed up the handset. "Yes," I said breathlessly. "John Bishop here."

A new voice at the other end said, "I wasn't too pleased when I came out and found you gone from my office." He sounded as if he'd been patched-in from out on the road somewhere—actually, the signal was so lousy that it sounded as if he was in a tin shed somewhere out in the Antarctic. But still I recognized the voice as Ben Steed of the River Springs Police.

I said, "I'm sorry about that. I had the impression you'd be glad to get rid of me."

"Is she there?"

"She's down in the car."

"Okay," Ben Steed said. "We have a slight problem."

I immediately recognized another of those phrases that they use to grease you up just before they shove in the bad news.

"This I don't think I want to hear," I said.

"I've got one helicopter in the air and right now it's bringing in those hikers."

"Can't you divert it?"

"If the kids were in good shape I could make them wait, but that's not the case. The rescue's under way right now. It doesn't make any sense to abort it. Can you see that?"

Yes, I could see it. It didn't help me and it didn't help Rachel, but I could certainly see it.

I rubbed at my brow with my free hand and said, "What about the local TV station? Don't they have a machine? I can't believe there's nothing else in the air."

"I've another copter on its way up from Asheville," he said. "Whichever one gets to you first will bring you out. How's she doing?"

"Not well," I said.

"I talked to your friend Kate O'Brien."

"What did she say?"

"She reckons you're upset but you're not out of control. Everyone apart from her says you're to be pitied and not listened to."

"How do you know that's not true?"

"I'd like to think I'm a better judge of character. Although it may have more to do with the fact that my wife's brother is the one who sold Cyrus his new butcher knife this morning. Is he likely to be a danger to you there?"

Was this the time to tell him that Behan had died? What the hell, it couldn't hurt. But then something made me hesitate.

"I really can't say," I said.

If he was dead, I'd be able to see him.

Ben Steed said, "There's a Rangers' helipad right alongside the tower. You probably can't see it under the snow but I'm telling you it's there. Is it clear enough for a landing?"

I looked down. I didn't know what I was looking for but I realized that the teardrop-shaped piece of ground had to be the landing pad. The Land Rover was standing right in the middle of it.

"Mister Bishop," he said patiently. "Is the helipad clear?"

"It will be," I said. "Just get somebody up here."

Thirty-seven

I went back down the tower. There were fresh tracks across the undisturbed part of the snow that covered the landing pad, but they were the marks of something small and they passed wide of the Land Rover. In all of the day's long journey I'd seen nothing living in the woods, but obviously there was life out there. I knew this was bear country. I wasn't too well-up on bear habits but I reckoned that at this time of year the bears were probably sleeping.

Rachel said to me, "Take your coat back."

"In a minute," I said.

"You'll get cold."

"I'm fine." And I was, for the moment, thanks to all the running up and down the tower. But I could feel the cold air on my sweat and I knew I'd chill down quickly once I stopped moving.

"I want to sit up," she said.

"Sure."

She'd slid down the seat a way, and I helped her to hitch up it. I tucked the coat in around her, like a quilt. Her face was as white as uncovered bone.

"I heard something outside," she said. "What was it?"

"Some kind of an animal," I told her. "I don't know what it was." I laid my hand on her forehead and she winced without opening her eyes. She felt warmer than I'd expected. Not feverish, but not right either.

I said, "We have to sit tight here and wait for a rescue helicopter."

"Wow," she said. "Suspense."

If she could manage sarcasm, then perhaps she wasn't as far-gone as I'd feared. She still didn't look too great, though. She was responding the way you do when you're conscious and alert, but your head's aching like a bastard and it'll get worse if you move it any more than you have to.

She said, "So this is what it takes to get you to sit still for a while."

"What do you mean?"

"You know what I'm talking about."

"Honestly, Rachel. You're going to have to help me out, there."

"You really don't get it?"

"No."

"You've been running since the moment she died. If you really want to mourn her, you've got to stop, first. How do you think it makes her feel when you won't?"

I didn't know how to respond. She was scaring me—not so much with what she was saying, because I was starting to get used to the hints and the surreal sense of meaning. More because of the way she was saying it. This wasn't the lucidity of someone who'd rested and regained a little ground and now was feeling better. It sounded more like the lucidity of the dying. Making perfect sense to themselves. But somehow, it's as if they've moved into another place to the rest of us and there's a different set of scenery there.

With an effort I said, "Why don't you tell me?"

But she turned her face away; just an inch or so of movement was all it took.

"I want to sleep," she said wearily.

"No," I said quickly, and I gripped her arm through the layers and shook her. "Rachel, no."

"I want to wake up and find it's all over."

"Me too, Rachel, but it doesn't work that way. Don't let go. You've got to hang on. Please."

She turned her face to me then, and she opened her eyes and looked into mine. Her eyes were clear. Startlingly so. I could see every thread and edge and shade in each of her pupils. There was a lot of green in there, but you couldn't easily pin them down to a single color.

"All right," she said. As if she had the option, and she'd oblige me for a while, but the eventual outcome would still be the same.

"Does it hurt anywhere?"

A slight shake of her head. No.

I think I'd have felt just a little happier if she'd said that it did.

~

I got myself properly repositioned behind the wheel before I revved the engine, sank the clutch, and put the shift into reverse. It wasn't the

Land Rover's favorite gear and it gave me a fight, gnashing its teeth on the first couple of tries before I finally managed to work it in.

Backing up was tricky, with no clear view behind me and only one door mirror still intact. I did my best to stay within my own tracks as I withdrew the thirty yards or so that it took to get clear of the helicopter pad.

After that I got out and cast around in the undergrowth until I found a fallen branch, and then with an effort to use this like a yard brush I made a start on clearing some of the snow from the target area. I gave that up before too long, but not before I'd started to uncover two big code letters, meant to be visible from the air and formed by yellow-painted blocks set flush into the turf. I didn't uncover enough to find out what the letters actually were. From what I could see, each of them would have to be about fifteen feet high.

But the snow was too deep, and there was too much of it. I had no chance of doing anything like a useful job. Surely the tower itself was enough of a landmark.

So I threw the branch away and watched the sky for a while. I was trying to be optimistic when what I really felt was a growing despair. I'd lost my faith in happy endings. What had happened once was going to happen all over again. I could keep the awareness of it at arm's length with more pointless activity, but there was nothing I could do to stop the inevitable. I made a fist and punched my thigh, hard, as if I needed to satisfy a hunger for some kind of punishment, but I was so cold that I could hardly feel the blow.

I wondered if I could bear to check on her again. I feared that she was entering that place where all the rules break down. Where the dying see as they've never seen before, where they speak as they've never spoken. Where they somehow become less the selves we know, but more the selves they really are.

My legs were trembling now as I climbed up to the observation platform once more.

"It's John Bishop," I said when I was able to raise the control center again. "What's the situation?"

"There's nothing new I can tell you, Mister Bishop," my nameless, bodiless voice of the airwaves said. "We're doing our best to get to you."

"Isn't there any way to get a vehicle up here? What about your National Guard? Haven't they got something?"

"Nothing we've got available to us can make it through. I know it's tough, but you've got to sit tight. We're trying to get hold of a paramedic to talk to you."

"I don't need a paramedic," I said. "I need a miracle worker."

Not again, I was thinking helplessly. *Oh, please, God, not again.* If I could have gone out into the open and yelled at the top of my voice and offered myself in her place with even the slenderest hope of success, I know I'd have done it.

"Hang in there, Mister Bishop," the radio voice was telling me. "The engineers are working on it now."

"On what?" I said with sudden suspicion.

There was radio silence for several long seconds, and I could imagine a hasty off-mike conference taking place. I thought he'd been told. Who was supposed to tell him? What should I say to him now?

The voice came back on and said, "Stay calm, John. We're going flat-out for you, here."

I said, "It isn't even in the air yet, is it?"

"John, don't be tempted to leave the tower. It gives us our best chance of finding you."

"Why would I leave the tower? Is there another way down from here?"

"No, John. Not in these conditions. I'm telling you to stay put."

I laid down the handset and switched off all the power and then I put my head in my hands and allowed myself one rotten, wretched sob. Then I dried my eyes and set to business. Before I left, I checked everywhere to see if they had a better map up there, but they hadn't.

I'm not sure at which exact point I'd made up my mind that I couldn't sit there and watch her die while waiting for a helicopter that would never turn up. There had to be some kind of land access to the tower. A service track or a road, however rudimentary. They didn't want to tell me about it because they'd assessed the situation and they were placing all their faith in airmobility.

But faith is a personal thing. And after what I'd been through, I was disinclined to surrender mine in deference to anyone else's.

In a situation very like this one, my disobedience had effectively killed my daughter.

And now, God help me, I felt I had no choice but to disobey yet again.

Thirty-eight

Rachel," I said to her. I was leaning close to her ear because she looked as if she'd slipped off away from me again, into a kind of listless torpor that I hoped might be some way short of complete unconsciousness. "Can you hear what I'm saying?"

She made no response.

I said, "Forgive me if this is the wrong thing to do."

Forgive me now. Because it will be too late to forgive me later.

Again, no response.

The only way off this ridge that I could see was a hikers' trail that dropped all the way to a creek and then followed it out. A hikers' trail wasn't a road, but it was the only route the map showed. Somehow I'd have to get the Land Rover down it. I'd like to say that I agonized over the decision for a while, but I didn't. The choice had been made and now I went for it.

My strategy was a straightforward one. We'd run downhill until we met the river. Then by following the river downstream we'd reach the place where it was bridged by the road back into town.

Picking up the trail was easier than I'd expected, because it had been blazed last summer by someone walking it with a can of spray paint. Every fifteen yards or so, a tree was marked. Sticking to the trail in a vehicle was another matter.

The descent quickly developed into a twisting, winding drive, crashing through snowdrifts and dead undergrowth, finding ways around places where the trees were grouped too closely or the ground fell away too sharply. Much of the time we were tilted at one perilous angle or another, and in some places I had to go so wide of my chosen route that I could never be sure afterwards that I'd picked it up again until I saw another of the blaze marks and knew we were still in business.

I don't know how it was that the Land Rover didn't just fall apart around us. It had to be one seriously tough old tank. One time we sideswiped a tree, and instead of stopping us in our tracks it was the tree that teetered and started to fall. Roots and dirt came up out of the ground in one enormous mass. I just managed to rev up and get us away from it before our back end got lifted and had us caught there.

One big advantage of the increasingly bumpy ride was that it made for an ordeal that even the dead would have found it difficult to sleep through. Whenever I heard anything of any kind from Rachel, or even imagined I did, I'd say something like, "That's it, Rachel. Show an interest. Here comes another."

The most I ever got back was an audible wince or a cry at the worst of the jolts, but I tried to tell myself that anything was better than a silence.

Lower down the mountain, the character of the snow began to change. There wasn't so much of it and it became thinner, more crystalline, more icy. Where there were drifts they weren't so deep, and their surface was a brittle crust that we plowed on through like an icebreaker.

In one place we lost traction altogether and the vehicle made an uncontrolled sideways slide down the hill for at least fifty or sixty yards. It felt the way you do when you run down a sand dune. Nothing's in check, but you're still getting where you want to go. You just have to cross your fingers and hope there's no mishap on the way.

The valley deepened, and became more like a gorge. The floor of the gorge was flattened and relatively navigable. We slalomed our way through the trees as if nothing could stop us, our wheels mounting the thickest roots and crashing down as we rode over them. We were probably a forest ranger's nightmare.

But we were making progress. We were, indisputably, coming down off the mountain.

In a winter glade with a small stream running down through it, we came to a place with a log weir and a rough-hewn wooden footbridge passing over. The bridge wasn't wide enough or strong enough to take a vehicle, so here I stopped and climbed out to scout for a place for the Land Rover to cross.

The stream wasn't wide and it didn't look particularly deep, but it was fast-running. That can be deceptive. I didn't want to get our wheels into anything I couldn't get them out of.

Then something caught my eye. Hung up in the weir, bright and shiny like a new addition to a magpie's nest, was what looked like a big piece of the chrome from Cyrus Behan's Dodge.

I went to the middle of the footbridge, and I crouched down and hung one-handed from the rail so that I could pull it free.

It was a part of one of the bumpers, twisted and smashed. I looked for anything else in the weir, but I could see only sticks and dead leaves.

Looking skyward, I realized that we were some way further down the very gorge he'd dropped into. Just as I hadn't been able to see to the bottom of it from up there, I couldn't see the top of it from here.

~

Well, this was good. Wasn't it? Tangible proof of our descent.

I listened for a while, but I don't know what I expected to hear. The only sound was of cold running water.

I used the trim as a probe to check the depth of the stream in a couple of places, and then I threw it off into the undergrowth where it disappeared from sight. Then I went back to Rachel.

"Guess what I just found," I said, but she didn't respond. I checked her quickly. She was still breathing.

We crossed just above the weir, where the stream was wide and fast but also shallow. We bounced in and out of the water and then it took me two or three goes to get the front wheels up the banking on the other side. We came back down through the trees and onto the trail and then once more we were on our way. I reckoned we'd be at the river within minutes, now.

But before that happened, the Rover's engine began to sputter and lose power again.

I trimmed the choke, dropped to a lower gear, tried everything I could think of, but still it died under me.

We rocked to a halt, and there was silence. I twisted the makeshift screwdriver and the starter made all the right noises, but nothing useful happened beyond that.

I couldn't understand it. One of the tanks still had fuel. Could there be a blockage in the valve, or some dirt in the pipes? If I couldn't get us moving, I was in big trouble whatever the reason.

So I looked at those gauges again. According to them, I still had most of a full tank on one side. If anything, the level didn't appear to have dropped at all. Which was odd. I felt around under the dash, and quickly established what I'd begun to suspect.

Neither of the gauges was actually connected to anything. All that I could feel back there were the bare terminals. There were a few cut wires behind the dash, but there was nothing that actually seemed to have a function. One dial was permanently stuck on full, the other permanently stuck on empty.

It made a certain Alice-in-Wonderland kind of sense, I suppose. You'd always be somewhere in between.

First I had to locate the tanks. I found them under the seats in the cab, of all places. The driver's seat squab lifted right out and revealed a recessed filler cap welded into the grey metal. I unscrewed the cap and peered into the tank. There was a powerful smell of gasoline but, as far as I could see, it was dry in there. It was a shallow space and I could see all the way to the bottom of it. I screwed the cap back in and replaced the squab.

The second tank was over on the passenger's side. I had to slide Rachel out of the way. I reached out for her and, in some kind of reflex, she wrapped her arms around me as I drew her over. I felt her hand grasp the back of my shirt like a baby's, hanging on tight.

I closed my eyes for a moment. I'd tell you that time seemed to stand still, but it didn't. In that moment it seemed to leap backwards.

In the end I broke away, and reached over her to prize out the other squab. The result was the same as before.

Carefully, I arranged her back as she'd been.

I crouched close to her.

"Don't worry about this," I told her. "Don't worry. I know there's a way. I just have to work out what it is."

As if that was the easy part.

I explored around in the back and found a metal jerrican there, secured behind the driving position with canvas webbing. It had no stopper and it was empty, but thanks to the engine block in the load space it had been protected from the shooting.

I climbed out of the back with it. I was thinking that whoever was responsible for the custom job clearly hadn't been too much troubled by thoughts of their own mortality. I mean…two fuel tanks under the seats, and a spare can behind the driver? One stray spark, and you'd go up like a Buddhist monk.

I set the can on the ground, and I checked once more on Rachel. I must have spent a minute or so talking to her, murmuring reassurances close to her ear. I don't recall exactly what I said. I don't suppose it matters.

It took me barely a minute to walk back to the footbridge and the weir. When I got there, with the can hooked on my shoulder one-handed like a crooner's jacket, I started the upward scramble alongside the stream to get into the higher, rockier part of the gorge.

I was praying that the Dodge's tank would have survived the fall intact, that the wreck wouldn't be in some inaccessible place, and that I wouldn't reach it and find that the only fuel to be had from it was diesel oil or something even more exotic.

I'd know soon enough. That piece of chromed trim couldn't have washed here from too far up, I reckoned. And I wasn't wrong. When I found the wreck it was no more than two or three hundred yards upstream.

I was gasping and lightheaded when I got to it, to find that neither Cyrus Behan nor his rifle were inside it or anywhere near.

Thirty-nine

When I did find the rifle it was about twenty-five yards away, in pieces all laid out on a flat rock. He'd field-stripped it, but the heart of the thing was shattered and there had been no point in him even attempting to put it back together.

It looked as if he'd tried, though.

I turned back to the Dodge. That was in a bad way, too. It was lying upside-down, fenders ripped off, wheels in the air, bodywork so rolled and ruined that you'd need to poke around in the snow and find a badge just to be able to say for certain what make it had been. It had come to rest on its roof. Part of the roof had been pushed in and all of the glass had been popped or smashed out, but the cab wasn't entirely crushed. Those big roll bars had done a good job of protecting it.

I went over to the cab and got down on my hands and knees to look inside it. What a mess.

No blood that I could see.

I saw his tracks, which led off up the canyon. There was no sign of any coming back down again. I could only imagine that he'd hoped to climb back up to where he thought we were.

Well, good.

With a broken wiper stalk I punched a hole in the Dodge's tank, and when the gasoline came out I put the jerrican under the stream and held it there. It made a rattling sound like someone pissing in a tin bucket. Faster would have made me happier. I had to stand there for several minutes, altering the position of the can every now and again.

I stopped when the can was about one-third full. With Cyrus still on the loose I wanted to get back to Rachel as quickly as I could.

The snow had begun to fall again, but not so heavily that I couldn't find my way. While the jerrican had been no lightweight before, it was considerably heavier now. I had to carry it two-handed, and it bumped against my leg with every step. A few times I slipped on the new snow and almost fell.

I didn't actually fall but I staggered, I stumbled. I hadn't realized how close to my physical limits I'd been getting. When I reached the stream, I could hardly keep my balance on the footbridge across it.

Dear Gillian.

Dear Rachel.

You both deserved so much better than me.

I think the cold had finally managed to enter into me. It had slid in like a razor so sharp that you don't even feel the wound. I was noticing it now, but now was too late. It had taken up a kind of residence and I couldn't drive it out. It was in my veins, like a setting concrete. It was spreading.

I wasn't shivering. I heard only silence in the forest, and my own hard breathing in my ears. No wind blew and nothing else moved. I felt so weary.

One step at a time, one foot after another.

I was back before I knew it.

There ahead of me was the Land Rover. I hadn't realized until now what a crazy, zigzagging progress we'd been making through the woods. Coming upon it was like catching up with some piece of game that I'd shot and then had to track until it fell. Now here it was; bullet-ridden, broken, silent. My driver's door stood open. The new snow was already beginning to cling to the bodywork.

She wasn't inside it. No-one was.

Forty

My first thought was that Cyrus had moved in as soon as I was out of the way. I looked all around the vehicle and saw no new tracks, but that meant nothing. The snow might have covered them over.

Had he been here? Had he taken her?

And if he had, *where* had he taken her?

I swung around, looking in every direction. The can was still in my hand. It banged into the side of the Land Rover and some of the fuel slopped out of it. I set the jerrican down and called out her name at the top of my voice. First shouting it out this way, then that.

Not even an echo. All sound was dead. But the light in that clearing was about as pure as light ever gets. Nothing can look bad where there's snow. Even the dead on a battlefield gain a poignant beauty in it.

I roared her name until my voice broke, and then as I stopped and listened again to the silence I was gripped by the thought that if Cyrus hadn't been here, and if he was still out there somewhere, then I was surely calling him in.

She couldn't have gone far. Given the way she'd been when I'd seen her last, I was amazed that she could to move at all.

On the edge of the clearing I found the coat that I'd covered her with. It lay in a heap as if it had fallen from her as she'd been walking away. One of the borrowed sweaters lay discarded a few yards further on. It was as if she'd begun to shed layers as she moved, like an emerging butterfly.

I took this as a sign of her direction, and went crashing out through the woods in what I hoped was her wake. I felt clumsy and crude and I pictured her ahead of me, floating in silence, covering the ground and making no mark. I fell once, heavily, and it drove all the breath out of me. But I got to my feet again and went on.

All the trees were tall and straight. All the ground was white. And the air…the air in that place was like no other.

I saw her then.

Her back was to me and I could only part-see her through the undergrowth, but I knew her by the clothes she was wearing. This season's favorite T-shirt, atmosphere-blue, making a figure so pale that she was barely there. She seemed to be crouched over something. Her hair had fallen so that it hid her face until I was almost standing over her, and then she pushed it aside as she looked up at me.

Everything stopped.

It was like the moment back in that seedy club with the mirror behind the bar, turning in the glitterball light. That brief acid-flash glimpse of the stranger who was no stranger.

It had passed in a second, back then.

But this did not pass.

Her face was like the kind of porcelain that makes you catch your breath. The tip of her nose was reddened and there were a few fine, broken veins in her cheeks.

"Hello, dad," she said.

I couldn't say anything.

She looked down at her hands. "I can't feel my fingers," she said, and when she flexed them all I heard a ripple of faint cracks. It was that popping of all the tiny bubbles that form in your joints when you haven't used them for a while.

"Me neither," I managed then. "That's the cold."

Moving stiffly, as if she'd all but forgotten how, she brought her hands up before her and tried to blow into them. I doubted she was making much difference.

"I wanted to show you something wonderful," she said.

I wanted to tell her that she already had.

"No," she said, as if I'd actually spoken the words out loud. "You'll have to see what I mean. Watch."

She turned her attention back to the ground before her and then, balancing herself with one hand braced, she reached forward and dug the other into the snow. She was cupping her fingers slightly, as if her aim was to lift out something fragile.

This was snow that had filled up the ruts between tree roots, making a series of shallow basins. Although she'd complained about her hands and she wasn't dressed for the outdoors, she wasn't shivering. It was as if she'd made an observation about the effects of the cold, but the cold itself didn't actually bother her.

I just stood there, saying nothing.

After a moment or two of working at it, she came up with an irregularly-shaped nugget of ice. It wasn't clean, pure or solid. It was more like trash ice, grey and porous.

She straightened up before me and covered it over in her hand, as if she was trying to use some of her body heat to melt it.

As we waited for something to happen I said, "Why did you do it, Gilly? You can tell me. I'm not angry now. I'm in hell, but I'm not angry."

"Poor dad," she said.

"Was it my fault? Honestly, you can tell me. I can take it if it was. I can't hurt any more than this."

She shook her head. "It wasn't anybody's fault."

"I don't know if I can handle that. I need someone to blame. Even if it's me."

"It was just a stupid thing that went wrong. It wasn't supposed to be some kind of a punishment. I never intended it to turn out the way it did. It just did."

"Was it because of something I'd done?"

"No."

She uncovered the ice, which looked exactly as it had before.

"It's not working," she said. "You try," and held it out to give it to me.

I knew that touch in an instant. If I doubted anything else, I couldn't doubt that. I recognized it too well. It was my last memory of my daughter's hand and it was the bone-cold of stone. It was no wonder that the ice wouldn't melt.

The frozen nugget lay in my palm and collapsed into water before my eyes. It took a matter of seconds.

At the heart of the nugget there was a dead bird. It was curled up and it was tiny, like a ball of feathers you might roll with your fingertips. It lay hunched in my palm with wet ice crystals all over it and I could see its beak laid along its wing, its eyes closed, the feathers bedraggled and drab. I could feel no weight to it at all.

It looked too small ever to have lived; but so perfect, so complex.

"What's the point of this?" I said.

And she said, "I'm not quite sure."

I was so shocked when it stirred in my hand that I almost closed up my fingers in a reflex and crushed it.

It tried to spread its wings, but they were too sodden. I felt its clawed feet moving in a little spasm against my skin. Its eyes were still closed and its head was still twisted down against its body.

She said, "I think it's something to do with there being no endings. Just new forms. And new beginnings."

Then suddenly it fluttered with impossible energy, spraying water like a shower of diamonds. It took to the air so close to my face that I flinched and turned away. I felt the cutting beat of its wings as it passed, and then it was gone.

~

We walked along together. I was filled with a certainty that if I were to look back I'd see my own tracks, but none from her…but I also knew that in looking back I'd break the spell, and it would all be over in that moment.

I have the memory that she told me some of the things I most needed to know, although the memory gets shaky when I try to remember exactly what they were.

I don't know what she was. I don't even know for certain that any of this happened at all. I can offer you no proof, no evidence, no explanation. The only remaining trace of the moment is my own enduring conviction, and I struggle with the nature of it still.

She'd called me. Or I'd conjured her. Or the answer lay in some nostrum from the Spirit Box, provenance unknown. Or nothing of what I remember ever happened at all.

Nothing can taunt you more than infinite possibility.

I remember the light and the way she looked and the way I found her, and I remember the touch of her hand, or perhaps that had stayed with me from before and would never leave.

That's it. I think.

The next thing I remember is that I was standing before the Land Rover with the jerrican I'd left beside it, and Rachel Young was curled up on the passenger seat with my coat over her. I looked down at her and I was gripped by an overwhelming happiness that I'd done nothing to earn. It was in me and through me like a warm light. It peaked and then it started to fade. When it was gone I knew that I would be unable ever to explain or reproduce it.

You could say that I'd dived from the heights and touched madness for that brief moment before the rebound drew me back. You could say anything you like and I wouldn't give you an argument. But nor would I give you one inch of the ground that I felt that I'd won. I'd touched something, that was certain. I knew what I knew.

Sometimes that's all that you need.

Slowly, more slowly than I'd have liked, I pulled out the driver's seat squab, and with my lifeless fingers I undid the filler cap and tipped in the fuel. For a can that had been so heavy, the amount that came out of it seemed pretty miserable.

I slotted the squab back in, and climbed up behind the wheel. I turned the screwdriver in the ignition. The engine turned over, but with no more of a result than before. But then I remembered to switch the feed tap over. It took a few more tries with the battery power now declining fast, but then it was trays and hammers again and then that rude engine roar.

I sat there with my hands on the wheel, feeling shocked and stupid, my heart ready to burst, capable of anything, if I could only remember what the next step ought to be.

Rachel tilted her head back and closed her eyes.

"Let me know when we get there," she said.

Forty-one

For the first few hundred yards we were moving along on a level somewhere high above the river. When I slackened off on the engine revs I could hear distant water, but I couldn't make out anything through the trees. The trail here was wide. The markers were infrequent but the line of the trail was unmistakeable.

As the trail dropped down, what before had been a general river ambience became more and more of a white water sound. It was like when an orchestra noise resolves itself into the various parts.

Suddenly, there it was.

The river was much wider than the map had made it seem, and it wasn't just one single body of water out there. It was an entire landscape of stagnant side pools, shelves of rock, rapids, island beaches of pebbles and stones and riverbank sand. Snaking down through the center of it all was a wide, dark and clear area where the main channel and the fastest part of the flow went on through.

Now I had a problem.

The river was moving between high cliffs on the far side, and high wooded slopes on this one. The problem was that my wide trail went straight down to the water's edge and then all but disappeared. I could see the line where it was supposed to go, but by then it had narrowed right down to a boot trail over the rocks off the riverbank. Between the river and the overhanging trees there were maybe two yards of rubble, and you had to go picking your way over that like you were clambering over dead buildings in an earthquake zone.

Good exercise for the legs with a backpack. On wheels, forget it. Handy as the Land Rover had been for us, it was no gazelle. I took it right down to the water and stopped there, looking for some way around this.

There was none.

So I thought, What the hell, and I did the only thing that I could. I drove us off the bank and into the river.

The shallows along the nearest edge were just deep enough to splash along in. This was fine. I reckoned we could risk going to a couple of feet of water before it started coming into the cab. The trick would be to keep to the slow-moving current on the inside of the bend, which ran just inches deep over a wide bank of shale. I was looking to get us back up onto dry land at the first opportunity.

Plowing along with the tires kicking up spray, it probably looked more hazardous than it really was. The river widened as we followed the inside of its curve. Further out it was all whitewater and rapids, but on these gravel banks it was more like a drive along the beach at low tide.

It would have been wrong to underestimate the river's power, though. Just coming into sight, out there on a low delta of river sand, I could see an entire tree that had been uprooted in some previous flood. It had been washed downstream and stripped clean and beached there, its root system plucked like a bird. Out beyond it, a broken-up shelf of rock was creating rapids.

After that we got into a very quiet and spooky stretch as the river moved between tall, dark stands of trees and the valley began to narrow in around it. I was still driving in the shallows, but from the ripples over the stones I was aware of the speed of flow increasing around us.

The sooner I was out of this, the happier I'd be. When I saw some big flat rocks tilting up out of the river like a ramp, I steered for them. They were jointed like a pavement, and erosion had rubbed them smooth. There was a jolt as the front wheels hit the submerged shoulder of the rock, but then the big engine hauled us up and out and we were on the dry again.

But then I had to stop, because it was a ramp that led nowhere. I braked the Land Rover at its awkward angle, and got out.

This had been somebody's picnic spot in the summer. In a dry cleft at the top of the rocks there was an old, cold burnt patch with a Folgers coffee can that looked as if it had been used to contain a small cooking fire.

But this was no good. This was an island of stone and we were effectively stranded here, with water flowing around us on all sides. All along the nearby riverbank, the way out of the river was blocked by a thicket of dead tree matter. Down by the water it was dark and sodden, like sedge. The stuff higher up was dry like tinder, but just as dense. I could see no way of getting a vehicle up into it.

I had to stop to listen for a moment, then.

Even over the sound of the river, I could hear something crashing around. Some kind of a forest creature up there in the undergrowth. Any other time, I'd have taken an interest. Right now I had too much to occupy me.

But even I had to pay attention when I saw Cyrus Behan tearing his way down through the brush on the slopes above the bank, apparently hell-bent on reaching us.

"Cyrus!" I shouted, meaning it as a warning, but either he didn't hear or he didn't care to acknowledge me.

He seemed to have lost it completely. He had a knife in his hand, and I guessed it was the one that he'd bought that very morning for the field-dressing of one Rachel Young. With it he was hacking right and left at any part of the foliage that threatened to get in his way. Wild-eyed, spit flying, he looked over-the-edge and impervious to pain. He looked as if he'd been rolled in dirt and brushed-down with razors.

I saw him slip and fall, and for a few moments he disappeared.

Then he popped up into sight again a few yards further down, and carried on exactly as before.

Vines and switches were whipping at him as he fought his way through. As they slashed at him, they only increased the manic fury with which he slashed back.

I heard a weak voice behind me say, "Is he there?"

"Yes, he is. Don't worry. He can't reach us."

"I don't want to see him," she said. "I want to go."

Looking at Cyrus trying to blitz his way down the bank, I couldn't blame her. He was the first authentic, out-of-control madman I'd ever seen. Watching him from this place of safety was like seeing some psychotic baboon throwing a major tantrum on its island at the zoo. He'd given in to a rage so overwhelming that it was like some self-sustaining, perpetual fit. He'd submerged into the depths of his own anger until no other part of him showed. This wasn't someone who'd stop and listen to argument. This didn't even look like a someone at all.

Something caught at him. His clothes were all hung up. I saw him struggle and roar and rip them free, leaving pieces behind.

The only thing to be done with this wild man was to leave him in the woods and get the hell out of there. Ben Steed's men could tackle him. They could come out here with ropes and nets and tranquilizer darts. Cyrus Behan was one seriously rabid raccoon.

I wasn't panicked. He couldn't get to us.

"He can't get to us," I repeated to Rachel as I climbed back in.

"Let's not bet on that," she said.

I put the gearshift into reverse, and backwards down the sloping rock we went. But getting off didn't prove to be quite as easy as getting on. I must have hit an underwater pothole because the entire vehicle lurched and tipped backwards with an alarming bang, and suddenly there was water pouring into the load space behind us. What I'd thought of as no current at all was now pushing at us hard enough to swing us around.

I slammed the shift into first and climbed us out of there. I could still taste the scare that it had given me.

At that moment, Cyrus Behan burst through the thicket above the river and dropped feet-first into the water.

That water was ice cold. The shock of it to his system must have been enormous. But it didn't stop him. He was under for seconds but then he came back up again, exploding out with his sights already set on us.

He was about a hundred, a hundred and fifty yards away. I hadn't imagined that he could get this close and I certainly didn't want to see him get any closer. I increased our speed and steered around the rock we'd just left and then I drove on downstream, getting deeper and deeper into the river and praying that the swell wouldn't wash in and drown our engine.

In the one good mirror I could see Cyrus fling himself around the rock and come plowing through the water after us. Then he hit a deep spot and fell flat on his face.

He wasn't down for long. Within seconds he was up again and struggling. I could see him hacking at the water with his knife as if it would somehow cut him a way through.

But the distance between us was increasing, and Cyrus wasn't taking care. The next time he lost his footing, he went completely. I saw somersaulting arms and legs as the current took him and rolled him over and swept him off to the side. He passed by us at speed. Then he was picked up by a fast watercourse and rushed through a chicane of rocks which battered him back and forth like a pinball, arms still windmilling in the water, and then he was lost to our sight.

Forty-two

I watched for his body as we moved downstream, but I didn't see anything of him. The river broadened out even more and the valley sides became increasingly sheer, like a canyon. We were still driving on the riverbed, in it up to our axles, the big vehicle scrambling and sliding whenever it got rocky and with us being rattled around inside it.

I tried to tell myself that this was the kind of thing some people did at weekends for pleasure, but it didn't help. Having said that, it was no tougher than some of the ground we'd already had to cover. The river was just one additional hazard.

And it was steady progress.

I reckoned that it was less than a mile further to the bridge and our prospective take-out point, and I was starting to wonder — could the worst of it really be over?

That kind of thinking made a trap that I'd fallen into before. The map had shown the river ahead of us as a big horseshoe loop, but there was nothing to say it would be a flat run all the way. If the river turned to rapids we'd be sunk, quite literally, and very quickly.

The water had started to come in by now. I had to tell Rachel to put her feet up on the seat because the floor of the cab was now awash. At first she didn't hear me. Then she had a couple of tries, but she couldn't do it. I had to reach over and lift them up for her.

She'd slipped down the scale of consciousness another notch or two. I didn't want to face it, but I was sure it was so. Her breathing had begun to rasp. She'd slide around when we hit something big, but she was doing almost nothing to protect herself. When that happened I had to grab for her while trying not to lose control of the vehicle.

Where I could, I steered with one hand on the wheel and my other holding one of hers. It was cold and I don't think she had the strength to grip me back. I couldn't even feel her pulse, but somehow I continued to sense the life in her.

We went on like that, using our riverbed for a road, with me watching for the bridge and praying that she'd last until we got there.

The first I knew of the falls was the sound of thunder building in the valley as we approached them.

It had to happen, I suppose. Shortly after that, I realized that about a hundred yards ahead of us was a deceptive change, a razor's edge across the river like a flat-earther's notion of the end of the world. I stopped the Land Rover in the lee of some boulders, and I left it there with the engine running while I went on alone to survey the situation.

Stepping down into the freezing water hardly affected me at all. I'd braced myself, but I was half-frozen already and I barely felt the change. The adrenaline was pumping, and I was burning it just as fast. The signals I was getting back from my body all felt like dangerous ones.

As I waded out, it got deeper. Reflex made me grab to protect my crotch when the current surged and rose. In a very short time I could feel it pushing at me and trying to take me off my feet.

The closer I got to the falls, the more urgent the undertow became. When I made it to some big rocks, I scrambled up onto them and crouched there, breathless, with icy water streaming from me and darkening the white stone. From here I could lean out and look over.

My heart would have sunk, had it not been stilled by the sight.

I felt no despair. It was as if the receptors for despair had been burned out of me, and their cut ends all sealed up with salt.

The river poured over the wide lip of the falls and then all funnelled together into a single, central torrent down the middle of a steeply-sloping wall of rock. It wasn't a straight drop but went down at maybe forty-five degrees, perhaps a little steeper. There were a few fallen trees across the way. The face of the rock was black and green, mostly black with slick moss. To either side rose a sheer canyon wall.

The waterfall ended down at the bottom in a kind of dump pool, where all the debris it had picked up seemed to be whirling around. Beyond that, after a short stretch of boiling white water, it became a river again.

"Oh, fuck," I said aloud.

What more was expected of me? It seemed that the harder I tried, the harder it got. The more I accomplished, the more I was given to do.

I floundered back into the water and made my way upstream toward Rachel.

It's not often that you can glimpse the face of God and know almost complete despair in the course of one afternoon. It was the ultimate emotional rollercoaster, all right. I felt that whatever deity I served, he was determined not to be impressed by anything I might achieve.

There has to come a point where you just roll over and concede.

But.

"Not yet," I said.

I got back into the Land Rover and I took Rachel's cold face in my cold hands and I said, "I'm going to go for this, Rachel, If I've killed us, I'm sorry. But we'll both go together. Forgive me."

Her eyes were barely-open and her lips were just sufficiently parted for her breath to get in and out. Ice-cold and spent, we were like two corpses already. I didn't know whether she could hear me or not. She certainly gave me no sign of it.

I stroked her face, and I stroked back some of the wet hair that had stuck down to her forehead.

Then I slammed the Rover into gear and, fighting the current and feeling it rock us as we turned, I got the vehicle completely about-face and then reversed slowly toward the edge of the falls. I got the rear wheels as close to it as I dared and then I stopped, and pulled on the handbrake. Even with the transmission locked I could feel the heavy vehicle being nudged around by the current, and I knew that it wouldn't take much of an increase in pressure to sweep us away.

I released the winch. Then I got out and ran the cable to a rock in the middle of the river, winding it around for a couple of turns like a rope on a capstan before anchoring its end to the firmest-looking tree on the bank. It sounds straightforward enough, but I was fighting the current all the way. When the cable was centered and secured I went back to the Land Rover and unlocked the freewheeling hubs.

Was there anything else I could do by way of preparation? I didn't think so.

After all that it was a simple matter of getting into the vehicle, checking the winch to make sure that the cable wasn't slack, and then backing right up to the edge of the falls and over.

My heart was filled with something, but it wasn't fear. When it came to it I don't think I even hesitated. I slipped the gears into neutral, kept my foot away from the brake, and instead of braking rode the cable control as the pressure of the current took us over.

There was a bad moment as we tipped back over the edge and our front end went right up into the air, but instead of doing a backwards rollercoaster plunge we were checked after only an instant of freefall as the vehicle dropped its own length. If the cable was going to snap or the winch give out, I reckoned it would have happened right then.

But it didn't.

The big torrent was only a few feet from our windows, and its spray came in through the hole where our windshield had been. Speech would have been pointless. It was impossible to be heard. We were rolling backwards and I was riding the winch control, paying it out like a fishing line. Now that we were on it, the rock slope felt even steeper than it had looked.

I had no idea what was going to happen when the cable reached its end.

But for the moment I seemed to see everything with an incredible sharpness of vision. My situation had all the textures and dimensions of a hallucination, but I knew that it was an effect that no drug could match and that only an exhausted, fucked-up and totally focused personality could achieve.

When I felt that we had to be getting near to the end of the line, I wrapped my arms around Rachel as tightly as I could. Then I braced myself between the seat and the dash in such a position that I could kick out and operate the cable release lever if I needed to.

It came without any warning, and I didn't have to do a thing. It just went, and suddenly we dropped. We smashed through at least one fallen tree as we plunged backwards.

I hadn't planned to hug her as hard as I did. I could easily have broken her. We were weightless for a moment or so and the moment seemed to go on for ever. Then we crashed rear-end first into the dump pool.

Everything was confusion. We were tumbling around then, completely out of control. We splashed, we bobbed, we turned. Iced water flooded the cab, and I felt Rachel's gasping reaction as it swamped us. I pressed her head into my shoulder and did my best to tell her it was all right. I knew she couldn't hear me. All I could hear was the battering of the falls against the bodywork. We were sinking fast and when the falls hit the roof we were thrust down even faster.

I was completely disoriented but I could feel that the vehicle was settling into the dump pool as it was being whirled around. There was a bump and a scrape that shook us from side to side. It was only afterwards that I realized that the pounding pressure of the falls was forcing us out of the pool, rattling us between the rocks and spitting us out into the lower reaches of the river like so much debris.

Out we came, backwards and bobbing, and somewhere further down we hit something on the riverbed and the impact spun us around.

If you've ever seen news footage of trucks and cars being swept away in flash-floods, you'll have some idea of how we were carried along by the river. Most of the time I just clung to Rachel and hoped that we wouldn't submerge completely or turn over. A couple of times we got a big shaking as we hit rocks and were spun again.

Then we slowed, and I could feel that the tires were touching ground every now and again as we bucked and bounced along. I put one hand out and tried turning the steering wheel, but the differences I made were unpredictable ones.

We covered a hundred and fifty, perhaps as much as two hundred yards in this way, and then the river widened out and dropped us back onto our wheels.

The engine was dead, of course. I even gave it a try although I knew I was wasting my time. We were still in water that was deep enough for the current to keep pushing us forward, but it wasn't anything you could realistically call progress. I could see ahead to where the river broke up and became all gullies and boulders. A raft or a canoe might get through there, but nothing the size of our vehicle.

But, come on. We'd come through it, we were alive, and we'd been carried some way in the direction we needed to go.

As I made my plans for us to abandon the vehicle, we were being propelled forward under the almost-horizontal trunk of a dead tree that had fallen out across the river.

The weird thing was, I could imagine that out of the corner of my eye I could see the statue-still figure of Cyrus Behan squatting on it, waiting for us to pass underneath.

Forty-three

It all turned real with the thump as he let himself down onto the roof of the cab. I looked up above my head and saw the sheet metal bending and flexing like a live thing as he shifted his weight around on it.

"Cyrus?" I said.

And then I said, "I know what you came for. Don't waste your time. You're too late."

Everything went quiet for a while. No sound but the onward rush of the river all around us.

"Cyrus?" I said. "I could have told you this sooner, if you'd given me chance. The drugs are in her body now. She's dying. There's nothing left for you to get."

Had he washed down here ahead of us? Or perhaps he'd fished himself out of the rapids and scrambled over the ridge to meet the river further along. Either way, it looked as if he'd just found himself a place and waited with total confidence for us to catch up with him.

I wondered what might have been going through his mind as he waited. White noise? Nursery rhymes?

Counting all the money he was never going to see?

I said, "Listen to me, Cyrus. There's nothing you can get out of this. By my reckoning the road's not five minutes downriver from here. Your best chance of turning this around will be to help me get Rachel back into town. How about it, Cyrus? What do you say?"

Cyrus Behan's answer, when it finally came, did little to raise my hopes of a reasonable outcome.

He said, "You're going to die today anyway. Stick your head out the window and I'll make it easy for you."

I closed my eyes and sighed. I was still holding Rachel. At least for the moment she was protected. Even if he were to swing over and lunge through the space where the windshield had been, he'd hit me before he could reach her.

But we couldn't stay like this for ever.

The next thing I heard was an echoing *ka-chung!* as the blade of Cyrus Behan's new hunting knife came down through the skin of the aluminum roof. He pulled it back again straight away, but the gut hook at the blade's end got caught and he had to work it back and forth in the hole.

"See?" he called down to me as he was trying to get it out. "With a blade this sharp, you won't even feel it."

"That's very encouraging," I said.

"Are you making fun of me?"

"You want me to stick my head out so you can cut my throat, and you don't think that's a joke?"

"I'm not a sadist," he said. "I'm not going to cut anyone's throat. I'm going to stick it in the back of your neck, like a Spanish garotte. The blade severs the spinal cord when it goes in. You don't see it coming and you hardly feel a thing."

One considerate human being, or what?

With one arm still around Rachel, I reached out and gripped the screwdriver in the Land Rover's ignition. It was jammed right in, but there was a little bit of play. It wouldn't be much of a defensive weapon, but it was the only thing to hand.

I said, "She's all but dead, Cyrus. You may not think the drugs are gone, but just look at the state she's in. I don't know what other kind of proof you could need. What do you call it when you tackle something completely worthless and then fail? Does that cancel out, or is it a double-stupid?"

"Nobody's going to trick me out of what's mine," he said.

"Cyrus," I said, "your life's only achievement is the misery you've caused others. Get this into your head. Nobody's tricking anybody out of anything. There's nothing for you. You're wasting your time. Look at her."

The screwdriver came free, bringing out half the ignition works and wiring after it. But I don't think he heard. The roof was creaking and I heard a *clump, thump* as he scrambled around on it and repositioned himself.

I realized then that he wasn't going to risk hanging his head over the side to look in at us, as I'd hoped, but he was going to squint down through the spyhole that he'd made with his knife.

Because it took me a moment to catch on to this I reacted late, but at least I then reacted quickly. I looked up, and saw the daylight being blocked out as Behan moved over the slash, and I rammed the screwdriver up through the hole.

It's about the hardest thing I've ever had to do. I didn't dare think about it, I just did it. The screwdriver went through up to the handle, but then the handle stopped it.

I knew I'd connected with something because there was an instantaneous howl that echoed all the way through the canyon.

Although I knew he was hurt, I doubted that he was finished. The racket he was making sounded far too healthy. I knew I'd have to act fast, so I opened the driver's door to scramble out.

That was more difficult than I'd expected, as well, because the river fought back. But when I'd got it some of the way open, the current got inside it and the door was snatched out of my hand. I swung up out of the cab and reached across the roof.

He was up there, but I didn't get chance to see what he was doing. I just grabbed the nearest part of him, and hauled. He thrashed around as he started to slide, but he'd nothing to hold on to; he came right over the edge and we went down into the river together.

My thought was that if I had to hold his stupid head under the water until he blacked out, then so be it. But what I hadn't bargained for was how strong he was. Unbelievably so, for someone who looked as if he never took exercise and lived on a diet of saturated fats. He was a lot younger than me, but in spite of that I'd expected to have some advantage.

If it wasn't for the fact that not one part of this was planned, I'd have said that I'd made a serious miscalculation. He had the upper hand almost right away. My screwdriver had skinned one of his pudding-face cheeks close to the eye, but that was all the damage I'd done him. I was fighting both him and the current, and I was losing against each of them.

I felt his elbow smash against the side of my head, and I lost all sense of up or down. The next thing I knew, I was being whirled around and then bodyslammed hard. But not by Cyrus. When I came up I was a dozen yards downriver and trying to get some purchase on the big rocks that I'd been swept up against. The river was trying to carry me on around them, while Cyrus was on his feet and laboring back up the flow toward the Land Rover.

The driver's door was open, pinned back by the river and cutting up a wash from its edge. I could see Rachel inside, lying on the seat where I'd left her. I couldn't see her face.

I started toward them and immediately lost my footing. When I came up again, he was in the cab with her. The door was partly in the way. Rachel must have been at least semi-conscious because I could see her head on the seat, turning from one side to the other although I couldn't see what Cyrus was doing to her. It was like watching the savage rape of a helpless but unwilling drunk. I was making nightmare progress, giving it my all and getting almost nowhere.

It didn't seem to be going right for him. I think he was trying to undress her and he couldn't make any headway with her sodden clothing.

I actually heard him say, "Help me, you bitch. Help me," and then the sound of a slap, which I didn't imagine came from any action of hers.

I was almost in reach of the door's edge by now. If I could grab it I could pull myself in. As he was moving around her I saw Rachel stir.

Then I heard her say, "Here, I'll help you," and then her hand came up from under and I saw her jam her thumb into the eye that I'd missed.

I can't say for certain but I'd swear it went in right up to the knuckle. She'd quite a long set of nails on her, too. Cyrus screamed like a chopped toad, and reared up clutching at his face.

There wouldn't be any better opportunity. I reached in and seized his collar and heaved him backwards out of the cab.

He landed flat on his back with his arms spread wide. The river engulfed him, and then spat him back up again. But when he bobbed up he was already several yards further downstream, floundering to regain his footing and having no success.

He was spraying, he was spluttering. He was having the same problem that I'd had, finding that the harder he tried to get onto his feet the more likely he was to fall. He did a five-second comedy routine and then he was barrel-rolling off showing head, legs, arms, head, spinning out of control and right into the same rocks that I'd been clinging to before.

With one difference. As if to punish him for fighting back, the river spun him around and swung his head against the boulders like a doll against a wall. I heard the crack when he hit. It was as sharp and as clean as a ball being hit by a bat. Suddenly there was no more pinwheeling of arms and legs; in an instant it was as if he'd been turned utterly boneless.

The current had no trouble with him then.

The river drew Cyrus Behan's limp and tumbling body to a space in the rocks, and funnelled it away with an instantaneous efficiency that made me think of nothing less than him being sucked down and out of sight by a flushing toilet.

I was still hanging on to the driver's door. With its help I struggled my way back to the cab.

Rachel had her hand to her head, her fingers spread, only the back of her forefinger against her brow. She was frowning. Her eyes were closed.

I started to say the wrong name, but then I caught myself.

"Rachel," I said. "He's gone. I think he's gone for good."

She grunted. She didn't open her eyes.

"Can you hold on? Can you hold on just a little while longer?"

The movement was slow and barely perceptible. But it was there. She was shaking her head.

"Oh, Christ," I said with suddenly-growing anger. "Don't you dare! Don't you dare do that to me!" And I dragged her half-out of the cab and somehow managed to get my shoulder under one of her arms so that I could then get my other arm under her legs and bring her out the rest of the way.

"Do you hear me?" I said. "You don't give up now. If I don't, you don't."

She did nothing to help me. Her head rocked forward onto her chest. Why had I thought that she was heavy back there in the cabin? She weighed nothing at all.

The fact that I staggered and stumbled forward with the current had nothing to do with it.

I knew where the turbulence was, and I steered wide of it. I kept talking to her all the way.

At least, I think I did. When Gillian had been small and a ruthless insomniac, there had been times when I'd lay stretched-out on the floor of her darkened bedroom busking one made-up story after another, in the vain hope of wearing her down despite already being worn out myself. At some point, exhaustion would overcome me and I'd doze off, but some switch in my head would stay open and somehow I'd keep on talking. Then I'd be awakened by a squawk, because my story had turned into an aphasic ramble with no proper words or meaning in it.

For all I knew, I could have been doing that now. Rambling on with the best of intentions, and no thoughts to back them up. Telling tales of life and wonder. Embroidering our private universe.

Grownups sharing dreams with their children. Like elephants dancing with butterflies.

Beyond these rapids, the river widened out and calmed so much that it was more like a rocky lake or a primeval lagoon. There were fallen trees just lying there in the shallows, and patches of greenery growing up on the rocks. The bank opposite looked as if it was an entire quarter of a mile away at least.

I saw something out there that may have been Cyrus. It might just as easily have been a bundle of old rags and trash, knotted, floating in a raft with the air trapped inside them. When the downdraft of the helicopter passed over them, ripples passed across the water like a visible shockwave and the rags began to flutter.

Looking up into the sky, I had to screw up one eye and squint with the other.

"Rachel," I said, "Look, Rachel, they've found us."

It wasn't the kind of rescue helicopter that had a winch. It looked military, and it was enormous. I knew then that I'd been right to move because there was no way it could ever have set down on the lookout tower's tiny landing pad.

It hovered out over the lagoon, and that was when I started to take proper note of the situation because, finally, that effing bridge that I'd been promising her for at least the past two hours was right there across the valley before us. I could see vehicles on it. I could see people on it. I could see some of them in reflector jackets scrambling down the riverbank from the road that ran across it.

And all the time, I just kept on going.

Two of them were in the water now, splashing their way toward me like galloping horses. Others were coming down to join them.

I was all but spent. I was stooping so low that Rachel was almost in the water. When they reached me and took her weight from me, I almost lifted off my feet and into the air. But I couldn't have been all that buoyant. Two of them caught me and stopped me from falling, and they all but did my walking for me as we followed the two with Rachel as they made toward the shore.

One mainly carried her, the other mainly steadied and guided him. They were moving faster, leaving us behind; between them they were almost managing a run. All I could see of Rachel was her legs sticking out, her feet kicking with the motion, her head nodding loosely.

By the time I reached the bridge, the helicopter had landed on the road. A man came slithering, scrambling down the banking toward me. I stared at him numbly and although a part of me knew it was Ben Steed, it was a while before the shattered mental apparatus that I was working with could do anything useful with the information.

They put a foil blanket around me. I was still moving. I felt a couple of those one-use heater pads being thrust into my collar, one either side of my throat to lie right on the jugular.

I tried to mutter my thanks but all that came out was, "Are they working on her yet?"

"What do you think?" Ben Steed said.

"I'll be fine," I said. "Tell them not to wait for me."

He took me at my word.

"Lucas!" he shouted to someone up at the cars. "Tell them to go!"

The helicopter was passing over us and we were battered by its downdraft as we got to the vehicles; the space blanket I was wearing almost got ripped away and it was only thanks to the others around me keeping a tight hold that it didn't. The bridge was the riveted metal span kind, hump-backed in profile like a dinosaur, and standing on it was the biggest snowplow I had ever seen. It dwarfed Ben Steed's truck and the other vehicles around it, of which there were three or four. They had their lightbars flashing and everything.

One of the vehicles was a Ford ambulance that looked like a big U-Haul truck. It was white with an orange stripe and had the words *Madison EMS Mission and St. Joseph Health System* on its side.

I assume they put me in that.

I really don't have any memory at all of the journey back.

Forty-four

The next thing I do remember is being in a school hall in Marshall where they'd made a temporary emergency center out of the gymnasium. Marshall is a one-street, old-fashioned small town squeezed between some railroad lines and the steep hills behind them. There's a traditional courthouse with temple steps and a silver cupola, and a few poky stores that seem to sell mostly paint and lawnmowers.

The gymnasium had been set up to receive the missing hikers. Someone had dug out the town's emergency plan and dusted off a number of folding beds, screens, and some basic paramedical equipment. The seriously injured would go directly to St. Joseph's Hospital in Asheville, either by air ambulance or by road. This was local backup offering the soup-and-blankets cure.

With the nine kids who'd already arrived and all the helpers, family and well-wishers who were milling around the place, it had the feel of a transit camp with a mobile phone chorus. They sped me through the crowd to a makeshift surgery where a young doctor checked me over for frostbite and then for signs of hypothermia. Was my speech slurred? Was my coordination poor? Did I have a tendency to misjudge my abilities, especially my strength?

I'd have said no to all of them had I known where I was inviting him to stick his thermometer.

I must have been in better shape than I felt. After a hot drink of something so sweet that it made all the roots of my teeth hurt, two nurses put me in a warm bath and then rolled me in dry blankets. They clipped something to my ear and taped something to my arm.

I didn't intend to sleep until I'd had some news of Rachel, but it didn't work out that way. They must have moved me from the chair. I woke on one of the folding cots at around four o'clock in the morning.

All I could remember at first was the dream that I'd had. I was in some kind of a boat or a canoe. I wasn't alone, but I'm not sure who was sitting behind me. It might have been Rachel. It might well have been Gillian. But although in the dream I never turned around and looked, something persuades me that it was probably Sophie.

We were being carried down a river and it was all very smooth. We came to Cyrus Behan's body along the way, hung up in the fork of a trapped tree-branch, the current lifting and rocking him in a semblance of lifelike movement. His eyes were open and his head was nodding and his mouth was opening and closing like a ventriloquist's dummy's. I expected it to make a clacking sound, but it made none. Our boat drifted by the body in silence, and it was deeply spooky.

That's all there was to it.

Despite the hour, there were people about the place and there was plenty going on. There was a local news crew with their camera hanging around because they hadn't got quite enough footage of teenagers looking shocked and scared and being tearful on the phone. I got hot coffee from an urn and some spare clothes from the volunteer fire department. I tried to make some calls to find out about Rachel, but no-one I spoke to could tell me anything.

Then I asked around until I found one of the emergency workers who was about to drive into Asheville, and asked him if he could give me a ride and drop me at St. Joseph's. Nobody tried to stop me or challenged me in any way. I don't know how long they'd all been going, but everybody else looked almost as tired as I felt. I left word for Ben Steed and then I climbed into the emergency worker's car and slept some more.

~

We got down into Asheville just a little after first light. Rain had been falling before we reached Biltmore Avenue, and as we drove along it felt like another world altogether.

St. Joseph's was a super-modern medical complex on the site of an old tuberculosis hospital, south of the downtown area. The scale of it was almost overpowering. It covered several blocks and there were satellite medical practices in the streets and avenues all around it. My driver took me down into the underground visitor parking deck, and dropped me by an elevator that he said would take me to the Emergency Room directly overhead.

I looked down at the floor as I waited for the elevator to arrive. I was mostly calm. I was too strung-out to be otherwise. Whatever they told me, I would accept.

Or I'd try.

When I stepped out of the elevator, the Emergency Room's waiting area was there before me. It had tubular steel seating and was decorated with enormous palm trees in pots. The seating was empty apart for one patient, a man in his sixties with a bandaged head and blood splatters down his white T-shirt. He was reading a magazine.

I asked the woman at the receiving desk about Rachel. Rachel Young.

She didn't need to ask my name, but said, "We've been expecting you. Why don't you take a seat. One of the doctors will come out to speak to you." She managed not quite to meet my eyes as she said it.

"You're telling me it didn't work out," I said.

"I'm not allowed to tell you anything at all," she said. "Please bear with me. Would you like our private room to wait in?"

"No," I said. "I've been through all that. When did she die?"

"Please," she said with a look that was both apologetic and imploring, showing me the phone receiver in her hand. "I'm calling him for you right now."

I could have pressed her further. But it wasn't her fault that she wasn't allowed to break the news, and a couple of extra minutes weren't going to change anything.

So I went over to one of the chairs and sat down. I didn't know what else to do with myself.

Someone else came into the waiting area after a while. I heard the elevator doors out in the corridor and then I sensed her standing there, looking around. Instead of going over to the receiving desk, she walked past all the empty chairs and lowered herself wearily into the one right alongside me.

She stretched out her legs and tilted her head back and said, without looking at me, "You *are* capable of staying in one place for more than five minutes, then."

"Sorry," I said.

It wasn't the Sophie I'd been expecting. She looked as knocked-sideways as I felt. We met here like strangers.

"How did you find me?" I said.

"Ben whatsisname," she said. "Ben Steed? I was coming to pick you up from Marshall but he said you'd be here. I said I'd believe it when I saw it."

There was no acrimony in this. None that I could detect, anyway. I'm not saying we were suddenly close again. We were more like a couple of opponents whom the game had worn down so much that their shared weariness was like a bond.

She said, "I talked to a couple of undertakers about the arrangements for getting her home. One was creepy but the other seemed all right. And I went shopping for her. They told me you'd written down all the sizes but I knew you'd be hopeless at choosing anything."

"Where did they tell you that?"

"When they took me down to see her."

"You're probably right," I said.

Without looking at me she said, "Later on I was in one of those parking garages right in the middle of town. I heard voices being raised on the next level up. Someone was arguing. It stopped me in my tracks, John. I'll swear to God that one of the voices was Gilly. I thought I was going to faint. I heard this car take off and then the next minute it was coming down through all the levels. She looked straight at me as it passed. It was only for a second but it was her. I know you won't believe me and I really can't explain it, but it was."

I said nothing.

She said, "I got in the car and followed her down. I should have been quicker. I lost her in the street outside but then I saw her car again at the next lights. I stayed behind her all the way to some house somewhere. She went into a driveway when I wasn't expecting it and by the time I'd turned around, she'd gone inside. I stayed there on the street for two hours or more. Someone must have called the police because one of their cars pulled in behind me and they wanted to know why I was watching the house. God knows what my explanation sounded like. One of them went over and brought her back. She was a twenty-three year-old married woman. You could see a resemblance, but…" she shrugged, helplessly.

Then she said, "But back there in the parking garage, what I heard and saw was our daughter. That won't go away. I know it wasn't so, but it still won't go away. I know she looked at me. Even though I can accept she could never have been there. Isn't that strange?"

I agreed that life was strange.

And then I said, "Where's your car?"

"Down in the basement," she said. "It's just an airport rental. I said I'd take whatever they had. Does this mean you're ready to go?"

"Bring it over and wait for me," I said. "I've got to finish something here."

"Don't be all day," she said. "You run away again, and I'll be taking her home on my own."

"I don't think I'll be long," I said.

~

A doctor came out through the double-doors as I was heading back over to the counter. He was wearing a white lab coat over the surgical green.

"Hi," he said. "Please come with me."

"Look," I said, "I know how it goes. I'll behave myself. Just tell me she died and I'll go."

He looked at me as if I'd just changed the subject on him with no warning.

"She just this minute came round," he said. "I was taking you to see her."

I rewound and ran his words again.

"Yeah," I said. "Right."

And, "Can you give me a moment?"

He said, "I won't lie to you. It was a close-run thing. We couldn't say for sure what we were dealing with. We gave her drugs to reduce the brain swelling and then we just had to do whatever we could to stabilize all her other functions. It's been a long night, but her blood pressure's now back up to normal. We're going to be watching her for a while. I'm not saying we're out of the woods, but I'm a lot less worried than I was."

I didn't know what to say.

"Well done," I said.

"It's what we do here," he said. "Still need a moment?"

I nodded.

He pointed to a door to the right of the receiving counter and said, "I'll be right through there. Don't take too long. We'll be moving her soon."

As he walked away from me, I took a breath and steadied myself. Okay. I was ready. I didn't quite know how I'd handle this, but I was ready.

The doctor was gone from sight now. The doors through to the medical area were still closing after him. As I moved to follow him, I became aware that someone new had come in and was standing at the counter. It was a man, fortysomething, his back toward me. You could read hyperanxiety in the very line of him and I wondered what he was here for.

I heard the woman say, "You'll have to take a seat. I think her father's with her right now."

And I heard the man say, "There must be some mistake. *I'm* her father."

I slowed down.

"Just one moment, please," the woman said, and picked up one of her phones.

While she was speaking to someone on the line, I moved toward him. She hadn't seen me and he wasn't aware of me, either. If I'd wanted, I could have drawn this moment out forever.

What a terrible power for anyone to have.

I touched his arm. He turned around and looked at me. His eyes were just like Rachel's. That same weird mix of greens and greys.

I would remember.

I nodded toward the door. "Through there," I said, and that was all the message he needed. There was nothing I needed to add that he wouldn't know soon enough.

And wherever my place was, it wasn't here.

"Thank you," he said.

He went in to see his daughter.

And I went the other way, out into the light to meet whatever this new day would bring.